The Signalman's Daughter

An Inspector Vignoles Mystery

Stephen Done

British Library Cataloguing in Publication Data:
A catalogue record for this book is available from the British Library
ISBN978-1-9164010-4-4

1st published 2022

The Vignoles Press
Stephen.done@gmail.com
www.thevignolespress.com
FB: The Vignoles Press

Set in Garamond
Cover paintings: Stephen Done
Cover design: Bill Citrine
Editor: Peter Elson
Printed in Poland by booksfactory.co.uk

Prologue

DCI Vignoles climbed the outside staircase and rapped on the door. Not waiting for a call to enter he turned the Bakelite handle, and together with DS Mellor, stepped inside the signal box and closed the door behind them.

A young woman in serge trousers and a short-sleeved man's shirt was busy heaving a signal lever. One sturdily shod foot was placed on the raised cast-iron frame to offer extra leverage as she pulled the lengthy signal wires running beside the railway tracks and then up to the signal arms at the top of their posts. She had a mane of pale curls held in place by a pair of tortoiseshell-coloured combs that glowed bright in the sun streaming through the many glass windows. A number of these were slid wide to reduce the oppressive heat that made it more like a hothouse for rare orchids than a place for physical work, and her regulation British Railways cap and jacket were sensibly hung on a peg behind the door

Signal woman Laura Green glanced at her visitors and if surprised by the appearance of two soberly dressed men in her private domaine, managed to conceal it. 'Hang on…' She released the catch on another lever and eased this forward to rest in the frame near the front row of windows, then tapped out a code that set small bells ringing. An observant young woman, Green had seen the sombre black car pull up outside and immediately suspected the Transport Police were paying her a visit.

'Gentlemen, I presume you have sound operational reasons for entering railway property or I shall have to ask you both to…' She finally looked away from her work. 'Gosh! DCI Vignoles. What a surprise.'

Vignoles tipped his hat and offered a smile in response, although this was his professional version reserved for communicating this was not a social call.

'What brings you here, Inspector?' Laura Green had met Vignoles on several occasions over her twelve years of service and in contrast to his restrained half-smile, she beamed broadly, first at Vignoles then slightly less confidently at his rather forbidding companion.

'DS Mellor.' Vignoles gave the grim-faced man a name. Mellor narrowed his eyes and gave a barely perceptible nod of his head but otherwise remained impassive. Without invitation, he pulled out a pack of Players and put one in his mouth.

'I hope you don't intend to smoke that? I get enough from the engines and that blessed stove that won't draw properly.'

Mellor shrugged his shoulders and left the cigarette unlit in the corner of his mouth. He sloped over to the desk where a ledger lay open with a record of all train movements orchestrated by the occupant of the signal box. He started to turn the pages but was firmly told to 'stop doing that' whilst Green wrote the time and description of the train now steaming noisily past on its way to Coalville. Mellor didn't move, making Green feel uncomfortable at having to almost lean against his body to complete her log entry.

'Miss Green. Laura. I apologise for our intrusion.' Vignoles watched the coal train chuff past the window and silently noted the number of the locomotive. He recognised it as a familiar Leicester North engine and even knew the names of the crew. Although interested, he was merely buying a few seconds as he prepared for an interview he was dreading. 'We need to ask you some questions.'

Green furrowed her brow for a moment but gave her attention to the passage of the train to check the guard's van was still attached at the tail, indicating the train was complete and in good order as it passed through her section of the line. 'As long as you don't distract me from my work, fire away!'

'It's about your father.' Vignoles cleared his throat. 'David Green,' he added unnecessarily.

She turned on a sixpence to look at Vignoles. 'Has something happened?'

'There has not been an accident. He is in good health.' There was a momentary pause. Vignoles was uncharacteristically uneasy.

Miss Green was one small cog in the vast railway establishment that spread to almost every corner of the nation and numbered many thousands of employees and all united by the powerful bond and camaraderie of working on the national railway. There were the usual fallings out and disagreements that happen in any large organisation and even some instances of crime between railway workers, but in spite of these occasional aberrations, it never sat easily having to question part of the 'railway family'. Even worse, Laura Green was almost literally 'part of the family' within the Detective Department, based in Leicester Central.

She was the fiancée of PC Simon Howerth and Vignoles and his wife Anna had already been told to expect an invitation to the forthcoming wedding, so his visit today had the potential to cause at the very least, a rift within his team that would be hard to repair if handled badly. Worse still, if his suspicions were proved correct then the Green family was about to be ripped asunder and there would be no wedding, let alone invitations and taking his wife shopping for a new dress and hat. The situation was potentially very serious and demanded he followed due process. Vignoles had considered bringing one of the WPCs who would be gentler towards Miss Green, but his detective sergeant needed to be here. It would be poor form to cut him out. He just wished Mellor would stop looking as though he was acting a part in a film in which he was about to grill a gangster's moll.

'I need to question you about your father.'

'I cannot imagine about what?' Her eyes warily flicked across to Mellor who had a notebook somewhat ominously open in one hand, pencil at the ready. He appeared to be studying her. She surreptitiously checked the buttons on her shirt were done up sufficiently high.

'When did you last see your father?'

'Last weekend, inspector.' She had adopted a more formal tone.

'Where was this?'

'At home. I mean at my *parent's* home in Woodford. Why on earth do you need to know?'

'Just a family visit, was it?' Mellor chipped in. Voice laden with the implication of something dark and sinister.

'Yes, I had the weekend off...' She looked from one to the other, a mixture of puzzlement and annoyance in her eyes at this intrusion into her private life.

'Don't mind my sergeant; he's more used to questioning members of the criminal fraternity from the less salubrious parts of London...' Vignoles darted Mellor a stern glance, then took his hat off. He was not only hot and the sweatband already damp, but felt Laura Green deserved a more casual approach. 'I appreciate these questions may appear strange, but I would be grateful if you would answer them.'

'If I must...' She turned away and stared at the range of block instruments arrayed on a shelf that ran across the front windows overlooking the junction. She was expecting the little pointer to start twitching any moment as a colleague in the next box along the line called her attention to accept an incoming train. The bells dutifully tinkled as if in response to her looking at them.

'How did your father seem at the weekend?'

'Seem?' She tapped a reply to the communication on her telegraph.

'Did he appear anxious or worried about something?'

'No...' She was concentrating on her work. That could explain the almost imperceptible catch, but Vignoles could not be sure and a slight movement told him that Mellor also picked this up.

'Have you noticed any changes in his mood recently?'

She did not answer and set to work throwing and releasing levels with a concentration demonstrating that whatever she thought about these questions, she was not going to allow them to divert her from vitally important duties.

'The DCI is waitin' for an answer, darlin',' Mellor was unsympathetic, and his London accent exaggerated.

Green wiped the levers with a cloth and turned to face them, her hands on her shapely hips. 'And I am going to answer, *sergeant*.' She glared at Mellor. 'He was his usual self, why would he not be?' Neither man spoke. 'Dad is reserved. Used to spending hours alone in a signal box, so if he sat quietly over lunch whilst mum and I chatted ten to the dozen about my impending wedding, then *yes*, you could say his mood was different. The poor chap was probably bored silly by us both going over every last detail about the big day, and if you think he's worried about something then it's probably about how much it costs to give his only daughter away. Give? There's an ironic word when talking about weddings!' She tried to make a joke of it, but it fell flat and she gave the polished handle another impatient rub. Two angry spots formed on her cheeks.

'Do you know this man?' Vignoles handed her a small photograph.

'He looks a bit like someone dad knew when he was young. An old schoolfriend.'

'A bit like or very like?' Mellor asked. 'Be specific.'

'I think he's the same.' She looked at it again. 'Yes, I would say so. Why?'

'Do you know his name?' Vignoles kept his voice calm and level.

'Richie something. I don't think I ever heard a second name. Just Richard. Richie.' She shrugged her shoulders. 'You'd be better asking dad.'

'We 'ave, but we want your side of the story.' Mellor

struck a match and lit his cigarette despite her earlier request, peering at Laura Green through the curling smoke. There was something menacing about the gesture.

'Has your father told you anything about Richard Grimes?' Vignoles asked.

'So that's his surname?' She shook her head. 'Not really. He has a photo of the two of them. Taken well before the war in Woodford on a sunny day like today. They look so young. That's a silly thing to say, as they are young in the photo. About seventeen or eighteen, I think. I like the way dad looks; quite dashing. He had jet black hair back then. When I asked him about his friend, he told me they'd lost contact and didn't say anything more. Neither of us mentioned him again.'

'Have you seen Grimes recently?'

'Seen him? Heavens no!'

'Do you know if your father has met Grimes recently?'

'He's not said anything to me.'

'If we told you Mr Grimes called on your dad at the family home two nights ago that would be surprising?'

'I suppose it would.'

'You sure he didn't say nuffin' last Sunday? An old school friend plannin' on dropping in sounds like news.' Mellor pressed the point.

'No. Perhaps it was a surprise visit?'

Vignoles had put the photograph back in his wallet and now carefully placed this in his jacket pocket, taking what seemed like an age in so doing. The sound of Mellor drawing heavily on his cigarette could be heard as a moment of ominous stillness descended. Even the birds outside the open windows seemed to fall silent as if listening.

'Miss Green, can you think of any reason why your father might want to kill Richard Grimes?'

A Suspicious Death

Chapter One

May 1956 saw the weather settling into a series of indulgent languid days of the kind where cows stood in meadows chewing the cud as their tails swished flies whilst the skies above welcomed back the first of the high-flying swifts with their little peeping cries. Fragrant honeysuckle entwined boughs of whitethorn and the shady sycamores were draped in seed capsules, each bearing a pair of translucent wings ready to fly like one of the novel helicopters that a lucky observer might occasionally glimpse hovering like a clumsy dragonfly. For this was also the dawning of what was being described as the brighter and cleaner 'Atomic Age'.

The crisply enunciated voice of the BBC newsreaders and the broadsheet leader columns declared that this second Elizabethan era was heralding 'Better times for all'. The National Health Service was up and running well and new schools were soon to be built offering brighter classrooms lit by 'see-thru' walls of glass whilst the lucky young scholars drank free milk from little glass bottles to ensure they developed healthy bones and teeth; the beginnings of a more egalitarian, tentative 'comprehensive' education system promising opportunities for all, be they boy or girl and irrespective of class and income. At least, that was the idea, though many opposed these dangerously libertarian ideals and the traditionalist grammar schools were mounting a robust fight-back.

Dazzling silver jet planes drew pale vapour traces across skies soon to be clear of the polluting coal smoke that still poured from countless house fires and factory chimneys and from the thousands of bustling steam locomotives that huffed and puffed goods and passengers up, down and around a bewildering network of railway lines.

The Clean Air Act was surely the writing on the walls of the filthy locomotive depots crowded with green or black steam engines, (though these were often so smeared in grease, soot and grime they took on a curious brownish-purple hue). These stabled iron horses were always surrounded by piles of friable ash and mountains of coal whilst breathing out pungent smoke that infuriated housewives when they hung out their brighter, whiter washing thanks to Hoover's new top-loading washing machines and the chemically and scientifically improved detergents.

In some parts of the railway system, diesel locomotives were starting to haul trains, although these were ugly, lumbering creatures with a tendency towards unreliability and they alarmed accountants with their high cost of construction, their numerous days out of revenue earning service and expensive spare parts. Whilst offering heated cabs, comfy seats and freeing the crew from clinkered fires and the need to shovel tons of coal for hours into a roaring firebox, the liquid 'Black Gold' of diesel fuel had yet to mount a significant assault on 'King Coal' and so, for now, steam locomotives kept the railway running.

Diesel engines were at least familiar, thanks to the increasing numbers of lorries and vans on the roads; far more mysterious and sinister was the thought of the silent atoms soon to split inside a curious structure that looked rather like an over-sized steel tennis ball nearing completion in an underpopulated part of Cumberland. When commissioned later in the year, Calder Hall would heat homes and bathwater cheaply and efficiently without the need for men to toil deep beneath the ground for filthy carbon. Or so the publicity brochures for the World's first nuclear power station claimed. Many remained uneasy. This was the same dangerous science that obliterated two cities in Japan and consumed the once beautiful Pacific paradise of Bikini Atoll whilst morbidly lending its name to a racy new line of swimwear in so doing. It took an especially dark sense of humour to find a connection between the grotesque mushroom cloud filling the Pacific at dawn and the sun-kissed female bodies barely concealed by triangles of fabric in the fashion magazines.

The two trainspotters seated on the wooden fence beside the main lines were eagerly awaiting their own glimpse of one part of this exciting modern world as it roared past in what promised to be a dazzling display of futuristic transportation.

A bottle of Corona Dandelion and Burdock pop was warming into a heady concoction of fizz and sugar to be savoured in small sips to make it last. They thought it tasted even better when flat and would occasionally give it a shake, then gently untwist the cap to let the carbon dioxide escape. As they waited beside the railway, they swung their feet and enjoyed the sounds of skylarks high in the sky and rejoiced in the sudden thunderous roar of three black Hawker Hunter jets screaming overhead in close formation.

'With my hypersonic ray-gun I can zap them from the sky!' One boy pointed his oddly shaped plastic gun at the rapidly diminishing planes and imagined them glowing green around the edges before vanishing into thin air at the press of the trigger.

'Pow! Pow! Pow!' His friend, dressed in a brown fringed jacket bearing a tin star, blue jeans with turn-ups and wearing a pale cowboy hat, pointed his cap gun at the jet fighters. 'I got one of them, pard'ner!'

'And I got the other two!'

'No chance against Cowboy Sam and Dan Dare the Space Cadet!'

They both took a swig of the dark brown pop.

'How long d'you think?'

'Got to be soon, we've been waiting for ages...'

'Better finish the last of the Caramac before it melts.'

'Good idea.' The milky-sweet chocolate bar was pliant due to the heat and their fingers left clear impressions in the last four squares as they tore them apart.

'We have to eat the evidence. Our fingerprints in the chocolate would be wizard clues for the police…'

Dan Dare licked his fingers and grinned. 'All gone! Now scrunch the wrapper and we'll bury it so no one tracking us will know we were here.' They both enjoyed imagining adventures and could switch between cowboys, secret agents, space cadets or soldiers advancing through Normandy, in a trice.

'What's that?'

Both boys fell silent, the Caramac wrapper instantly forgotten and carelessly discarded.

The sound carried on the warm southern wind. A train was approaching. It sounded unlike anything that had passed in the last hour. This was not one of the familiar V2 or O2 types they now sneered at and dismissed with downturned thumbs or took potshots at from their toy guns. Nor was it one of the glamorous A3 express engines named after racehorses and which both boys still admitted to admiring. This time there was a curious constant high-pitched whine above a deeper throaty roar not unlike a memory of the passing Hawker Hunters. The singing of metal on metal and ticking of coach wheels over rail joints could now be discerned. The whine grew to a scream as though every kettle in the village was boiling frantically.

'Corrrr!'

'Wow….'

The white and silver beast was blinding in the sun; brash and gleaming like something dropped from another planet. It was a world away from the work-stained freight engines that plodded past on lengthy coal trains in a fog of exhaust. It even rendered the elegant express steamers old-fashioned. The American-style curved prow of this futuristic beast was equipped with a central headlight and the raked windscreens of the cab allowed the boys a perfect view of the driver and second man 'second man,' both dressed in neat overalls and peaked caps. Men in white lab coats stood at the back of the spacious cab, clipboards in hand.

'Like looking into a rocket ship…'

'Yeeeehaaa!' Cowboy Sam waved his hat wildly, but the men in the cabin were too intent on monitoring the shining beast to respond.

The striking gas-turbine locomotive flew past in a whirlwind of hot exhaust that made the air bubble in a ripple streaming from a port set into the roof, the turbine whining inside whilst a an ominous tell-tale trail of liquid streamed in viscous rivulets from a mesh grille on the side, staining the glossy white paint with something like over-stewed tea.

'She's leaking…'

'She won't make it home!'

'Fuel is running low, captain!'

'Will we make it back to Lunar base?'

'I'm fighting hard to mend the pipes, captain…'

'But we're losing speed!'

The boy's lived out their fantasy in a series of mutually shared images borrowed from the science fiction films they loved to watch in the Saturday matinees in the church hall.

As yet blissfully unaware of the leak, the powerful locomotive hurtled onwards, the dynamometer car coupled behind was filled with hunched figures studying dials and graphs as the rake of empty coaches clattered behind.

'We just looked into the future.'

'Sure did, pard'ner!' responded Cowboy Sam in his best John Wayne accent.

They stared, wistfully, towards the now vanishing train as the skylarks took up their tumbling trilling songs once again.

* * * *

Meanwhile, back in Rugby, the enduring love affair with steam locomotion was still alive and kicking and the British Railways Locomotive Testing Station was being lauded as the nation's epicentre of steam traction development.

This installation possessed a hall containing a rolling road that allowed steam locomotives to be wired up to monitoring equipment like patients in a hospital bed. After being firmly shackled to the spot, these steaming giants were then set free to spin rollers under the driving wheels for hours on end whilst feeding measurements of speed, tractive effort, thermal efficiency and streams of other data analysed by teams of intense men with pencils behind their ears and heavily framed glasses on their noses. It was noisily impressive and more than a little thrilling to stand at close quarters whilst a powerful steam engine turned the rollers at maximum effort. These tests made for good publicity photographs, with the blur of wheels giving an exhilarating sense of power as smoke poured out the chimney and up through the roof vent hood. It was captivating to observe the contrast between the bright windowed offices with their banks of flashing lights and the twitching needles in dials screwed onto desktops and the raw power of the engine storming like a Fury.

Yet, even here, the creeping threat of modernity could not be repelled. A steam locomotive bearing the name *The Ranger* on a brass nameplate was standing on one of the covered stabling tracks that led into the smaller of the two main blocks making up the Testing Station. Just cold ash where there should be a roaring fire in its belly, as it waited to be reunited with its tender. During the last fortnight, this steamer had been pushed aside to allow a new locomotive to take its place. There had been some exhilarating sessions that had impressed the watching engineers and boffins, but these were off-set in about equal part with the levels of frustration induced by spectacular failures of their innovative machine. But ever was the way with prototypes. The directors of Tomkins-Dunkler accepted the setbacks with equanimity but were now impatient to see their expensive creation out on the mainline.

'Time is money, Harvey. She's spent long enough going

nowhere fast behind closed doors. The board want to see her put through her paces with a train behind.' Harvey Race, the project director, had received similar telephone calls from the Tomkins-Dunkler head office in Birmingham every day and most had ended with the same pleading command from the company's chairman. 'We appreciate the teething problems, and these are to be expected, I suppose. However, we really must see her stretch her legs to show our financial backers. Your team can address any minor niggles along the way.'

'Not exactly niggles, sir. There was another overheating issue today...'

'Yes, you do keep reminding me, but I have good news. You will be pleased to hear we've not been idle. We're sending over some chaps, even as I speak. From English Electric and with brand new electrical gubbins. An improved version of that clever box of tricks that keeps playing up...'

'That is good news. We've had all manner of problems. It doesn't help that none of us apart from Cartwright and his sparks understand how the darned thing works!' Race had grumbled, as he usually did, and drawn heavily on his pipe. 'It keeps sending out the wrong instructions and everything goes belly up!'

The chairman laughed indulgently. This was his customary mid-afternoon call and he was enjoying a postprandial whisky in the boardroom which was making him affable despite the considerable investment riding on the project. The chairman and Race enjoyed a good relationship. 'I'm sure Cartwright can soon swap the gizmo around and then just you see her go... Now, take note; we've got clearance for a straight run to Marylebone and back along the London Extension tomorrow and every day next week, so have the chaps on standby...'

The following day, the temperamental locomotive in question stood outside the sliding doors which opened onto the hall containing the rolling road. Its modern lines in stark contrast to the pre-war design of *The Ranger* which was ignored by everyone and looked forlorn and unloved. This new and fantastical beast did at least exhaust steam from a vestigial chimney, although this was concealed by the air smoothed body, whilst the driving wheels bore a striking resemblance to those of the Royal Scot class steamer with which it was sharing the facility. In all other respects it looked more like something from the centre-fold artwork of *The Eagle* and perhaps driven by Dan Dare himself across the mauve and blue imagined mountain passes of Venus or the red deserts of Mars. It possessed driving cabs at both ends and the raked windows set above a centrally mounted headlamp which accounted for its American look. The white sides were smooth, with grills, inspection panels and small windows set flush into the metal cladding. Three stylish longitudinal 'stripes' of polished stainless steel ran the length of the locomotive. When the sun slid from behind a cloud the effect was dazzling and the wiser technicians reached for sunglasses and in so doing echoed the sinister images of servicemen compelled to watch terrifying atomic detonations. At such moments it became a shimmering block of white and silver with a number plate of yet more burnished metal and a dark blue background bearing the legend TD-GTX1 and a nameplate halfway along the side that declared this first Tomkins-Dunkler Gas Turbine Experimental locomotive was christened *The Difference Engine*.

Named after Charles Babbage's experimental adding machine, the directors felt this captured their optimistic vision of pushing the boundaries of what was possible and their belief that theirs would be 'the engine that made the difference'. It was to be the solution that would rid the world of coal and smoke and usher in a faster and more efficient form of railway haulage. The outrageously impractical colour scheme was designed to communicate a message of clean modernity. Ladies no longer need fear for their dresses and businessmen could arrive at their meetings with suits and white shirts unsullied by coal smuts. It remained to be seen if this confidence was misplaced. The roof was at least painted a more practical dark grey. At platform level, a passenger would see only air-smoothing worthy of a De Havilland *Comet* jetliner. It was sure to turn heads. Down at rail level, the low-slung body casing covered almost the top half of the coupled driving wheels, which were painted electric blue, whilst at each end, curved metal fairings dipped low over four-wheeled bogies. The whole effect was of massive weight and a brooding presence as she simmered quietly, still hooked up to various wires and fuel hoses snaking across the concrete apron.

However, *The Difference Engine* was both a beauty and beast. A temperamental machine that often refused to start and then once up and running would develop any one of numerous electrical faults or spring a leak and force an emergency shut down of the turbine. However, tomorrow was to see a run on the big railway and engineers were scurrying around like ants and there was a tense atmosphere developing, not eased by the presence of Richard Grimes.

Grimes was working for the prestigious publication *The Railway Magazine* and the only member of the press allowed privileged access to the project. His camera shutter constantly clicked and he never lost an opportunity to ask prying questions. 'I hear there's a run to London tomorrow?'

'Then you heard correct.' Chief electrical engineer Ellis Cartwright was carrying a stack of folders containing technical data from the test runs on the rolling road.

'Confident it will hold up? I heard there was another blowout...' Grimes had been excluded from the morning test and smarting from the snub.

Cartwright continued to walk, a look of irritation on his brow. 'One way to find out. That's why we call it a *test* run.' His voice was acerbic.

Cartwright didn't care for Grimes even if he did work for a fancy magazine. They'd known each other since school and Cartwright, whilst two years older, had never forgotten that

Grimes had relentlessly mocked and bullied him back then when he'd been a weedy, spotty and bespectacled youth.

'I heard there are problems with the robot control again?'

'With the what?' Cartwright stopped and gave Grimes a withering look.

'The electric robot that tells the engine what to do...'

Cartwright rolled his eyes in disdain. 'It's not a *robot,* idiot. Highly advanced electrical switching gear, but there's really no point trying to explain it to a layman...' He walked on.

'Is it true there's a new version on the way?' Grimes trotted after Cartwright.

'You'd best ask the lovely Miss Lessiter,' Cartwright replied over his shoulder, voice heavy with disdain. He was in no mood for sharing restricted information. 'I'm sure she will be delighted to tell you not to stick your bloody nose where it's not wanted!'

'What had you best ask me, Mr Grimes?' Doris Lessiter was the immaculately presented Head of Public Relations for Tomkins-Dunkler. She was trying not to betray she'd overheard Cartwright's impertinent comment.

'Doris... A vision of loveliness as always.' She was an archetype of the beautiful, yet cool blonde loved by directors of *film noir*.

'Drop the sweet talk, I'm off sugar.' She gave him her frostiest look. 'If there is technical information the company wishes to share, I shall supply the necessary briefing sheet, otherwise, as I have repeatedly reminded you, you will not ask members of the technical team about such matters.'

'Then I look forward to you keeping me abreast of new developments.' His lingering over the word 'abreast' whilst slowly inspecting Lessiter's undeniably fine figure made her skin crawl.

Grimes was an unattractive creature. Lessiter thought he looked older than his forty-nine years, with greasy hair desperately needing a trim draped over a fraying shirt collar and a copious expanse of belly straining buttons and trouser belt. His eyes constantly roved in an unpleasantly forensic manner. And then there was his camera. He was forever pointing this towards her in spite of being asked not to do so. It would be better to avoid the man altogether, but Lessiter was under instruction to keep Grimes from looking into places he shouldn't. The enforced proximity this demanded coupled with Grimes' unbridled lusting was a source of amusement amongst the otherwise serious technicians. Cartwright was not alone in making undeserved comments implying a close relationship between the two. Lessiter could not imagine anything worse and impatient for Grimes to get his story written and photographs in the bag. His assignment seemed worryingly open-ended and Grimes kept coming back each morning like an eager puppy dog. Perhaps once they'd got a few runs to London under their belt he would be called back to the magazine office. However, she prided herself in her professionalism and refused to rise to the lewd comments and in spite of the warmth of the day, managed to not look neither hot nor bothered. Which was perhaps more than could be said for some members of the engineering team.

Henry Gimball, the assistant project manager, was visibly fretting. A born worrier, he was prone to barking orders all day long, however his daily briefings with Lessiter were usually polite affairs. Lessiter walked over to Gimball who was flipping through a sheaf of notes clipped to a board before his fingers nervously harrowed his dampening hair into ridges.

'Mr Gimball?

'Yes, Doris.'

'I heard Mr Cartwright say there are problems with the control system and the engine broke down again. I'm worried about how this will look.'

'Don't fret, pet!' Gimball gave her a kindly smile, his North-Eastern accent soft and pleasing to the ear. 'We've been sent a newer version by those clever fellows up in English Electric.'

'Is this something I should be reporting?'

'Not yet. And keep Grimes away.'

'Gladly!' Lessiter was now looking across the apron towards the elderly wooden-bodied dynamometer car of North Eastern Railway vintage now being coupled to the engine. A more striking contrast between glossy air-smoothed metal and half-century-old varnished teak and gold leaf lettering would be hard to find. Men in white coats were stringing cables between the two vehicles in preparation for the test run. But where the devil was Grimes? He had an irritating habit of 'disappearing' and this made her uneasy.

'I don't want that blessed man taking pictures and asking questions when they fit the new part. It's hot technology and we need to keep this under our hats.'

'Understood, sir.'

'He is restricted to pictures taken lineside from now on, or perhaps a three-quarter view here. There is no need to allow him access inside the locomotive.'

'I shall make sure of it.' Lessiter was inwardly cheering. She was ready to square up to Grimes with his leery looks and wandering hands and tell him how the land lay. Lessiter reached for her own reporter's pad and pencil from inside her handbag. 'I think we should draft something in advance of tomorrow's run…'

'Fair point. Well, she's powerful!' Gimball grimaced as he recalled a catastrophic shredding of turbine blades during an earlier trial within the factory in Birmingham. However, he smiled reassuringly, masking his inward sense of irony. 'We're fighting to contain the incredible power and effectively transfer the massive torque she produces to the railhead. We've had a few small setbacks, but purely because of the sheer punch she packs!' Not exactly the whole truth, but Gimball knew how to play the publicity game. He turned and faced Lessiter. 'We've created a powerful vision of the future and technology needs to catch us up!'

'Golly gosh...' Lessiter scribbled furiously. This was Good News. Any mishaps and setbacks could be blamed on *It Being Too Powerful!* She used capital letters to reinforce the point in her notes. 'Gas turbine power is the way forward...' The Way Forward. She also liked how that sounded and could see it at the top of her next briefing sheet.

'We believe so. As you know, the Western region has been trialing their heavy old brute for years, but that's old hat. Too cumbersome and it stinks like a leaky petrol station. They don't call it the *Kerosene Castle* for nothing!' They both laughed. 'What we have here in *The Difference Engine* is a leap forward. Ah ha! And if I'm not mistaken, these must be our bonny lads from English Electric...'

A Morris van pulled to a stop and two young men hopped out and looked at the bizarre marriage of teak and gleaming metal. One whistled softly as a lab-coated technician hurried across and they opened the back of the J-type van. Gimball visibly relaxed. 'I have no doubt our gas turbine will drive a stake deep into the heart of the coal industry...'

Lessiter nodded sagely. She needed to be careful how this was reported. The coal unions would not react kindly to such claims. She might need to rein back a little on this point. She snapped her notebook closed and looking up, noticed that annoying photographer was pointing his camera at her *again*. How long had he been there? She didn't like the way the single unblinking eye of the lens was staring at her with his beady eye pressed to the viewfinder behind. She made the visual equivalent of a snarl and turned away. At least with his hands on his camera he couldn't be groping her bottom. She didn't trust Grimes as far as she'd like to push him. Under a speeding train, preferably...

Chapter Two

As Doris Lessiter considered how to tackle the unwelcome attentions of Grimes, Laura Green was in a happier state of mind. She was blissfully unaware of the impending catastrophe brewing like a summer thunderstorm. A storm as yet unseen and unheard but which would soon loom ominously over the horizon and shatter her world.

She lay on a tartan blanket further cushioned by the dry grass of the railway embankment. It was a lonely spot safe from prying eyes in spite of the close proximity to Leicester and just out of view from the passing trains. Both she and her fiancé Simon Howerth came from railway families and so the sights, sounds and smells of the railway were literally ingrained into the pores of their skin and seemed always to scent their hair, no matter how much the liberal attention of shampoo and hot water. They both loved to lie close to the railway in a private embrace, able to hear the comforting sounds of the steam trains thundering past and making the earth move beneath them. And so, on this gloriously hot day, Laura Green lifted her arms above her head into a position of open invitation and half-closed her eyes, listening to the singing of the birds and the distant bleating of young spring lambs.

They had a rare weekday to spend together, with both booked onto late shifts that evening. Howerth manning the Detective Department offices in Leicester Central for the night and Green in her lonely signal box at Desford Junction as cover for a colleague's absence through illness. Howerth was pleased she'd chosen to wear her signal woman's uniform for their romantic rendezvous. It was a purely practical choice as it allowed her to go straight to work and so could spend longer together. However, if Laura in uniform was not exciting enough, she'd already unhooked and removed her bra after a short wriggle and allowed her shirt to fall open and frame her lithe body. Simon's hands caressed and gently kneaded her soft flesh.

'Is it my imagination, or do you feel even more lovely than I remember...'

'You have an overactive imagination...'

'You feel very real right now.'

'As long as you like what you see.'

'Very much!'

'Then what are you waiting for?' Laura murmured. She guided one of his hands to the belt on her trousers. 'Why don't you take them off...There's no-one around.'

'*Laura*!' Simon's breathing was growing faster. 'You are keen...'

'Just being practical. I cannot clock on at work with grass stains on my clothes and neither should you.'

'I can be careful.'

She opened her blue eyes wide and looked at him with burning intent. 'Who asked you to be careful!'

Simon needed no further encouragement.

'And you won't want *that*. Not today. Not now.' Simon hesitated, with a packet of condoms in his hand. 'In three weeks, I lose this uniform forever and become Mrs Laura Howerth and I fully intend to do my duty as your wife.' She spoke with an exaggerated expression to her voice and even made a mock salute as she lay almost naked on the blanket, eyes alive with humour and desire.

'I say! But I still think it bad form you have to get the heave-ho just for getting married.' Simon was removing the last of his clothes.

'*C'est la vie*!' She threw her arms wide. 'Those are the rules and nothing we can do about 'em. And besides, time and tide wait for no girl. If we're going to start a family, then we'd best get on with it...'

'You're not old!'

16

'Twenty-seven is dangerously close!'

'You look beautiful.' He gorged his eyes on her smooth skin and the pink rosebuds of her nipples.

'I can see you think so.' She giggled. 'Giving up work might have its compensations. I want to walk down that aisle as pregnant as any woman can be!' Her eyes dropped to admire the form of her future husband bathed in sunlight. 'So, you had best keep your side of the deal!'

Laura was in a joyous mood, but she wasn't telling Simon - not *just* yet - that she was already with child. The latest wedding dress fitting had almost given the game away. She suspected neither the seamstress nor her mother had been fooled. Mum had raised three children and Laura had discovered that a simple calculation working back from her eldest brother's birthdate and the date of their wedding anniversary told an inescapable truth. Her mother had asked her to twirl around whilst perched on a chair before quietly observing 'you've put on a little around the tummy area…' The seamstress had nodded sagely and suggested she 'let an allowance in the seams around the bust.' Laura was sure all three were complicit in sharing the secret. *An allowance.* Laura liked the way the two wise women had exchanged glances over this word. As she once more closed her eyes the better to savour the moment, she decided that sometimes a little secret could not hurt.

It could be allowed.

Chapter Three

'Mr Grimes, a word, please.' Miss Lessiter was looking pin-up pretty in a pale blue twinset that fitted like a glove. As this was the day of the first test run to Marylebone, she was eager to present the correct image upon their arrival in London, an event bound to stir up interest.

'The directors have made the decision you have sufficient images of the locomotive's inner workings and the team working thereon. They ask you to concentrate on suitably impressive images of our engine in action on the mainline. Lineside shots are the order of the day, henceforth,' she icily intoned.

'I'd hoped to snap some of her being prepared for the inaugural run,' pleaded Grimes.

She gave him the benefit of her smile; all red lipstick and coolness in the eye. 'That will not be possible. I suggest you find a suitable vantage point as we shall make just one round trip per day.'

'This is short notice. If I had known…'

Miss Lessiter was not to be swayed and was quietly taking delight in giving him his marching orders. 'I have prepared the estimated timings passing key stations on the run to London.' She handed a sheet of paper to Grimes. 'You have time enough if you start now.' Another flash of her painted smile. 'We shall repeat the same sequence until Friday. By then, if not before -,' she raised a perfectly manicured eyebrow '- you will have sufficient material for your article. We are eager you make the deadline for next months' edition.'

'I understand.' Grimes fiddled with the strap on his camera case.

'Now, if you will excuse me, I have a lot to prepare. I must stress that with immediate effect, access to the Testing Station and *The Difference Engine* is restricted.' Miss Lessiter spun about and trotted off as Grimes watched.

'Got yer marching orders?' Ellis Cartwright appeared beside Grimes. 'About time. We've had it up to here with you snooping around...'

'Sod off, *Speccy*.'

'Is that the best you can do, *Grimey*?' Cartwright sneered at Grimes, contempt in his voice. 'No one's called me that since we were at school. You're pathetic, do you know that?' He laughed unpleasantly. 'At least I made something of my life. I wear these 'specs' to do my job as Chief Electrical Engineer. What have you achieved?' He managed to sound like he was addressing a lower form of life. Grimes held his tongue, but his jaw muscles twitched. 'A jobbing photographer? Not even a good one.' Cartwright made to walk off.

'I work for the best in the business!'

'No. You *used* to. Occasionally. I've not seen anything in *The Railway Magazine* in well over a year.'

'How would you know?' Grimes sounded less confident.

'Because I've subscribed since I was in college,' Cartwright gave a triumphant smile. He leaned closer, voice low and almost a hiss. 'I know the truth about you...'

Grimes balled his fists and scrunched the timesheet he'd been given in so doing. 'That makes two of us,' his voice was just as low and loaded with loathing. 'I know all about you...'

'Don't know what you mean.'

'Then wait and see.'

'You're full of wind and gas...'

But Grimes had turned his back and replied over his shoulder. 'You'll find out. When I'm ready!'

Cartwright swore at Grimes' back. He noticed his colleague Mercer was watching the exchange with curiosity. 'He drives me nuts. Just a second-rate chancer,' Cartwright offered by way of an explanation.

'Can't say I'll miss him either,' Mercer agreed.

Chapter Four

Privately, Grimes was far from unhappy in being ordered to the trackside. He'd gathered all he could working up close with the engineering team and the recent exchange with Cartwright warned him it was time to take a step back. It would be sensible to lay low from now on and gather the missing information he needed behind the scenes and out of sight. Banishment to the lineside gave him the perfect excuse to change tactics. He could bag a couple of decent shots each day and still have enough time to follow up the loose ends and tentative leads he'd uncovered. He was still some way from building a solid enough case to take to the police but knew he was getting close. This was the shake-up he needed. He'd taken too long and dipped too deep into his depleted financial reserves getting this far. He now needed to move things along more quickly. Staying holed up in that rented room in Rugby for another week was unbearable. It was time for action. Grimes was walking faster than usual towards Rugby Central station, mind clear about the day ahead. He needed to get to Loughborough, and *The Difference Engine* could go hang for today.

A little over an hour and a half later, Grimes exited the booking hall at Loughborough Central. This was built to one side of the road bridge that spanned the station with its many tracks that lay below. He turned left along Great Central Road, keeping the allotments to his left until he reached Little Moor Lane. This narrow road crossed a typically humpbacked canal bridge and offered access onto the towpath beside the Grand Union Canal. Immediately, the atmosphere changed. It was quieter and the sound of birdsong increased as he walked beside sluggish canal water that saw virtually no traffic these days and was becoming clogged by algae and duckweed.

The towpath however was still well-used and he made quick progress and was in time to see the tail end of his departing train cross the lattice bridge that spanned the canal at a skew angle. The canal now swung left and made its secretive way through the town, passing house backs and blank walls of manufactories and shuttered and empty warehouses. The sound of the town going about its daily business was hushed and virtually invisible, except when he walked beneath the Nottingham Road and Meadow Lane bridges. He paused to take a photograph of the path leading from the canal up onto the busy road that stretched out of town towards the Falcon Engineering Works. He got glimpses of the impressive collection of buildings and associated railway sidings of this famous locomotive works. It would be an easy route to work for someone living on a houseboat berthed along the canal. This confirmed his thinking. Just another small piece of the jigsaw puzzle he was assembling.

Walking on, he reached the Chain Bridge, but chose not to cross. He did not need to follow the canal into the cul-de-sac of what must once have been a busy quay. Even from a distance, it signalled dereliction. The water was foul and brackish and there was litter strewn everywhere. The banks packed with stands of rosebay willowherb, stinging nettles and viciously spiked arms of blackberry bushes crossed the access path. Two rusting narrow boats lay partly submerged, abandoned and unloved. It was a forlorn place, with trade stolen first by the railway and now by the many lorries roaring across the road bridges.

Grimes walked on and soon out into the open country and the depressing mood of dereliction lifted almost immediately as he walked in sunlight past mature trees and rolling fields. It was the kind of walk a young woman may well have been happy to take on the arm of a man she trusted. She would have been pleasantly surprised to be able to walk beside this gently flowing tea-coloured canal amidst idyllic English countryside after only a relatively short train ride to Loughborough. It had been a fine summer's day and as she linked arms, the man she was with might have pointed out the moorhens and named the wildflowers as he drew her closer to his lair...

He took a couple more photographs. They would help reinforce his thought process. Help him visualise the course of that fateful, one-way journey in a series of images. He knew he was right. It was just a case of proving it.

Ahead lay another humpbacked bridge, allowing access to the far bank where the flowing River Soar joined the canal. The combined waters opening into a wider pool on a bend where the tiny Black Book also joined forces to lend more speed to what was now a fully flowing river. Grimes surveyed the scene. He reached into his camera bag and extracted a packet of photographic prints. Most were recent images he'd taken and had printed at Boots the chemists in Rugby, but amongst them was one older print. Yellowing at the edges and with one corner dog-eared, but the amateur photographer had used a decent camera and taken care of the exposure. Grimes held it up and although many years and a world war had passed since the shutter had clicked to capture that fleeting moment in time, the trees were easily identifiable as was the curve of the riverbank. There was the indentation in the far bank large enough to berth a single boat. There was the run of wooden fence that offered both view and access into the field beyond and the short walk to the distinctive clump of trees standing on a grassy mound. This was an ancient tump. It was thought to be an iron-age construction although the original function was long forgotten. Trees grew in a copse on top with the gaps between filled with thick, wild vegetation and ignored by the farmer.

If Grimes used a magnifying glass to inspect the photo print it was just possible to read the faded name painted on what, even back then, was an ageing narrowboat. *Blackbird*. A skein of smoke rose from the chimney in the cabin roof.

Someone was home.

He took a photograph from the same spot. He'd like to find a way across and explore the tump. Inspect the ground beneath the trees and choking vegetation, but he would need the use of a boat for that to cross the river. This could wait. After so many years it would be just a mass of tangled undergrowth and leaf mould. It would need a professional team to do a thorough dig to ensure it was done properly and under supervision. He must not tamper with the scene of the crime and potentially damage any evidence. And he could not bear to be the one that uncovered her remains.

Standing there, he was sure he was right. That was where she lay. He felt a pricking in his eyes and a violent surge of anger. He wanted to kill the man responsible for this. Devise a slow and unpleasant death.

He took a deep breath and tried to calm his emotions. This was not a time to lose his cool. He would see justice was done. For now, she could lie there a while longer. If there was any consolation, it was at least a peaceful spot.

* * * *

June 1928. Rosalind Tustain watched the fields of cows and sheep roll past the train window, shadows of the puffs of steam rising and falling over the hedgerows and fields, the telegraph wires rising and dipping rhythmically in time with the beat of the engine.

Was this crazy? Was she being foolhardy to travel out of Woodford for a secret rendezvous with a man? But they knew each other, had known of each other all their short lives and after all it was not far to Loughborough. It made sense to meet there. They were both too well known in Woodford and she preferred to escape the watching eyes and gossiping voices. People would talk if they as much as walked along a road together. That was the reality of living in a close-knit community. It could be suffocating. A gentle walk in the sunshine along a canal to take tea on his houseboat was an appealing proposition. A houseboat! She'd never seen one of these, let alone stepped aboard and it sounded slightly exotic and even a little bit romantic. A brew of tea on a Primus stove onboard and then walk back to the station. She'd made it very clear what time her train departed from Loughborough Central and he'd promised he'd make sure she was on it. 'Scout's honour, cross my heart and hope to die' he'd said in a rather childish manner, but which had also made her giggle. She turned the little cardboard Edmunson return ticket in her hands. Just over two hours together. Not so long and surely no harm could come of a stroll by a canal?

Perhaps she *might* let him hold her hand. A peck on the cheek as a greeting *could* be allowed, and if he behaved himself and acted gallantly, maybe a little squeeze and a longer kiss before she boarded her train home. Why not? She smoothed her dress and admired the generous swell of her breasts and wondered if she dared undo the top button. Her shape was unfashionably curvy, and she would never fit in one of those 'flapper' dresses the rich young things wore in Paris and London these days, but like her best friend Margy said; 'Boobs like *those* don't go out of fashion, Rosie.' Tustain enjoyed the effect they had on men whatever their age. She could coax almost anything she liked out of a man just by setting her shoulders back and adopting a winning smile.

That's how she'd got this date.

Agreed, he was no film star pin up, but she'd known of him for most of her life and he seemed a quiet, thoughtful kind of man and had a decent apprenticeship with a big company in Loughborough. He had prospects and was going places. A world away from the rough lads in Woodford who were either sons of railwaymen or farmers. He was nothing like Grimey or Green, who were a right pair of lads. She shook her head slightly, but a wry smile formed as she thought about those two tearaways. Drinking and smoking and wolf-whistling at her and always trying to steal a kiss - or a grope. It was Grimey who made the running, but his mate was never far behind, even if he was quieter. Margy reckoned it was the quiet ones you should be wary of... Having said that, she'd been furious with Grimey that time on the bridge. She should have pushed him over the side and under a passing train. She could have murdered him there and then - and of course there was that gawping idiot Green; just standing and looking and no doubt loving everything he saw. And he'd seen plenty...

All right, Grimey *was* better looking than her date today and he *was* quite a charmer in his irritating way. And didn't Grimey know it! When he wasn't drinking, he could be amusing and good company and once she'd got over her initial embarrassment and humiliation of the 'bridge incident' she and her girlfriends had laughed uproariously about it. And perhaps she'd even quite enjoyed the dangerous thrill of it, looking back. Not that she'd ever admit that to them! Perhaps that's why she'd gone back for more... On her terms of course and demanding the cost of a new dress as down payment before any hope of even a single button undone. But no, there was no future with Grimey. Tustain had no intention of marrying him and the constant subterfuge of their secret meetings that were essential to avoid scandal, whilst fun at first, were already starting to lose their appeal.

Getting away on a train out of that small town where everyone knew everything about everyone, or liked to think they did, was quite liberating. She felt freer already. The ticket was inexpensive, and she'd only be gone for the afternoon and should be able to get back without anyone noticing. Anyway, she was very nearly eighteen and could take a train ride if she wanted. Why was it anybody's business if she did? And besides, he was two years older and wiser than Grimes and Green. It was just a walk along a canal. Dipping a toe in the water, so as to speak. She smiled to herself at the image and thought herself clever at dreaming it up.

She'd be home for tea and nobody would be any the wiser and that included Grimey. Ok, she *was* standing Grimey up, but there was nothing she could do about that without causing a scene and making complications. It wouldn't do any harm to keep him on his toes and she could always tell him a white lie about not being able to get away. And she *had* left him a note and that funny little pebble that looked a bit like a heart. Not that she was giving her heart to Grimey. Just something to make him think nice thoughts about her ready for the next time she felt the urge...

Chapter Five

It was a day made for escaping the smoky confines of the office, and WPC's Lucy Lansdowne and Jane Benson were seated outside a cafe on King Street, a few steps from New Walk. This was busy with many citizens of Leicester enjoying the dappled shade from the trees lining the pedestrian thoroughfare that ran as straight as the Roman road it followed. A canvas awning was opened over the front windows of their cafe and in a move the WPCs considered very '*continentale*', the proprietor had moved several small tables and chairs outside so customers could enjoy the clement weather. Their heavy uniforms of black serge, dark hats and buttoned-up blouses with ties at the neck ensured they were feeling the heat and they were delighted to be able to sit in the shade and fresh air as they ate their cold lunch.

The workload for the last few months had been largely routine, and the Detective Department office had become more relaxed than usual. A shared lunch away from the office was not going to be frowned upon.

'Jane, I've hardly said more than good morning and good evening to you for what seems like weeks!'

'It's this pilfering case I'm working on. It's taken a lot of footwork and then checking absolute *mountains* of paperwork. Tedious stuff, but it needs doing. Mellor tasked me to collect every scrap of information I can find to build the case. It means I spend most of my days in Annesley engine shed.'

'This is the engine oil theft?'

'That's the one. Two rogues siphoning off a small percentage of every delivery. Virtually unnoticeable, but as they use hundreds of gallons a year even this adds up to a tidy illegal income.'

'But not a workplace you would choose...'

'Better believe it, Lucy. The engine shed is huge and utterly filthy.' Benson sipped some tea. 'I don't want to put you off your sandwich, so I won't mention the latrines.'

Lansdowne made a pained expression. 'Best draw a veil over that, please. And what about our beloved sergeant? He's given you some free rein?'

'Actually, he has. The sarge drives us hard and is tough as old boots as you know, but at least he gets the job done. I'm enjoying having some leeway and being trusted to get on with the job. I suppose it helps that nothing dreadfully serious has come up for months.'

'I know what you mean. I've sorted, tidied and organised our filing system so it's a model of perfection. I'm desperate for a good murder!'

Benson laughed 'Be careful what you wish for. Our two detectives do seem very mellow these days as a result of this pace of life. And Simon has been a help. I send him off on any amount of donkey work and he's happy enough.' She sipped some tea. 'Did you know he was getting married?'

'I'd heard something,' Lansdowne replied. 'Although he seems coy about discussing it.'

'Typical man.' Benson smiled. 'Can't get a word out of him about anything interesting, but ask him about a steam engine's workings or railway operations and you can't shut him up!'

They laughed.

'He's marrying into a railway family so at least his poor wife will know what she's taking on.'

'A signal woman, I think?'

'That's right. Laura Green. She's a relative of our Mavis on reception.'

'No joking? Maybe that's why Simon is being coy...' Lansdowne pondered.

'Laura works not so far from here at Desford Junction. But she's having to give it up.'

'Because she's getting married?'

'You know how it goes.'

'I do.'

A pensive silence fell between the two women for a moment. Benson spoke first. 'Lucy, are you *really* breaking off the engagement?'

'I am.' Lansdowne stared at her half-eaten sandwich. 'With a heavy heart. It's not been an easy decision, but then if I am honest to myself, it has been brewing for a year.'

'You've been wavering that long?'

'Not acknowledging it more like. Living so far apart it was easy to just sweep any worries under the carpet and pretend everything is fine and ignore the problem. Push it aside for another month and avoid facing the reality when we meet. I've done that for long enough.'

'Is it just the separation, or something more?' Benson sipped her tea.

'I was in love with Frank. Perhaps I still am. He's done nothing wrong.' She paused. 'We entered into this agreement honestly and became engaged and intended to marry and settle down, maybe have children.' Lansdowne looked wistfully at a young couple walking arm in arm along King Street. 'I wanted to share my life with him. I'd had enough of my pokey digs that smell of boiled cabbage and waiting in my dressing gown in the mornings for my turn in the icy bathroom or sitting alone in the evening with a mug of cocoa.' She smiled at her friend. 'You know how it is.'

'Don't I just!' Benson replied with passion. 'I once thought being independent and getting a pay packet would give me freedom and space to express myself, but instead, I stare at dingy house backs and watch a succession of residents walk to the outside privy or count starlings on the ridge tiles. That is, until a certain Mr Hawkes crashed into my life. He's shaken everything up. I can even count starlings on a London rooftop now!' They both laughed. 'I know he's not the marrying kind, Lucy and I knew that from the start. But you both seemed so clear about what you wanted?'

'I know. Frankie Wainwright, the young and ambitious architecture student with the promise of a decent career and matching salary and the thought that one day we'd even build our own home with central heating and a wonderful kitchen and bathroom. A house like you see in the Ideal Home Exhibition catalogues. But it was just a dream...'

'There's no harm in having a dream.'

Lansdowne chewed on her sandwich for a moment. 'I'm not so sure now. The contrast between dream and reality starts to grow wider as the months pass.'

'But where's the problem? Frankie moved to West Germany and from what you've told me is securing good contracts rebuilding the place. Why not join him?'

'He's doing very well. He's got a natural gift. I knew he was clever, and it makes me proud to hear how he's taken to civil engineering projects like the proverbial ducks take to water in Bradgate Park...'

'So?'

'So, I encouraged him and delighted in his letters and it became clear he wanted me to join him in West Germany. Become his wife and settle down in a dull place called Dusseldorf. He showed me photographs. It was pulverised by the bomber boys and now being completely rebuilt. Never a picture book before, it looks grim and austere now, if you ask me. All concrete and glass and whilst Frankie thinks it 'modern and exciting', I find it soulless. It's a dreary part of the world and I'm not sure I'm cut out to be a devoted *hausfrau* amongst the relentless reconstruction of broken railway bridges and the building of blocks of flats. I'm sorry to say it, but I'm not sure I want a child of mine growing up German. Gosh, that sounds a bit awful...'

Benson looked at the trees and sunlight playing on New Walk, then the other way towards the grandiose form of Fenwicks department store on Belvoir Street. The stylish shop was all Arts and Crafts inspired gables and bargeboards, stone mullioned windows and doorways and delicate metal railings around balconies bathed in sunlight. It looked like a glorious baronial hall. 'When you put it like that, I can see your point. But you're a blue-eyed blonde. You'd fit in perfectly!' Benson laughed and winked.

'Don't I know it? But we shouldn't make fun and the past is the past.' Lansdowne managed a wry smile. 'How selfish I sound. Frank is doing important work and I believe him when he says most of the people he works with are thoroughly decent. I really *should* join him and make a home together and be thankful.'

'But you won't?'

'No...' Lansdowne fiddled with the teaspoon beside her cup. 'I love my work here too much. For all I complain about the hours and the loneliness and my landlady's God-awful cooking, it's having a proper, decent job that makes me who I am. I love my work and I'm proud to do it. I even like wearing the uniform.'

'Me too.'

'We're darned lucky you realise, Jane? Apologies for my language, but I get hot under the collar when I think about it.'

'Easy enough in this weather...'

'If I leave and become Mrs Wainwright, then that's it. I can never go back. I forsake my career forever. Do you know we are the *only* two WPC's left in British Railways? There are plenty of women in secretarial roles of course, but just us two in uniform, fighting crime.'

'Seriously?'

'If I go, then I leave you standing alone. I'm not prepared to do it.'

'Lucy, you don't give up on your engagement just because of me.'

'I'm not. Believe me. I made the decision some time ago as I sat in my crummy little room with the gas fire that barely works and realised that I'd miss it more than I cared to admit. I was reading a book at the time that reminded me of what we have. It made me realise we're the lucky few. The war gave us a chance and we took it, but we live in a very different world now, and despite the many empty promises, I fear we girls are being pushed out of the interesting work — and not just in policing.'

'What was the book?'

'It came out a few months ago. I saw it in a book shop and the cover drew me in. It showed a good looking woman standing in front of a warplane. It tells the story of the girls who flew in the Air Transport Auxiliary. They delivered Spitfires, Stirling bombers and every other plane imaginable to the airfields throughout the war. Many of the ATA were women. Brave and brilliant pilots and equally able as the men, if not more so in some cases.'

'I've not heard about them.'

'And you know why that is. An uncomfortable truth more convenient to sweep under the carpet. The author is Veronica Volkersz and she's still flying, but knows her days are numbered. Commercial licences cost a packet and women cannot afford to gain or renew them as they can't be sure to get a flying job to repay the cost. The commercial companies don't like women pilots regardless of their abilities, so that's it. A closed shop. Male pilots only. It makes me angry.'

Benson sipped tea as she considered what she'd heard. 'Things are closing in. I've felt it. We could be detectives. We both *should* be detectives by now — but it's not allowed.'

'Mellor took your place as DS.' Lansdowne sounded bitter.

'Don't be silly.'

'It's true! We all know that job had your name written all over it. The DCI was as unhappy about the decision as anyone else.'

'I'm not sure about that...' Benson replied. 'Never mind, that is water under the bridge and we're still fortunate.

Vignoles is sympathetic and gives us a freer hand than many others and even the sergeant allows us some slack. We must make the most of it. Perhaps that's why I hooked up with an unmarriageable man. No danger of getting hitched and forced to hang up my uniform.'

Lansdowne laughed. 'Let's see if we can't break through the office door and make detective grade.'

'I'll drink to that.' Benson drained her teacup.

Chapter Six

Grimes stepped off the train at Rugby Central and climbed the stairs into the booking hall and out onto Lower Hillmorton Road. He was no detective but knew enough of the way the police worked to appreciate that more hard evidence was needed. He'd bagged a few more pictures today that would be added to his file and visiting the location had convinced him he knew where her remains were buried. It was an overlooked spot despite being marked on a map. Just a stand of unremarkable trees on a slight hump in a farmer's field and there was no compelling reason for anyone to tackle the stands of stinging nettles and duck under the rusty barbed wire that encircled the tump. It would be odd if even one person fought their way in from one year to the next. It was a clever choice. Grimes was also sure his suspect had been living on a boat moored against the river bank a short distance away at the time of her disappearance. It was just down for him to prove it.

Grimes headed off on the short walk back towards his digs, hands in pockets, his head full of thoughts. He should have taken more care. Rooting around in an unsolved murder case was not a game. Stirring up the filthy sediment of murderous intent should not be tackled lightly, and Grimes would have been wise to proceed cautiously and cover his tracks. He was walking along a quiet suburban street that petered out in a dead-end and a dusty path across wasteland towards the boundary of the former LNWR mainline. If Grimes had been more alert and looked around to check the street, his follower would have been exposed, but he seemed lost in his thoughts and remained oblivious to the threat.

He stepped into the hall of his landlady's house and saw a message pinned to the noticeboard in her handwriting. Someone had telephoned for him. Almost nobody had the number and the house telephone was something the landlady reserved for dire emergency or interminable calls to her sister most evenings. Miss Lessiter was one of the few who knew his temporary address and must have shared the number. He grimaced as he read the note. The editor of *The Railway Magazine* wished to speak with him urgently. The landlady would never agree to him calling from there and Grimes had no desire for anyone to overhear the bawling out he was surely about to receive. The editor, Mr BWC Cooke, would still be at his desk if he hurried.

Unbeknown to Grimes, his follower was almost rumbled by his sudden reappearance at the front door. Grimes however once again kept his head down and hurried back to the station where there was a telephone kiosk outside the entrance. It was unoccupied and Grimes was soon dialing London, shaking pennies into his free hand as he did so. This was going to be awkward.

'Mr Cooke, I understand you wish to speak…'

'I do.' The voice was cold and austere as it cut him off mid-sentence. 'I have had a most curious conversation with a certain Miss Lessiter. Charming woman. Very efficient. She gave me to understand you have made claims to be representing *The Railway Magazine* and assembling some kind of feature on the TD-GTX1 at our behest. Please explain how she has been given this false impression?'

'Mr Cooke, I apologise if there has been any misunderstanding…'

'There has. Your apology is not accepted.'

'As a freelancer who has worked for your fine magazine on numerous occasions…'

'Three occasions, hardly 'numerous'. The last time was eight months ago.'

'Was it really? Gosh, time flies.' Grimes laughed but received a stony silence in return. More pennies pushed into the slot. 'Mr Cooke, you know how it is in this trade; one has to work hard to secure work and take that one photograph that commands attention and...'

'Yes, yes...' A heavy sigh of resignation could be heard down the line. 'Just tell me, what *have* you been doing whilst taking our name in vain?'

'I admit I may have over-egged the link to your magazine to win their confidence, but I have secured some good material and a fine set of images I intend to offer to yourselves. As an exclusive! A unique inside glimpse into this innovative gas turbine.'

'You misrepresented our good name and falsified your status by implying you were on our payroll.'

'Perhaps when you see the images you will feel it was worth taking the chance?'

'Mr Grimes, you are not the first nor I suppose will be the last freelancer to stick their neck out in this manner.' The editor's voice sounded weary. 'Let me make it plain. I do not condone your actions. You are fortunate Miss Lessiter was understanding and we were able to come to an equable arrangement. You will send everything to me, copy, negatives and prints, and I shall see if there is anything useable. If it is, you will receive a flat fee. If not, it goes on the fire and you will walk away and consider yourself lucky.'

'A fair offer,' Grimes forced himself to remain polite.

'I understand there are test runs all week. One action shot will suffice. I expect everything you have obtained delivered to my desk by Monday morning. Is that understood?'

'It is.'

'Very well, good evening.' The line went dead.

If nothing else, Grimes needed a story that packed a punch. He'd invested heavily and needed to earn some money from the magazine.

Chapter Seven

Grimes flopped on the creaky bed in his rented room at the back of Winfield Street in Rugby. He'd shrugged off his uncomfortable shoes with the thinning soles and lay propped against a pillow that leaked feathers. He was tired after a full day and had much to think about and the awkward call to the editor had given him a headache. He needed to get a 'money shot' and get it fast. A photograph that would win Mr Cooke over and earn him some much-needed funds. Not only must he get this image by the end of the week, but he couldn't afford to allow this to get in the way of his true reason for being in Rugby. He was close to solving a cold case that lay forgotten to all but the family and those once close to the beautiful young woman cruelly robbed of her life. He'd worried away at this on and off for years and wanted some form of justice for her.

The rougher the better…

But could he really kill the man he considered guilty? Would that not just make him equally bad in the eyes of the law? As his head ached and his unfit body lay like a beached whale, he knew this was not a realistic proposition. He needed to order his thoughts, update his file of documents and photographs that lay inside his suitcase beneath the bed and decide what should be his next move. When he felt the case was proven he would go to the police with his evidence and let justice be served.

It was hard to think straight. His landlady, Mrs Meldrum, had returned home whilst he had been telephoning Mr Cooke and was boiling something malodorous for his evening meal. When he'd opened the front door the second time she'd poked her head out of the kitchen to tell him what he already knew about the message then slammed the door closed in a cloud of pungent steam. He could hear pans clattering in a manner that communicated ongoing disapproval about taking messages for unloved lodgers. It was neither relaxing nor inspiring.

Through the open bedroom window, he could hear the sound of children larking about in a park on their way home after school and the passing of a fast goods on the former Great Central line that ran across the bottom of the garden on an embankment. This proximity ensured he was also suffering from a lack of sleep as the night freight trains shook the window frame. Even more frequent were the hooting trains on the busier West Coast mainline, but these were at least muffled by distance and the trees now coming into leaf. He closed his eyes and gave a few minutes to decode the different sounds of the railway, concentrating on the huffs and puffs and ring of metal wheels on rails all of which was more soothing than the aggressive clatter of pans on the stove. It almost lulled him to sleep. However, a sudden strident whistle sounded like an alarm call and served to snap Grimes out of his daydreaming. He opened his eyes and looked up at the tobacco-stained Anaglypta wallpaper pasted to the ceiling and the hideous lampshade hanging by a furred brown cable.

Grimes hauled himself into a sitting position and the bedsprings complained. He was overweight and unshaven, but this at least was excusable as there was never any hot water, let alone one of those mythical baths the landlady claimed was available once a week. Excuses aside, he was letting things slip. Too many bags of chips had been eaten from the wrapper washed down by numerous pints of beer. He gloomily contemplated his rotund figure and the shabby bleakness of his room only marginally improved by the golden glow of the late afternoon sunlight. Flirting with Miss Lessiter was a charade to deflect attention amongst the Tomkins-Dunkler team, but also his only source of pleasure these days. Who was he kidding? Fantasising about bringing the lovely Doris back *here*? It was ludicrous. With her crisply ironed blouses, clouds of perfume and film-star make-up, looking like Rugby's reply to Hollywood's Grace Kelly, she was the kind of girl who'd expect to be wined and dined and treated like a lady. A Babycham and prawn cocktail in one of those swanky new Berni Inns at the very least! He could not imagine her peeling off that twinset to reveal sheer stockings and expensive underwear whilst avoiding the ragged holes and indeterminate stains in the garishly patterned carpet. There was no chance she'd allow him to make the bed complain even if he could smuggle her upstairs.

Where did it all go wrong? There was a time he could charm any girl he wished into his bed, or so memory told him. Back then he'd been tolerably fit with a taut physique and a fat wallet in his jacket, snappily dressed and brimful of swagger. He'd taken a wrong turning or two somewhere down the road. He ran a hand across his face and reached for the fresh packet of photographic prints. He fanned them on the eiderdown and took a moment to rest his eyes on a few pleasing images surreptitiously taken of Doris. She was scowling in one after catching him in the act. It just made her look more attractive. Dammit, she had good legs. He put these aside and looked at the others. But what did they tell him? What did they *prove*? Was he just wasting his time?

Grimes opened his little suitcase and extracted what he optimistically called his 'case file'. On the first page was a list of names, numbers and addresses he'd copied from a telephone directory in Loughborough. He had an idea to try and trace one or other of the two senior officers who'd worked the original investigation. Both were retired now and he had to hope neither had left the area. It was a long shot but he had a list of five bearing the same surname of the detective sergeant on the case in 1928. Two shared the same initial. He stared at the address beside each in the vain hope they could tell him which, if either, were correct. He really should take the plunge and place the calls and hope he struck lucky, but something held him back. It was too late in the day now. He was going to ask a man he'd never met about a long-dormant police investigation and would need to establish some measure of trust if he was to get any joy. He doubted if either of the now elderly former detectives would welcome having their evening disturbed by his questions. He'd put this off all week and knew he would do so again. He needed to work out exactly what to say in a few succinct lines that would persuade a time-served professional to take him seriously and agree to meet.

Grimes was resigned to another day passing without making this vital step and instead just placed the new photographs between fresh blank pages of his bulging file ready to be pasted in later and closed it. Too many thoughts were swirling around his head for yet another difficult telephone conversation. Memories of a time that felt like a lifetime ago and yet still so painfully vivid were crowding in.

He thought about his old mate Davey. David Green. Two hot-headed lads living it up as best they could in their curious little railway town where the best fun to be had was drinking bottles of stolen beer, smoking fags, watching the trains go by and eyeing up the girls. And Rosie had been the loveliest of them all...

Grimes stood up and impatiently paced the room. Was he responsible for what happened? There were plenty in Woodford who thought he was. That was why he upped and left in the autumn of 1929 and rarely ever returned. He'd been too casual with Rosie. Off hand and arrogant, just wanting a kiss and a fondle . . . and a bit more. She'd not taken him seriously and had been tempted away only to meet an awful fate. He couldn't bear to follow that line of thought to its conclusion, only allowing an image of the tree-topped grassy knoll beside the Soar to stand for all that must have followed.

For years he'd just felt intense anger and betrayal that had eaten away inside like a canker. An ugly knot of jealous fury that Rosie could accept a 'better' invitation. An invitation to walk off and meet the man who would take her life. Not that he'd exactly set a gold standard. He'd made a bad first impression and even if they'd later kissed, made up, fumbled furtively behind the sand drying hut in the loco depot and stolen kisses after dark in that secret meeting place. Later he got even more than he dared dream of, rolling in the grass on that glorious occasion, and to think that daft twerp Davey Green even copped them at it. What an eyeful he'd got! Ok, it had added to the thrill... knowing his best mate, who he knew lusted after Rosie as much as he did, had seen her stripped naked and straddling him. Luckily her eyes had been closed or else she'd probably have screamed and leaped off him at the worst moment... It was a delicious memory, but try as he might to hold on to it, it shredded like a cloud of steam...

It was obvious Rosie had been taking what she wanted on her terms, deliberately playing him as a foolish cuckold even as she moaned in pleasure. She didn't really want him, just used him for her own gratification. Perhaps this was all he deserved? He'd been inebriated that day on the bridge, and he'd acted like a brute. The sun and alcohol and then the vision of Rosie in that thin summer dress that left little to the imagination meant desire had got the better of him. If he could just turn back time and start over, perhaps things might have worked out differently.

Perhaps she'd still be alive?

The smell of gravy and cabbage assaulted his nostrils and he realised he couldn't stomach another of his landlady's unpalatable meals. The sudden urge to leave the house prompted a flash of inspiration. He had an idea how to set up the perfect shot to win over even the most sceptical picture editor! He needed to see Davey. He was in his thoughts this evening, so why not go over there? After so many years it would be rude not to call in whilst he was working the same line. Offer an olive branch and put the past behind them, then twist his old chum's arm to help get what he needed. He'd always been able to get Davey to agree to his ideas no matter how outrageous. The soft lad never stood up for himself. Aside from the time Davey landed that punch just as he was about to rip Rosie's dress off…

Grimes grabbed his jacket and wallet and ran down the stairs, shouting that he was 'going out until late' and not bothering to wait for the angry reaction this was bound to elicit. He'd be out of the place by the weekend and would ride out the wrath of Mrs Meldrum.

Chapter Eight

David Green gave a nod of greeting as the night duty signalman stepped into Woodford Halse Signal Box Number 4. Green rang a series of bell codes in answer to the melodious tinkle that sounded moments before his colleague arrived. He then pulled off a couple of levers and gave the handles of each an unnecessary wipe with the cloth used when touching these almost sacred levers mounted in their heavy cast-iron frame. A signalman never allowed sweaty flesh to tarnish the polished handles. Satisfied his train was set to enter the section safely, Green made an entry in the logbook, checked the clock on the wall, noted the time and signed himself off. 'All yours, Geoff.'

'Thanks. Anything to report?' The new signalman had hung his jacket on the peg beside the door and was running his expert eye over everything from block telegraph equipment to the measure of water in the kettle.

'All fine and dandy. We had that flashy new turbine through again not long ago.'

'That so?' The new signalman signed himself in and took command of the ever-present polishing cloth in readiness for action. 'A strange design to my way of looking. Call me an old stick-in-the-mud, but it's got a way to go before it convinces me it'll replace a trusty V2 or A3.'

'Streaming oil the last time I saw her. It was ruining the paintwork!'

'Who ever thought it was a good idea to paint it *white*?'

'I reckon it was the Union. Ensures more cleaners are employed.' Green was sarcastic.

'You could be right, but we can't get enough cleaners for the steamers as it is. I presume it broke down again?'

'Had to pull over and waiting for a tow. Woodford has sent out an ex-War Department beast. A bit of a humiliation, eh?'

Green grinned. 'The rescue engine has only been gone forty minutes so you'll see *The Difference Engine* pulled back to Rugby, tail between its legs!'

'And a dirty steamer doing the work...'

Both men laughed heartily. Green wished his friend 'goodnight' and stepped down to his waiting motorbike. Slipping on a donkey jacket and fastening the chin strap on his helmet he kicked the motor into life and roared off for the short run home. He could easily walk and save petrol, but the motorbike was his one indulgence. His pride and joy, dating from a time when he'd been posted further up the line and the significant hike each way made easier with this lovely machine. He found it hard to let it go despite the close proximity of his work and would sometimes take a deliberately circuitous route home just to let the engine have a bit of a roar and feel the wind on his face. It only used a drop of petrol each day even if he did burn some rubber off on the quiet country lanes around Woodford. After just a short run this evening along a few empty lanes, he parked his motorbike outside the terraced house he and Julie had lived in for the last 30 or so years.

One of many almost identical houses dating from the turn of the century when Woodford-cum-Membris had expanded from a sleepy village of rustic ironstone dwellings and transformed into a bustling railway centre filled with farmers and locomotive drivers, seedsmen, cattle dealers, wagon repairers, tarpaulin sewers, engine fitters and signalmen living cheek by jowl in a curious mix of the heavy railway industry and a bucolic agrarian existence. The high-speed railway aside, Woodford Halse was not an easy place to find. Despite being an important junction, few travelled there as a destination, most just passing through and perhaps wondering where exactly they were, before pushing it from their minds as they hurried on to places like Banbury, Hull, London Marylebone, Nottingham Victoria or even Manchester London Road.

Ten minutes later and Green was sitting at the deal table

in their back kitchen pouring a strong cup of tea. His wife was peeling potatoes into a sturdy pot filled with water. The range was glowing in spite of the benign warmth of the evening and the back door stood open to allow the promise of approaching summer to drift inside. Green contemplated his rows of growing cabbages, beets and carrot tops and considered putting in an hour of weeding after their meal.

'Laura's coming over at the weekend.'

'That'll be nice.' Green sipped his tea and felt content. 'Simon also?'

'Depends on his work. She says he's quiet at the moment, but you never know what might come up.'

'There's no rest for the wicked or for those who bang 'em up!' David Green grinned. 'Hope he can make it. He's a good lad. I've worked with his father since I joined the railway, so I reckon I know him about as well as Derek knows his son.'

'It's a perfect match. I hope they can get their name down on one of those new council houses they're building in Leicester. A bright new house with all the 'mod cons' would be the perfect start for them all.'

'All?' Green raised a querying eyebrow at his wife.

'For now...' She gave her husband a knowing smile. 'You get to the top of the waiting list if expecting.'

'Steady on! They're not even hitched yet.'

'High time they got a family started. Laura's given enough over to the railway. If you ask me, this wedding's not come a moment too soon...' She gave her husband a knowing look.

Green digested the implied revelation. 'We lost no time having our first.' He looked pensively across the kitchen into the golden embers of evening light on the garden.

'What is it?'

'Nothing.' He paused before continuing. 'Laura took to signalling as if born to it. Like I did and like Simon's dad an' all. It's a lonely existence. Just yourself and the block bells and a brief wave or smile from a passing crew. There's the odd phone call, but otherwise nobody to speak a word to for eight hours a day. You need to be comfortable on your own. I just hope she doesn't find the demands of a husband and a baby and the inevitable gaggle of young mothers in a new estate all too much. She's used to her own company and not one for too much distraction.'

His wife smiled to herself as she put the spuds on to boil. 'You've had four growing up in this place and I've not seen you suffer. You don't spend every night down The Gorse drinking your wages away and avoiding your family. You've been at home almost every night for years despite all the noise of growing kids. And she might take a liking to growing roses and dallying in a garden shed for hours like her dad.'

'Aye, you could be right!'

Suddenly a dark shape appeared at the opened door, silhouetted by the brightness of the evening sunlight. A knuckle wrapped on the door frame in a harsh, yet oddly familiar tattoo. Julie Green took a sharp intake of breath. 'You startled me sidling up like that...'

Green peered at the silhouette for a moment in silence. 'Grimes?'

'That's no way to greet an old chum, Davey!' The man at the door laughed.

Green stood up. 'Julie, you remember Richie. Richard Grimes?'

She wiped her hands on her apron and shook hands. 'Oh, my goodness. How nice to see you again, Richard.' She said his name as one might a difficult word, unpractised and unfamiliar.

'May I?' But Grimes did not wait for the invitation and stepped into the kitchen. Green looked uncertain, suddenly wrong-footed in his own house.

'What brings you back?'

'Do I need a reason?'

'You've not set foot here since...'

'April 1943. I had some leave and spent a week here,

remember? And then there was that day in 1947 we all met at the White Hart when I was passing through and changing trains.' Grimes gave a broad grin, his eyes alert and flicking between silent wife and uneasy husband, aware of the impact his unexpected appearance was having on the cosy domestic scene. 'I've been busy. Travelling the length and breadth, even to Europe.' Grimes moved as if to take a chair and sit. 'I've seen the world. Broadened my horizons.'

'You'd best step into the parlour. Julie's busy with the evening meal.'

'Don't mind me!' Grimes fired back with a wolfish grin.

Green opened the door into the hall. 'We can talk in here.' It was a command, not a request. Green was trying to reassert control.

The front parlour was a cold and unloved room; polished and preciously tidy, it exuded an air of inhospitality despite the armchairs, small side tables, gleaming fire surround and smiling porcelain figurines on the mantlepiece. An ugly clock ticked mournfully, and a row of unread books patiently awaited someone to remove them from behind the glass doors of the sideboard. The dusty bottle of sherry had not been touched since last Christmas. Grimes flung his heavy frame down in one of the chairs and crossed a leg over the other in an extravagant demonstration of a man at ease. Green decided to stand with his back to the empty fireplace as if warming his legs.

'You could have sent word.'

'That frosty formality again. Signalling's done nothing for your social skills! Heck, I'm parched.'

Green stared impassively at Grimes for a moment. A vein throbbing in his neck. 'Julie will bring us a beer through.' There was the soft sound of glass clinking in the other room even as he spoke.

'Perfect. A drink together, just like old times…'

'I hope not.'

Julie Green entered the parlour and quietly placed two

bottles of Hook Norton bitter on a table with two glasses. She'd removed the caps and a gentle scent of hops was already being released. She closed the door behind her. Grimes ignored the glass and supped from the bottle. 'Ah... reminds me of that time we filched some of these from the Fleur de Lys. Remember?' Green concentrated on pouring his beer carefully down the inside of the glass. 'We got properly ratted! Sitting on the bridge watching trains and putting the world to rights. They were good times.'

'We stole the beer. It still rankles.'

'Just four bottles out of a crate. They're still in business and they'd never have sold us them 'cos we were too young.'

'That's no excuse.' Green drank and hoped it would knock the edges off the ill-feeling he still harboured for someone once called a friend. 'I drink there once in a while and still feel a twitch of bad conscience.'

'Yeah, well you always were Mr Goody-Two-Shoes.' Grimes instantly regretted his mocking tone.

'Instead of what? Being more like you?' Green was not smiling. 'Your reputation was hardly saintly by the time you left. People talked. It wasn't nice what they said.'

'Talked about what?'

'You know damn well about what.'

The atmosphere grew chillier.

'About Rosie?'

'I don't think we should talk about her. Not after what happened...'

'After what?' Grimes gave an innocent look at Green. 'Just lads larking about! Her dress got torn and we got a lovely eyeful...'

'That was bad enough, but that's not what I mean, and you know it. Because of what happened later.'

'And what do you think happened later?' Grimes glared at Green and felt his mouth go dry.

'No one knows. Not me, not the police, not her family. No

one. She went missing. That's it. They never found her.'

'Perhaps they weren't looking in the right place?'

'Obviously.' Green felt a cold shiver down his spine. 'Do you know something?' He felt the room rock slightly. His head swim for a second or two. Just one bottle of beer, so it was not that.

'Yes, that she's out there somewhere and the man responsible is still walking free. Stands to reason.'

'You seem very sure about it.' Their gaze met and held for a moment. Both men wary. 'Why are you raking this up? Let it lie. What I do know is the family never got over her disappearance. They never will. For the rest of us, after so many years no one talks about her anymore. Maybe that's best...' He stared at the carpet feeling confused an angry that his evening had been so rudely interrupted and awkward and unpleasant memories rekindled.

'Best for who? The man who did her harm?' Grimes was angry with himself and needed to regain his composure. What was he doing bringing Rosie Tustain into the conversation for God's sake? Was he crazy. He knew what he knew, but now was not the time to reveal anything. Everything was too delicately poised, but after spending so long immersed in the case then seeing his friend again had brought it all to the surface so vividly it was hard not to speak out. He needed to change tack quickly. 'Hey, Davey. We were best mates! We had some good times. Don't deny it' He spoke with a forced enthusiasm, desperate to move the conversation on.

'We were little more than big kids then. Water under the bridge.' Green sighed deeply.

'Trains under the bridge, more like!' They both managed a smile. Grimes raised his bottle in a gesture of friendship. Green took a moment, then raised his bottle, although there was little beer left in either.

'What line of work are you in these days?' Green wanted to drag the conversation back to the present and hopefully cheerier subjects. He noticed Grimes was unshaven and his clothes were shabby. He used to be one for splashing out on smart togs and had looked a proper 'spiv' in the latter part of the war and after. Time certainly changed a man.

'I'm a journalist.' Grimes popped a cigarette in his mouth and let it bounce there unlit whilst he spoke. 'Photographer *and* journalist.' He patted the leather camera case still slung over his shoulder. 'I've got a Leica in here. Beautiful piece of kit. Cost a packet.' Green said nothing. He wasn't in the mood to sound impressed and was puzzling over the contrast between an expensive camera and a worn-out shirt and life-expired shoes. 'I work for *The Railway Magazine*. Freelancing, but it pays well when I land a picture or story.' Grimes proffered the carton of cigarettes and Green accepted one. Grimes struck a match and lit both their cigarettes then blew a plume of smoke into the air. 'That's partly why I'm here.'

'I knew there would be an ulterior motive.'

'Don't be cynical.'

'What do you want?' Why was he not surprised? The same old tale…

'I'm working on a feature on the experimental gas turbine. You might not have read my articles, but you must have seen the TD-GTX1 scream past today?'

'I signalled her through from Rugby and back. It looks like it landed from another planet.'

'Makes a cracking photo.'

'Do you think she's a serious proposition?' Green was feeling happier talking railways. He'd finished his beer and felt calmer. Grimes might be arrogant and culpable of some dubious actions in the past, but it would be churlish not to seek the opinion of someone who worked for the oldest and most prestigious of railway journals.

'Shows promise. Some niggling problems, but to be expected. Just eighteen months in and *The Difference Engine* is already out on the mainline.'

'It broke down.'

'It did?' Grimes did his best to hide his surprise. He was forced to extemporise because he'd spent the day in Loughborough and was unaware of this development. 'As I said, there are a few teething issues - but soon fixed.' He hoped.

'The test runs to London are why you're here?'

'I need a big story and photograph before the weekend. Something dramatic.'

'How can I help?' Green shrugged his shoulders. 'I just signal her through twice a day. If it runs.' He was trying to rediscover the young man he once knew in the overweight and shabby figure filling the armchair.

'Do you remember I always said everything would come good if you put your trust in me?'

Green snorted derisively. 'I can't forget. My life became a lot easier once you left Woodford.'

'Thanks for nothing.' Grimes paused a beat. 'I have a small favour to ask.'

Green stifled a groan.

Chapter Nine

Laura Green was in her signal box at Desford Junction and which guarded the location where the single track mineral line to West Wharf in Leicester branched from the busy Coalville line. She was looking forward to another day signalling scurrying passenger trains and a near constant succession of coal trains through her section of the Coalville line and in-between these, dealing with one or other of the two delightfully antiquated locomotives that gently puffed and pulled short trains of wagons along the ageing branch line. These trains were mainly open wagons of coal, terracotta tiles or laden with bags of manure, but whatever the load, trundled at little more than walking pace along the mouldering track that was being steadily consumed by weeds. It was to be a typical working day that included tea making and staring out of the big windows at the birds in the trees and beasts in the fields on the far side of the hawthorn hedgerows.

Laura was feeling content, although with a tinge of sadness. Did she really want to give all this up? Signalling the traffic along the railway had been her life since she was barely eighteen. Willingly accepted back then to help the national need for workers to keep the railways running during wartime, a time when even young women - hardly more than a schoolgirl in her case - were welcomed to the cause. Attitudes had hardened since those heady days and the unions were closing ranks and making it clear women were no longer considered part of the modern railway. Quite why modernity meant removing women from a job they'd done with aplomb was unexplained. They wanted her out, and what made it more galling was the fact they were struggling to find a replacement. It made no sense.

After the murder of the crossing keeper at Black Spinney

Crossing a couple of years back, the poorly remunerated post left vacant by the death of the female 'keeper, remained unfilled. Perhaps nobody wanted to live in the attached cottage which retained a sinister atmosphere to this day? The train crews now had to stop, open the gates themselves and after taking the train through repeat the exercise behind them. It was a lightly used line and a quiet country road, so the inconvenience was little more than that. However, someone would have to take her place in the Desford Junction 'box. It was too important to be unmanned.

A noisy magpie chattered on a branch outside. Laura looked for its mate but couldn't see it. *One for sorrow.* She shrugged her shoulders. It was just silly superstition. She turned away from the window to survey the interior, heavy with the scent of lavender polish and the disinfectant used in the sink and toilet downstairs and felt inordinately proud of 'her' little cabin. Laura was effectively the only person to use the box in the daytime apart from on her rest days and felt jealously protective. Her father had visited her here one memorable day. He'd sat contentedly with a mug of tea and watched her work for an hour or so, saying little as was his way. Only when he got up to leave and whilst putting on his motorcycle helmet did he rest his hand on her shoulder and speak. 'You've done well, Laura. I can be proud of you as one of us.' He meant as one of the signalmen on British Railways. It meant everything. She found herself brushing away an unexpected tear. *Silly goose!* She studied the entries in the logbook as a distraction. She was not going to indulge in sentimentality. She was soon to become Mrs Howerth, the happy housewife. It was her choice and had nothing to do with narrow-minded opinionated men acting out their vision of a 'fairer' world.

There was hiatus before the next train and she sat in the armchair closed her eyes and pushed aside any lingering regrets and allowed herself to remember the delights of that sweetly scented embankment with the hot sun on her naked skin...

* * * *

Laura's father, David Green, was also at work. His was a busier day, with continual train movements to handle in the Number Four box at Woodford Halse. He saw fast 'windcutter' coal trains clatter past in waves of percussive bangs and crashes as the steel-bodied wagons bounced over rail joints leaving a shadow of coal dust in their wake and the local passenger 'stoppers' filled with shoppers and all manner of other workings around this important junction on the former Great Central mainline. Not all traffic passed in front of his signal box, but as one of four controlling the running lines, junctions, locomotive depot, wagon repair works and the extensive marshalling yards, the four signalmen were constantly working in synchronicity; opening or closing pathways to allow trains to cross or be temporarily sidelined to allow something more important through. Trains such as the fast fish vans from Grimsby must not be delayed, as the London markets needed the daily catch to arrive unspoilt.

Then there were the important expresses linking London with the midland and northern industrial heartlands, including the famous *Master Cutler* and *South Yorkshireman*. These named trains always brought a sense of anticipation as they stormed their way north or south with the legendary Gresley A3 pacifics looking polished and buffed with their brightly painted nameboards hung across the front of their boilers, hauling gleaming coaches filled with businessmen and bustling white-jacketed waiters in the restaurant cars. Green was particularly fond of these beautiful locomotives which were named after famous racehorses and which suited them well as they hurried their glamorous trains on their way.

It was both physically and mentally demanding working

this 'box, but Green was long practised. He loved the relentless focus that forbade daydreaming. There was a strict logic to every movement, and these came in a sequence that was learned by heart so he could anticipate every pull or release of a lever, every bell code to offer or accept a train. There were also unusual and surprising interruptions to this ordered plan, with extra workings and trains delayed for any number of reasons to keep him on his toes, but these just added spice to the day.

Visitors inside a signal box were not strictly forbidden but should be infrequent and the choice of visitor carefully vetted. Green had, somewhat reluctantly, eventually agreed to Richard Grimes' request to call in and make the most of the vantage point the signal box provided to take photographs of *The Difference Engine*.

'I've got my fill of three-quarter views or spinning on the test plant rollers.' Grimes had chosen not to explain he was banished from getting close to the locomotive whilst outlining his plan the night before.

'The test plant must be interesting.'

'Not really. She screams like a banshee and we have to wear noise protectors over our ears, but aside from a glimpse of whirling wheels there's little to see and after five minutes I want to escape!' Perhaps Grimes had a point, Green conceded.

'I need a grandstand view and your signal box is perfect.'

With a heavy heart and a nagging sense of foreboding, Green had accepted. Grimes was now in the signal box pacing around and starting to get on Green's nerves. 'Pour yourself a cuppa and sit in the chair. I can't think with you behind my back...'

Grimes sat but looked ill at ease. 'Davey, I've been thinking...' Green felt a cold tingle down his spine. He knew there would be more to this. 'As I said, I need something to make me a quick buck.' He said it with a mock American accent. 'It would suit me if you held her here. Stopped her getting a clear path for ten minutes or so...'

'Pardon?'

'Pull the special over. Put her into the loop and hold her to let something pass.'

'Don't talk rot. We've been told to give her a clear path for the trials.'

'But perhaps something goes wrong? Another train taking too long to clear a section... a breakdown... you're in charge. You decide. If you say she needs to pull over, she does.'

'We don't play games. It's not a Hornby-Dublo trainset where you can do what you like!'

'But you *can* do it...' Grimes' voice had a wheedling quality.

'But why would I?'

'It won't hurt anyone. There are no passengers. Just a stupid experimental gas bag that won't make it into production. No-one is waiting at Marylebone for her to arrive, despite what the company think.'

'Why do want the engine held? Why would that make a good story?'

'I've learned the turbine is prone to over-heating if stationary for any length of time. A flaw in the design. I want to witness what happens when it boils over and capture it on film. I want the story as it unfolds. A massive scoop and under my name.'

'You want me to deliberately cause it to overheat?' Green was incredulous.

'It has a safety valve! I'm telling you it will do this at some point further down the line, just not where I'm waiting with my camera. She boils over at the drop of a hat. You said it yourself, yesterday.'

Green gaped, speechless. Yet again Grimes was leading him into agreeing to something he'd never signed up for. Just like old times.

Both men watched as a work-stained V2 class engine snorted past with a line of box wagons, the three-cylinder sound as its syncopated rhythmic beat pounded through the opened windows. Green raised a hand to the driver. 'Are you up to something?' Green asked.

'Yeah, taking photographs of trains.'

'Is there something else you're not telling me about? Because this sounds fishy.'

'Still don't trust me.'

'I don't. Not after...'

'Over thirty years and still angry.'

Green fixed Grimes with a hard look. 'That says it all.'

'It says nothing! I grabbed a kiss and got a slap from you. So what?'

'I nearly knocked you over the bridge...Sometimes I wish I had.' Green looked at his block instruments, seeking refuge in the little dancing pointer and polished teak cabinet and little tinkling bells that reflected the sunlight. 'She might still be alive if I had...' His last words faded into *sotto voce*.

'Say that again?'

'Forget it!'

Grimes stood up and balled a fist but jammed it in his pocket to try and still his mounting anger. 'You think *I* killed her?'

Silence.

'Bloody hell...'

'I dunno. I know stuff. Heard things...whispers, rumours, then you just left and never came back. You ran away. It looks like the action of a guilty man.' Green felt his face burn. He'd said aloud what he'd thought for years and was regretting it. It was a truly terrible thing to pin on his old school friend. The atmosphere was electric. Grimes was pale.

'You're a bloody idiot David Green. Just as bad as the rest of them. I never thought you'd turn on me. Never.' Silence stewed in the heat between the two men. 'Well, since you asked, I *know*. I investigate and ask questions before making accusations. And I know better than to hurl vile insults against a friend. If you believe I did it, then go and tell the police. Go on! Oh, but no, let's keep quiet and say and do nothing and become bitter and twisted!' He spat the words out.

Green listened to a bell code, but instead of accepting the train offered into his section, he stood staring blankly, out of the windows, hands automatically wiping the lever handles. Neither man spoke. Their breathing which had started to race as tempers flared, now eased. After what felt like an age, Green reached up and tapped out a response. 'I'll take my time with this and with the trip goods working following behind. I'll drag my heels. I can find you ten minutes with this train stopped in the loop. If that's not long enough - not my problem.' He didn't look at Grimes as he spoke.

'That should be enough.'

'Just take your pictures, then leave.'

'I'll be out of your hair the moment she blows her top. I'll be gone and won't embarrass you again.'

Green said nothing. He felt confused. Ancient memories, like dying embers being fanned into flames. He just didn't need any of this. It was unsettling. Inconvenient. What was he thinking? He'd accused his friend of murder and this was *inconvenient*. He needed to pull himself together. This kind of muddled thinking was dangerous, and he needed a clear head to do his job. Taking a deep breath or two he shook himself out of this ugly frame of mind and concentrated on his work. He'd agreed to do as Grimes asked, so he'd best do a tidy job so nothing could come back to bite him.

It proved easy to be tardy clearing paths for several slow train movements and an especially down-at-heel J39 class engine with a short run of wagons behind played into his hands. The engine was in appalling condition with a boiler streaked with limescale and the smokebox door had paint burned off to reveal orange-coloured rust. The yellowing smoke barely lifting from the chimney told Green the fire was misbehaving, and the inexperienced young fireman was struggling. Green held them outside his box and talked to the exasperated driver. Green suggested they took time to get the fire clean and make more steam before he let them advance. The suggestion was gratefully received. By the time they were back on their way, Green had introduced more than enough delay into the timetable to cause a problem for the rapidly approaching test train. He might be criticised for being too indulgent with the sickly train but doubted anyone would query the situation. Most of his compatriots held *The Difference Engine* in a measure of disdain and he suspected some might even cheer at its demise…

A telephone rang. He turned to Grimes after a short exchange on the line. 'Running late, as requested.' He dropped the distant signal. This would check their speed as it told the driver they didn't have a clear path ahead. 'Best get your camera ready, Richie.' Using the old familiar name was an olive branch. A peace offering. Green would do this one last thing and be done with Grimes once and for all, so could afford to show a little warmth. Green pulled the home signal to danger.

The high-pitched whine was like the approach of a swarm of angry hornets. Then the extraordinary white engine eased around the approach curve leaning inwards due to the camber of the track, sunlight illuminating the polished white and burnished metal. The gas turbine looked eye-catching as she drew closer in a roar and towering shimmer of hot exhaust.

Grimes clicked the shutter and wound on the film in his camera, then moved the lens to capture Green with one hand on a lever, the train visible outside the windows. 'Man and machine…'

Green would rather he'd not been photographed, but for a few fleeting moments they recaptured something of their long-lost friendship. Carefree lads once again, watching the trains. It was just a brief moment, fading rapidly like a dream upon waking. The reality of the train's complaining brakes and the face of the driver poking out of the cab window looking back towards the signal box brought Green into the here and now. After a few minutes held at danger, the train guard dropped to the six-foot way and walked to a telephone mounted on a signal post and when Green picked up the telephone, asked what was going on.

'An engine needed to make steam. Had to let her brew up and took an age to clear the section. I'll have to put you into the loop...' The guard agreed. It was no skin off his nose, and he trudged back to the train. By the time the guard hauled himself back on board, *The Difference Engine* was already starting to make alarming noises.

Grimes now left the signal box to drop down to the trackside and not a moment too soon. Green set the route for the train to pull across onto the loop, but as the two-tone horn sounded and the engine attempted to roar into action, it merely crawled forward at a snails' pace whilst billows of steam issued from every louvred grille along its flanks and roof. The hiss of steam was continuous as the train finally gained walking pace before coming to an ignominious halt some 50 yards from where they'd started. The big white whale issued one last sigh of desperation as the turbine closed down and the unhealthy sounds started to quieten until it sat in almost silence with just the drip of hot water, ticking of cooling metal and a blackbird angrily chirping in a nearby tree. It had been a spectacular demise and Green could not be blamed for causing it. There had not even been time to pull the train clear of the mainline. Green felt no guilt in the part he'd played as he closed the section to ensure nothing could enter and smash into the stricken train from behind then telephoned his colleague in the next box to explain the line was blocked until a rescue could be arranged. Grimes, meanwhile, was getting what he needed and doing it away from the signal box.

Half an hour later, Woodford shed had rustled up a steam engine to drag the locomotive and train out of the way, and after depositing the coaches in one of the marshalling yards, the dead locomotive was ignominiously hauled to the engine shed and shoved out of harm's way, deep inside and out of sight.

Chapter Ten

Despite promising he would have nothing more to do with him, the unwelcome return of Richie Grimes was filling David Green's head with long-repressed memories that refused to leave him alone. Too many awkward questions kept swirling around his head and no matter how hard he tried he could not clear his mind.

Why had Grimes chosen to speak about *that* particular day on the bridge? Why that day - of all days? Why even mention Rosie? Her name was highly charged; like a perfectly wrapped parcel of dynamite ready to explode in their faces with just the tiniest jolt. Her name was almost never heard in Woodford now. Those old enough to remember her shared a communal guilt that she was never found, a sense of shame and guilt that they had failed to protect one of their own. The pain the Tustain family continued to endure had once been the source of outpourings of compassion and support, but after so many long years and an intervening world war was now something to avoid and it made others feel embarrassed. It was generally held that someone local was most probably to blame for what must surely be an abduction and murder, yet, in spite of the many rumours and suspicions that had done the rounds back then, no-one had ever been held to account and her body had never been found. Green was puzzled. When there were so many innocuous memories that Grimes *could* have chosen, why did he rake this one up? Was she preying on his conscience?

Green hardly dared allow himself to follow this line of thought. What if Grimes knew what had happened to Rosie? What if he...? Green shook his head as if he could somehow shake these ugly, dangerous, disturbing thoughts away. All he managed to do was find himself back on that bridge when the beer took hold of their senses...

*   *   *   *

It was one of those glorious May days that lingered long in the memory. The sky above Woodford almost cloudless and filled with birdsong. Being a Saturday, they were free to roam and soak up the heat of this early taste of summer. A brewer's dray was standing outside the Fleur de Lys pub, the horse with its nose in a bag of hay as barrels of Hook Norton dropped onto a sack and then down into the cool cellar. The two draymen had already placed a stack of wooden crates of bottled beer to one side, preferring to get the barrels out of the way before taking these into the bar. There was a problem in the cellar, and the two young lads Davey Green and Richie Grimes could hear the landlord and one of the men having a discussion down below. Whatever the problem it dragged on and the second man now growing impatient stepped off the wagon and dropped out of sight to join them. The coast was clear. In a moment they had filched a pair of bottles each from the top crate and by the time the draymen reappeared blinking into the light, the bottles were in the saddlebags on their bikes and they were bowling out of Woodford at full pelt. Sitting on the bridge spanning the railway, they watched the trains speed by inhaling mouthfuls of locomotive smoke and talking about their fantasy of an exciting life filled with girls, bags of money and a plentiful supply of cigarettes and alcohol. The beer was making them lightheaded and careless.

Rosie Tustain walked into view just as the second bottles were drained and tossed carelessly onto a train of coal wagons passing below. She was acknowledged as Woodford's prettiest and the object of every young man's attention and drawing many a passing glance from those older and supposedly wiser not to harbour lascivious thoughts about her youthful body. Her light brown hair was looking its silky best in the sunlight and the same weather had inspired her to choose a sleeveless summer dress with just a cardigan draped over her shoulders exposing a daring expanse of décolletage that her mother must surely have disapproved. If worn buttoned up, the fashionably thin cardigan would have offered some modesty, but Tustain was both aware of her good looks and worshipped the sun, thereby creating a vision of female loveliness impossible to ignore.

'Going anywhere interesting, Rosie?'

Having little choice but to pass them close by she politely stopped. 'None of your business if I am, Richie Grimes.'

Green would be lying to pretend he did not harbour desire for Rosie and it was obvious his friend felt the same way. However, it was Richie doing the talking. Of course. Green felt a spark of something dark inside. A twist in his guts and a flush of jealousy. Why could he not find the confidence to stop this gorgeous girl in her tracks and get her to smile in answer to his inane enquiry? It wasn't as if Grimes said anything special, it was just that he had the confidence to go for what he wanted. And he wanted Rosie Tustain. Green knew he would have let her walk by, saying nothing and even averting his eyes in spite of being equally keen to talk with her and desperate to receive a winning smile from her.

Gaining confidence, both lads slid off the bridge parapet and stood close to the beautiful young woman. They stood too close, but the alcohol was urging them on. Green could hardly take his eyes off the slight sheen to her golden skin where her cleavage started. Grimes managed to manoeuvre so the young girl was now standing between them, her back to the wall and unable to walk on unless she pushed one of them aside. Rosie Tustain was now batting aside a series of flirtatious comments from Grimes, still with a hint of a smile, but she fidgeted with the cardigan, now holding it tighter around her neck until she realised this was not helping as she was just enhancing the view down her cleavage by bringing her arms together. Her voice remained light as she fended off Grimes with ease. It was time to walk on and bid them goodbye but the beer and her revealing dress was proving a dangerous mix and now Richie Grimes was becoming overconfident.

Green would later convince himself he had purely altruistic reasons for introducing a new topic of conversation to deflect the conversation, but the top button of her dress had come loose as she tried again to readjust her cardigan and was fixating on rapid rise and fall of her breasts as her breathing quickened and he was just as eager to keep her there. Green mentioned they were waiting for a specific train to pass. It was a throwaway comment, but railways were practically all he knew about and like everyone in Woodford his life was dominated or touched by the railway. Even Rosie Tustain's father worked on the engines, so it felt like safe ground. She seemed grateful for this innocuous shift, but somewhere between asking if her dad was in the depot today and watching her shapely pink lips frame the reply, his friend made an unwise move.

A lurch, a grab, a stumble backwards and she was pinned to the parapet and he was kissing her, the cardigan falling helplessly onto the railway below, her bare shoulders fully revealed. Grimes' kiss was inexpertly executed and rough as his hands gripped her arms, pressing her against the sun warmed stone and she was finding it impossible to twist her lips away from his. He fumbled for a breast and gave it a squeeze, but in doing so she found space to wriggle free and push him off with surprising ferocity. She'd grown up working evenings and weekends on her uncle's farm and was no weakling. She aimed a slap at Grimes' cheek and it struck home with such force it made him blink back tears. Although she'd gained a moment of advantage, the stinging humiliation mixed with beer-fuelled desire urged Grimes on and he lunged for her, a hand catching the thin straps of her cotton dress and in one move he'd ripped the fabric, whether intentionally or accidentally was hard to tell. The thin cotton tore easily, rent open down one side so it fell unhindered to her waist, revealing that she had nothing underneath.

Green was aghast as he watched. This was wrong. He knew it was bad and it had to stop, and yet the thrill of seeing her young body exposed left him transfixed and mute. He must haul his friend away, pin his arms to his side and tell Rosie to escape. This is what any right-minded person should do - but instead he just stood, open-mouthed and useless as the poor girl clutched at her ample chest in a desperate attempt to cover her nakedness, face burning with shame as tears streamed down her cheeks. Grimes was now saying awful things, dreadful phrases that even Green was shocked to hear. What he was going to do to her. Grimes was like a wild animal, trying to pull the girl's hands away from her breasts and then hauling her dress further down to her hips, where thankfully it snagged. Only now did Green snap out of his pathetic torpor and spring into action. Tustain's distress was obvious and the scene unfolding was sickening. He wanted it to stop. Green swung a fist at Grimes and struck his friend squarely on the side of the temple with a powerful blow that sent him reeling. He followed this up with a low but viciously hard punch into the solar plexus and Grimes doubled over, clutching his stomach, vomiting beer and bile onto his shoes. Green kicked his friend hard on the backside so was now his turn to be thrust against the bridge parapet. Rosie Tustain was trying to run whilst gathering up her ruined dress to cover herself. She looked back just once over her shoulder, hair awry and face streaked. If Green had hoped his efforts at rescue were to be rewarded, he was mistaken. The look in her eyes held such contempt Green had to look away.

'I'm sorry!' He called after her. She ran. He was implicated in this appalling assault and that baleful look told him she was not going to be generous. Her father, fireman Tom Tustain, was a strong man; rough and uncomplicated and not the sort to be crossed. Perhaps worse, she had two older brothers, equally powerfully built and known for their quick tempers. Green knew they were both in for a hiding. It was going to be vicious, unpleasant and deserved.

Or was it? Resentment started to build even as Green looked at his friend who was still clutching his stomach whilst making a low animal moaning noise as he threw up once more, this time over the side of the bridge. There was a red welt on his cheek. It was Grimes who'd stopped Rosie and it was he who'd forced a kiss and mauled her then ripped her dress. He'd played no part in this. Bloody typical! Green knew he was going to share the blame and the beating and yet he'd not started any of this. He'd tried to stop it. He felt a surge of self-righteousness inside. It has been bad, but could have been worse. It wasn't fair. The Tustain girl was pretty and Green would love a kiss from her, but he'd rather she chose to offer one, not force it. A kiss given freely surely tasted better than Richie's ugly attempt.

He turned his back on Grimes and walked away from the stink of sweat, vomit and creosoted railway sleepers.

* * * *

Signalman Green parked his motorbike beside his house and entered the walled back garden and into his shed. Leaving his helmet on the workbench, he searched for a short while until he found a small metal tin at the back of a shelf lined with jam jars filled with nails and screws, a packet of rat poison with dire warnings about the danger of death from ingestion and some rusting cans of paint. Pocketing the tin, he walked straight back out onto the street and towards the depot without so much as a glance towards the house.

He'd debated whether this was the right plan of action during the hours since the train had been hauled clear. He'd seen Grimes hitch a ride back to the depot on the train and suspected his old school friend might still be on-site, even now, ensuring he got everything he needed for his important article. Green had promised himself to be done with Grimes once and for all, but the wind on his face and opening the throttle and making the exhaust roar on his Norton motorbike hadn't cleared his mind as he'd hoped it might. That dark, sinister thought had crept inside, unwelcome and uninvited like a black rat. He wished he could administer a dose of that poison and kill it off. He'd get no peace until he could find a way to drive it away. He had to find Grimes one last time for a showdown. It was time to end this.

Once and for all.

The Woodford engine shed was a large construction mostly in functional red brick but with stone lintels and mullions on the shed master's office bay window and a large clock mounted above the stabling lines, thereby ensuring it was thoroughly stained with soot and rain water, although not much more so than the whole building which had a deathly grey pallor all over. There were tall wooden doors that always stood wide for easy access to the eight sets of rails leading inside, these holding several steam locomotives within the noxious interior. In the golden evening sunlight outside, more engines gathered variously hissing and dribbling hot water. A few had sluggish curls of dirty smoke drifting from their chimneys whilst being readied for night duties, but most gently cooled in the dusty warm haze, their work over for the day. Their tenders were refilled and boilers topped with cold water and baby-soft ash was being shovelled from out of their smokeboxes in preparation for the morning when their fires would be fanned awake and heat breathed into their bellies. A few men were dotted around the depot wheelbarrowing ash, others raking glowing coals into pits beneath the engine wheels or hammering something with a ringing sound of metal on metal. A fitter losing patience with a recalcitrant nut or jammed valve as he dreamed of cleaning his hands in Swarfega before quenching his thirst in the railwayman's favourite, The Gorse. It was nearly time to hand the yard over to the small complement of men who looked after this stable of iron horses for the night and none of the tired day workers had the inclination or energy to take notice of a stern-faced signalman walking with a purposeful air into their domain. If they did glance up, they knew his face. A Woodford man, born and bred. One of them. If he wanted to walk around here instead of hurrying home to his wife, what of it? He was a railwayman and knew how to handle himself in a dangerous environment. Back to raking hot clinker and belting the hell out of that blinking nut...

Green had no trouble spotting *The Difference Engine*. She'd been placed deep in the shed on a line furthest from the foreman's office. It was probably the only space free at short notice, but as a dyed-in-the-wool 'steam man' perhaps it offended Mr Saunders' eye? Or was he trying to save 'face' for the crew? Green could imagine them smarting with the humiliation of being dragged broken and useless into this fiery pit of hot ash, coal, clinker and smoke by one of the uglier steam engines on the roster. A place where everyone had been brought up with the sounds and smells of the steam locomotive and which bred tough men reeking of sweat and toil and engine oil, all gazing with incredulity at bespectacled chaps wearing ridiculous white coats and looking as though they might make up medicine prescriptions or sell ice creams. Railwaymen were never shy of making fun and exploiting another's mistakes and Green could imagine the joshing to have been unsympathetic.

Green stood for a moment beside an ex-War Department engine and rolled a cigarette. This was the same loco that had come to the rescue of the gas turbine. However, he'd no interest in it this evening, nor did he much care about gaining a closer view of *The Difference Engine,* although that was his plausible justification for being on shed. He was angry. His was a seething resentment brewed for something like thirty years and now in danger of boiling over. He was ready to burst. His pulse racing and fists clenching. He needed to order his thoughts. Take some deep breaths. He had to be the smart one here. Blundering into a confrontation with Grimes would be a disaster. His one-time friend might have aged but he'd not changed. He was still as slippery as an eel...

Green watched and waited, assessing who was working around the shed and who had remained with the gas turbine. He presumed most of the engineers had returned with the empty coaching stock to Rugby about an hour ago. However, one or two might stick around as night watchmen. They would be easy enough to spot unless they'd sensibly decided to abandon their lab coats. More importantly, he suspected Grimes had not accompanied the team back to Rugby. He was sure Grimes was up to something more than just taking a photo of the engine shrouded in steam, and whatever he was really up to, it was bound to be bad. Green knew enough about Grimes to realise that he should no longer be so gullible and think the best of him. Taken on face value, Grime's story made sense and there was a logic to his plan that had succeeded rather well. But Green was not convinced. He felt for the little tin in his jacket pocket. Years had passed when he'd managed to forget it all about this, tucked away with his nails and screws and bits and bobs in his shed, safe in the knowledge there was little possibility of anyone discovering it. However, it only took a slight jolt of the memory for him to be reminded what he had kept. He should have thrown it away years ago. Destroyed it. Burnt it from his memory, or at least placed it forever out of reach. But he knew it was evidence. He knew it was connected to that poor missing girl and it was time for its dirty secret to be revealed.

The sun was setting and the deeper recesses of the shed growing dark. It would not be long before the big pendant lamps in the roof space would be switched on. Grimes was in there. Green tossed his cigarette away. He wanted another chance to punch Grimes in the face. But harder this time. As he drew closer, he caught sight of a figure furtively snooping around at the far end of *The Difference Engine*. Despite the distance he knew who it was.

'Damn you, Richie. I want you gone. I want rid of you...' He was muttering angrily under his breath as he strode forward into the shed, fists balled so hard his knuckles were white. He was fit and lithe from a lifetime hauling those heavy signal levers, whereas Grimes was overweight and out of shape. It was not an even contest, but since when had it ever been?

Chapter Eleven

'Davey, what brings you here?'

'I could ask you the same. Your train has left for Rugby.' Green locked eyes with Grimes. 'You do have permission to be on railway premises?'

'I wanted a photo of the engine…'

'Still need permission.'

'Come off it!' Grimes laughed, but stopped, seeing his friend was not smiling. Green appeared tense and nervy, poised as if ready to spring and kept flexing his fingers in an ominous manner. They were standing on the far side of *The Difference Engine* in a narrow gap lined on one side by heavy wooden workbenches pressed against the side wall of the shed and piled with heavy tools and lumps of metal. The air heavy with the tang of metal shavings, machine oil and sulphurous fumes. Dusk was advancing and the shed darkening. 'Hey, but the plan worked. I should have some cracking shots. Thanks to you.' Grimes cracked a smile, trying to break the tension in the air.

'Make sure you keep any mention of me out of print.'

'Don't worry. Is that why you came looking for me?'

'Not exactly.'

Grimes gave a furtive look around, one hand nervously fiddling with the leather strap of his camera in its case slung over on his shoulder. Perhaps Green was getting under his skin? 'Then why are you here?'

Green pulled the enamelled tin from his jacket. It had once held a rectangle of toffees; perhaps a rare Christmas treat from years past. He flipped open the lid which hinged along one side. 'Remember this?'

Grimes' eyes widened like dinner plates. 'What the…? How the hell did you get that?'

'That's not important.' Green lifted out the baby blue Alice band that had lain curled inside since the summer of 1929. It was still as fresh as the day it had been taken off having never seen daylight. 'Recognise this, Richie? Of course, you do...'

Grimes stared, appearing mesmerised by the humble scrap of cloth dangling between them, but suddenly snapped into life. 'You thieving bastard! *You* took it? I-I don't believe it...' Grimes made to grab the headband. 'Give it! You've no right to it!' But Green was ready for this and lifted it high and away, neatly dropping it back in the tin and snapping the lid closed. His laugh was mocking, Green discovering he was almost enjoying his friend's discomfort. Grimes lunged once again but Green nimbly stepped back, but as he did so jostled some heavy tools overhanging the workbench sending a massive monkey wrench clattering to the floor. 'Oh no you don't!' Green stuffed the tin safely back into the inside pocket of his jacket. 'It even comes with a love-sick note breaking off the date and a heart-shaped pebble. Sweet.'

'You double-crossing bastard! That's private!'

Green stepped further away then bent down and picked up the wrench. A railwayman never left things lying where they might endanger another especially in a cramped space and diminishing light. He hefted the massive wrench in one hand for a moment, surprised at the weight.

'What you going to do with that?' Grimes adopted a sneering tone, his question ambiguous about whether he meant the Alice band or the monkey wrench. He didn't look intimidated. 'You make me sick. Stealing private things then keeping them like...like some twisted little pervert! Why would you do that? And now what?' Grimes eyed the wrench. 'Going to do me in, is that the idea?'

'Christ sake...' Green shook his head in exasperation and carefully placed the wrench back on the bench. 'No, I'm not going to "do you in." But perhaps I *should?*' They stared at each other 'That would make it a life for a life, an eye for an eye. Isn't that what it says in the Bible? A kind of balance. Come on, tell me why you had her hairband? She hardly left the house without it. So how did you get it off her?'

'Go to hell!' Grimes sneered. He turned away for a moment as if gathering his thoughts and when he spoke again it was in a quieter tone. 'I worried myself sick wondering where that tin went, way back then. Thought my dad had chucked it out. And to think *you* had it all the time. My best mate. Some mate you turned out to be.'

'It had you worried though? Why was that? Worried someone had found out about the two of you?'

Grimes made another lunge towards Green, but the signalman was the fitter of the two and danced out of the way.

'I saw you. In the fields. Together.'

'And I saw you spying on us, remember?'

How could he forget? Green was seething inside.

'I saw you, peering through the corn like a naughty schoolboy,' Grimes suddenly looked smug. 'Did you like what you saw?' His voice was mocking with a more youthful edge than before. 'You're strange. Weird.' He spat the words out. 'A little peeping Tom!'

'I didn't plan to see you. God knows I didn't want to see her like that with you.' Green looked sickened by the memory. 'I was surprised. Shocked. After what you'd done to her and after the pasting we got from her brothers and the way she snubbed you and made sure everyone saw. It was impossible. But there you both were. Kissing and...'

Grimes gave a sly grin. 'And all the rest! Not just the once, either. The prettiest of them all and in my arms and happy about it.' Despite everything, Grimes still managed to look self-satisfied.

'I still can't believe she wanted to,' Green was bitter.

'Better believe it, Davey.' Grimes stopped. 'You're jealous. Bloody hell, I think you're still jealous after all these years.' He laughed, unsympathetically. 'Mind, I don't blame you. She was absolutely gorgeous...'

'Shut yer trap or else!'

'No, *you* shut it and listen.' Grimes was unsmiling and glared at Green. 'That time when you caught us at it. That was the last time. I never saw her again.' The bravado seemed to drain away from Grimes even as he was speaking. 'After she got dressed, she was sorting her hair and was going to put that band back on but changed her mind and gave it to me. A little keepsake.'

'Even after how you behaved on the bridge?' Green still couldn't comprehend it.

'You saw us. Was she crying out for help? Was she scratching and fighting? You're mad with me because you always were too slow and too boring to ask for what you wanted. Always playing the second fiddle. Standing in the shadows, a dumb little creep who steals things...'

Green felt bile rise in his throat. 'Rosie Tustain went missing two days later. Never seen again. The Police said she was wearing that band.'

'Well, they were wrong. She gave it to me, so she couldn't have been.'

'That's not good enough. It doesn't look good for you. Didn't then, doesn't now. I found where you hid the tin. I followed you four or five times and watched you take it out and look it. All this after she'd vanished off the face of the earth.'

'I missed her. More than I can bear to say. She left a note and heart shaped stone at the secret place we met. We left notes there so nobody would see us in the village together. Said she needed to see me, but there was a delay. She was busy in the day but would try to meet later. You've got the note, so you know that. She left it on the day she vanished, but never turned up. I waited deep into the evening. I suppose I've waited most of my life, but she never came back.'

'You want me to believe that sob story?'

'Of course. Bloody hell, you don't actually think I...?'

'I didn't want to. I couldn't bear to back then, but it ate away at me. You and her doing it in a field - then suddenly she vanished. And you changed after that. You were never the same after that day. You acted strange. Secretive and bad-tempered and we argued all the time. You acted like a man with a guilty conscience.'

Grimes was pale, beads of sweat on his brow. 'I didn't harm her.' He dropped his voice melodramatically to a whisper. 'I was a bit drunk and acted stupid on the bridge. But I knew she wanted it... She liked it.'

'Like hell she did. She got her brothers to beat us up.'

'She wanted to make a point. Show me she was no push over. But you saw us. I bet you liked her and wished it was you underneath her! That young body bouncing up and down...' Grimes laughed, but it was a cruel and mocking version. 'I had her and you didn't. You lost and you're still bitter.'

'You always were a selfish sod.' Green was furious. It came back to him in a searing vision that he'd tried for so many years to repress.

He'd been walking on his own along the edges of the many fields that surrounded Woodford, lost in his thoughts, wishing he could find a way to win a kiss off a girl like Rosie, rather than a humiliating beating. That had knocked his confidence. Taken the wind out of his sails and that day he'd not wanted the company of his arrogant friend, just wanting to be alone. And then he'd stumbled upon them.

* * * *

He'd seen Rosie first. She was quite shameless. Completely naked and moving rhythmically whilst making a slight moaning sound. Her lithe body fully on view, hair hanging loose down her back with just a pale blue Alice band the only thing she wore. Green had almost been unable to breathe.

She was such a vision of loveliness and Green felt a sharp stab of intense jealousy override any feelings of desire. Who was the lucky man with his trousers around his ankles lying on his back? Green knew he must not be discovered looking. Rosie Tustain would never forgive him staring at her a second time. He must turn about and get away, but instead, he took a few more steps closer whilst crouching low so the corn might help hide him from view. It was Grimes. She was making love to his best friend. How was this possible? How could she do *that* with him after what had happened on the bridge? It was impossible…

Grimes had heard something, caught a movement, and turned his head, his hands on Rosie's perfectly shaped hips keeping her moving in rhythm. His touch reassuring, so she might not open her eyes and leap off in fright. He winked and gave Green a wicked smile…He knew who was watching and couldn't help but revel in it.

* * * *

'I don't trust you. You used her and then you…'

'Did what?'

Green couldn't speak the words, but it was clear what he was thinking and the look on his face was equally murderous.

'I never hurt a hair on her head, Davey. Believe me.' Grimes suddenly realised the situation was serious. 'Listen, I want to get the man who did. I know who did it. I've worked it out! That's why I'm here. I'm close to proving it. It's taken me years, but you must trust me on this. Help me get the bastard who took her life and you'll see I'm not the monster you imagine.' His voice was imploring, eyes pleading. 'Just give me the tin and what's inside…'

Green had been almost ready to believe Grimes. He wanted to believe him, but that last wheedling request burst the fragile bubble. He looked at Grimes with his lank hair and bad teeth, the shabby clothes and the desperation in his voice and it made Green recoil. 'Rot in hell! It's time you confessed to the police. Tell them everything. Admit it all. You can die with a clear conscience at least. I'll give you until Monday, or else I'll do it for you. In the meantime, I'll keep hold of the tin.' He spun about and walked briskly away, his neck tingling as he anticipated the assault that surely would follow. Nothing happened.

Chapter Twelve

Grimes stood still for almost a minute watching as Green walked away. That brief glimpse of the long-lost toffee tin and Rosie's Alice band had pierced his heart more keenly than a filleting knife. He slowly walked to the end of *The Difference Engine*, one hand seeking support from the massive bulk of the engine as he was feeling unsteady from the shock of the encounter. A set of concrete steps lead down between the rails into an inspection pit beneath. He needed to sit down and regain his equilibrium. He cautiously descended the steps and sat on the second from lowest and unslung his camera case and laid it beside him. He rested his hands on his knees and took some deep breaths with his eyes closed.

His head was spinning. He was getting a headache. Davey thought he had taken Rosie's life. Perhaps almost worse, Davey had believed this all those years and never said anything. No wonder their friendship had withered and died. Grimes knew her brothers had suspected him at the time, though nothing had ever been proved. Of course not, he was not her killer. He'd been questioned by the police, but so had just about every male in the area, including Davey. He'd never been a serious suspect with the police. However, the Tustain brothers had made his life a living hell from one day to the next. They'd been sly and effective in their unwelcome attentions, determined to make him suffer and after a few months of this Grimes knew he would have to move away and never return.

It was little wonder he'd acted oddly back then. He became withdrawn and secretive and lost some of his bravado and swagger. He knew others had seen the change, and especially Davey. His old friend had caught the mood and suspected he was guilty and saw the change in his personality. It made sense, yet all the time *he* was the one suffering, he was the one wracked with guilt, anger and frustration. He was desperate to find her, desperate to bring her home and yet felt unable to admit this to anyone. Well it was time to reveal the truth. He needed to clear his name of any lingering suspicion by nailing the guilty man. He wanted to be the one who would point the finger and say *'J'accuse!'* like they did in cheap paperback thrillers. The family could finally lay her to rest whilst the man responsible had a date with the hangman.

Grimes closed his eyes. As his mind calmed, a wave of sleepiness washed over him as the adrenaline rush subsided. The drowsiness dulled his senses. He no longer noticed the background clattering of fitters labouring and whistling or the hiss and wheeze of a distant engine passing in the yard. Nor did he hear the sound of footsteps approaching, the slight noise as the heavy monkey wrench was hefted by a gloved hand. He knew nothing about the rapid descent of this same dead weight as it smashed into the back of his skull.

The Inspector Calls

Chapter Thirteen

Tim Saunders had been shed master at Woodford Halse for twenty years. He'd seen most things in his time and even a dead body was not the worst of it. A mortally injured man with appalling wounds and bleeding to certain death was probably more distressing. Working in a busy engine shed in blackout conditions during the war meant he had seen the inevitable accidents happen, and some had been horrific. Then there had been the curious case of the body tipped out from the Cenotaph type coal hopper. Had a structure ever a more appropriate name? That was back in 1946, and whilst remaining a source of the occasional story, time had largely reduced it to a curiosity and lost the power to shock. So, when a startled looking engineer dressed in a ridiculous white coat rapped on his door shouting, 'He's dead!' Saunders took a moment to ask the excitable young man to gather his thoughts and calmly tell him what he thought had happened.

'You're sure he's dead?' Saunders already had his telephone in hand, ready to call an ambulance.

'He looks it. He's just lying under our engine. Flat out.'

'We'll let the professionals decide.' Saunders gave the man, who breathlessly gasped that his name was Cartwright, an appraising stare. Was he a reliable witness? Maybe the victim was unconscious and in need of urgent help. Was there something he was not being told? Saunders was not friends with a DCI for nothing. He knew to take a few moments to gather his thoughts and observe the man whilst he dialled 999. Having made the connection and been assured an ambulance would be on its way from Banbury as soon as possible, he stood up and called into the next office for his deputy to join them.

'Lead on Mr Cartwright and remember to breathe.' In the

potentially dangerous environment of an engine shed it was essential to remain calm. Running about in an agitated state would only result in a further accident. However, Saunders had a gloomy feeling about this. He'd never met Cartwright until now but was sensing the man was correct in his assessment. Saunders was likely to be calling his friend Charles Vignoles. The only question was whether to try his office or his home number at this time of the evening.

* * * *

'Charles? Tim. Not a social call, I'm afraid. A fatality at the shed. And an odd one.'

DCI Charles Vignoles felt his hand grip the receiver that bit harder. Years in the service never diminished that first jolt news of a death always brought. Harsh reality would soon bring him face to face with the ugly scenes of a tragic loss beneath a train, or perhaps crushed by heavy machinery or between wagons and then would start the series of depressingly mundane actions to reconstruct the events resulting in these unromantic endings. Most of the time it was brutally obvious with no mystery attached. A drunk straying on a busy line at night; the missed footing of an over-confident shunter hanging from the side of a wagon propelled at speed; or yet another lonely suicide jumping from a bridge. Just yet another sad story to be documented, written up and passed to the coroner. However, there was always the possibility of it being different. A puzzle. A messy mystery offering more than just sliced flesh, spilled guts and pints of surprisingly red blood that would lift it to another level. Vignoles immediately sensed there was something in the air this evening.

His friend was a tough old boot not given to adorning his speech with more than bare facts. Saunders ran a busy shed and issued commands all day for practical solutions to pressing problems, so Vignoles could sense that Tim Saunders smelt a rat when he elaborated.

'He banged his head under an engine - but too hard for my liking.'

DS Mellor was unimpressed when Vignoles telephoned him straight afterwards. 'That's it? Not much to go on, guv.'

'I've known Saunders since '43. If he thinks something is not right, I trust his instinct. I want us there before ambulance men and do-gooding first aiders mess up the scene.'

Mellor remained unconvinced, but if Vignoles wanted to waste time on a geezer who'd taken insufficient care in an inspection pit, so be it. 'We'd best take the motor. I'll get us there quicker.' He was already jingling the car keys.

'Agreed. Pick me up. I'll be waiting outside Belgrave and Birstall Station.'

* * * *

Vignoles was standing head bowed, an unlit pipe in his mouth whilst staring at the body of Richard Grimes. Occasionally he looked up and played a torch around the many bulky shapes and protuberances cluttering the massive underside of *The Difference Engine* just above their heads. He played the beam onto 'V' shaped hangers supporting various metal rods and levers that formed part of the braking system and then at one especially nasty looking corner of a traction motor. There was a plethora of potential points on which a man could strike the back of his head with sufficient force to cause a nasty wound and perhaps knock him to the floor. But sufficient to kill?

Mellor agreed. 'First off; he's hit the back of his head. That's what the doc says and we can see the wound. It was a right whack. That means he must 'ave been leaning forward or bending down and then stood up sharpish.'

'An action likely to give an unpleasant bump and perhaps cut the skin, but insufficient to kill...'

'Right. An' secondly, what was he lookin' at? What's so interesting about this bit of floor he needed to stare at it? I reckon someone's made off with whatever it was.' Mellor was warming to the idea this was a crime scene.

Vignoles looked at where Mellor was playing the beam of his torch. The inspection pit was remarkably clear of detritus and the floor just a patchwork of oil stains and ever-present coal dust and ash. 'Have you moved the body?' Vignoles now looked between the big driving wheels of the engine to address the doctor standing close by. The doctor's beautifully polished hand-made shoes looked out of place.

'Dear me, no, inspector. I am well enough versed in this kind of business to know that you, the detectives, must survey the scene unblemished. I was able to ascertain that this fellow had moved from the land of the living by checking his pulse and temperature exactly as he lay. That very visible wound to his head would fell an elephant.' The doctor was an effete character previously known to Vignoles and his opinion respected. 'The warmth of the body is consistent with his demise being close to the time he was discovered, give or take a few minutes.'

'I'd like to turn him over. I want to see if there is anything underneath the body.'

Mellor wedged himself against one side of the narrow pit, whilst trying not to get his sharp blue suit filthy. He gave Grimes a hefty pull upwards, making one limp arm drag along the brick floor and his pale, waxy face roll unpleasantly to one side. The eyes were open and held a fixed stare that suggested complete surprise. 'Looks like 'e never knew what was comin'.'

Vignoles grunted agreement as the doctor looked down from between the wheels.

Vignoles shone his torch along the floor and over the chest of the dead man. 'Can't see anything.' He searched jacket pockets and both trouser pockets. 'Lower him back to how we found him.' Vignoles addressed Mellor, then adjusted the lay of a lifeless arm using his gloved hand. 'Let's get out of here and get a better look. Ask the photographer to do the best he can down there.'

'Wallet…' He handed this straight to Mellor, who rifled through it.

'Journalist. Name of Richard Grimes. A small amount of dosh, but not worth killing for.'

'Keys…handkerchief. A cloth for polishing spectacles or the lens of a camera…

'He's a photo-journalist.' Mellor added.

'Then where is his camera?' Vignoles replied. 'We need to find it.'

Mellor instructed a uniformed constable to start a search and went back to the contents of the wallet.

'Anything to indicate where he lives?'

'Not in here.'

'He may have been part of the group who came in with the gas turbine.' Saunders, who had been looking on, finally broke his silence. 'The engine was held at signals and managed to blow herself up.' Saunders gave an ironic lift to one side of his mouth. 'There was a crowd of technicians who came in with her, though I couldn't identify most of them. It was the assistant director and one of his men who spoke to me and it was that chap over there who found the body.'

Cartwright was sitting on a bench against the back wall some distance away with a blanket around his shoulders and nursing a mug of strong tea. A constable stood by preventing anyone crossing a hasty cordon erected using lengths of rope strung between locomotive buffers and the legs of sturdy workbenches lining the walls.

'We need names and addresses and the whereabouts of everyone on the turbine project and who was here today.' Vignoles issued the orders. 'Our man there should be able to help. It's likely Mr Grimes was following their progress.'

'They won't have wanted him reporting it blowing up…'

Mellor chipped in.

'True, but I can't see them killing him to stop the story either,' Vignoles was eyeing Cartwright whilst he spoke. He looked the kind of intelligent fellow who'd spend most of his waking hours devoted to his project. Was he capable of striking out and murdering someone because it suffered a setback? It seemed unlikely. 'Doctor, you will do a PM?

'Most certainly, inspector. On the face of it, a case of "blunt instrument to the back of the head."' He raised a cautionary finger, 'but I shall need a more detailed appraisal before I could say if the blunt instrument in question was stationary or being deployed by someone with malicious intent...'

'You think he was struck?'

'All I shall say at this present moment is that I need to find convincing evidence the poor fellow could accidentally throw himself back with sufficient force to cause that wound.'

'I take your point. We will carefully study the underside of the engine in daylight and look for blood.'

'I'll work on him midday tomorrow.'

'One of us will be there.' Vignoles raised his hat in farewell. 'Mellor, get uniform to search for possible heavy blunt instruments. Gloves on and tell them to be careful not to destroy fingerprints.'

The two detectives surveyed the many workbenches piled with oversized tools and Mellor shrugged his shoulders. 'Take 'yer pick!'

'Tim, we need to fingerprint everyone working here today for purposes of elimination. Yourself included...'

Saunders nodded understandingly and sent his deputy away to compile a list of those known to have been on site. 'First impressions, Charles?' Saunders now felt free to speak about what was unfolding within his domain.

'As you suspected.' Vignoles gave a nod of appreciation to his friend. 'It would have been reasonable to have him moved and perhaps even try resuscitation. Once away from the scene, his death may not have aroused suspicion. Just another workplace accident.'

'Was that the intention?' Mellor was speaking rhetorically, his roving, restless eyes turning to the interior of the engine shed, surveying the layout and the relative positions of the various engines stabled there. 'Set up to look like an accident...'

'We must consider that.'

'Seems reasonable to imagine a nosy journalist sneaking underneath the engine to see where he shouldn't. It's cramped and dark down there and a good place to stage an accidental death?'

* * * *

'Mr Cartwright, what were you doing before you discovered the body?'.

'A last look over before locking the engine up for the night. We'll have to drag her back to the works to get her up and running, but if we're lucky, we might be able to fix her up here. But that's for Mr Race to decide once we've assessed the damage.'

'Mr Race?'

'Project Director.'

'And where is he?' Vignoles asked.

'Back in Rugby with the rest of the team.'

'You were alone with the engine when you discovered the body?' Mellor continued.

'Yeah. It should have been me *and* Phil. Phil Mercer, but I sent him ahead to sort lodgings and find a decent pub and some fish and chips. That felt like a priority, to be honest.' His tummy rumbled loudly. 'He's probably wondering where I've got to.'

'When we've finished, DS Mellor will accompany you into town and you can introduce him to Mr Mercer. Explain how you discovered the body.'

'I first went inside the engine compartment. At number one 1 end - the one nearest us - as it was open, the other end was locked.'

'Was Mr Grimes onboard?'

'Nope, just me. It would have been against company policy for him to be inside. He knows…he knew… he was not allowed unless accompanied by Miss Lessiter, and then only by prior agreement.'

'Who is Miss Lessiter?'

'Press Officer for Tompkins-Dunkler. She was in charge of keeping a close rein on the photographer.'

'And did she?'

'On the whole. He was cheeky. Tried it on a bit.'

'With Miss Lessiter?' Vignoles raised an eyebrow.

'He was all over her like a rash,' Cartwright was disapproving. 'Fancied himself as a ladies' man but I don't think he had any luck. Easy to see why he failed as Doris is a real looker. You've seen the state of him. She'd have to be desperate…' He stopped. 'Sorry, I shouldn't say things like that about a dead man.'

'Grimes was working with the project?' Vignoles asked.

'On an article for a railway magazine. He was always trying to go where he was not supposed to and asking prying questions. I think he wanted to catch us off guard and give away information.'

'You have information to give away?' Vignoles was interested in the direction this was going.

'I suppose we do. It's a new project with some novel ideas.'

'What specifically? This is a police investigation and you can be assured of our discretion.'

'Some of the kit onboard is experimental.'

'Electronics?'

'How do you know that?'

'A guess,' Vignoles replied.

'Uh-huh. English Electric supply this kit and they're eager

to protect their ideas.'

'They wouldn't want a journalist telling the world?'

'Of course not.'

'There is something about the engine worth killing for?' Mellor had walked across to join them. He seemed eager to speak to Vignoles.

'I hope not!' Cartwright looked shocked.

'When you were inside the engine did you see or hear anyone close by?' Mellor chipped in.

'No. I mean, there were the sounds of others working. Like now...' The relentless battle of man against unyielding metal continued somewhere distant.

'You sound unsure?' Vignoles pressed Cartwright.

The engineer seemed to be weighing something up. 'I was concentrating on what I had to do and not taking notice of anything else...'

'But?'

'But I thought I heard voices. Raised voices for a few moments.'

'When was this?'

'When I was inside the engine compartment.'

'An argument?'

'Perhaps... I was not trying to listen in...'

'Did you recognise the voices?' Vignoles asked.

'Look, inspector, I really could be wrong about this.'

'Tell us what you heard, and we will decide if it is important or not.' Mellor demanded.

'One of them could have been Grimes. The other was unfamiliar.'

'Grimes was arguing with someone near the engine?'

'I think he was.'

'You have no idea who the other man was?'

'The engine compartment has tiny windows, I couldn't see.'

'But you looked?' Vignoles queried.

'I tried. I caught a bad view of someone. Their back. He was in a uniform. I couldn't see his face.'

'What sort of uniform?'

'Smart. The sort a station master might wear. Or maybe a signalman or porter. A railwayman.'

'You did not recognise them?'

'Sorry...'

'That is still useful Mr Cartwright. How long was it after this possible argument between Grimes and the other man before you went underneath?'

'A couple of minutes.'

Vignoles and Mellor exchanged looks. This was significant. 'What made you go underneath?' Vignoles asked.

'More checks.' Cartwright shrugged. 'I wasn't expecting to find anything, but it's how we are on this project.'

Vignoles accepted his explanation and asked him to continue.

'I stepped into the pit, clicked on my torch and there he was. Couldn't miss him. I thought he'd just banged his head and was out cold...'

'Did you touch the body?' Vignoles asked.

'I went close. I saw it was Grimes and called his name. I shook his shoulder to try and wake him. But there was no response and then I saw his eyes...' Cartwright was pale. 'I didn't like the way they were just staring, so I went for help. It was better someone who knows what they're doing looked at him.'

Vignoles nodded assent. 'You went to find Mr Saunders?'

'I looked for someone in charge so they could get an ambulance.'

'Did you see Mr Grimes' camera?' Vignoles asked.

'No?'

'Is the locomotive still unlocked?'

'I'd best lock it...' Cartwright made to leave.

'I will lock it after I've finished,' Vignoles held out his hand for the keys.

'It's against company policy. It's forbidden for anyone -.'

'There is a dead man under the company's property. We're British Railways Transport Police on British Railways property. We decide who takes a look inside.' Mellor's voice was hard. 'If DCI Vignoles wants the keys you hand 'em over or we might wonder why you don't want us to see inside.'

Cartwright looked worried. 'My boss will throw a fit...'

'We'll square everything.' Vignoles accepted the keys and sounded conciliatory. The man had had a nasty shock at the end of a trying day. 'You need food and a pint. Mellor, take Mr Cartwright into town and get a statement from Mercer whilst you are there.'

'Wilco. But there's something you need to see first...'

Chapter Fourteen

'We've found a possible murder weapon.' Mellor explained as he led Vignoles to the far side of *The Difference Engine* and towards a sturdy bench cluttered with tools. 'Howerth picked this out,' Mellor indicated a huge monkey wrench. PC Simon Howerth stood guard, pleased at the approval in Mellor's voice but trying not to show it.

Vignoles peered closely at the wrench but did not touch it. 'Is that blood?'

'I reckon so.'

Vignoles nodded. Even under the imperfect illumination of the roof lamps he could see a clutch of fresh fingerprints. 'This was recently handled.'

'Look like good fresh dabs on the handle and blood on the end.'

'We need a fingerprint team up here. Get everyone in the depot printed. This requires preserving exactly as it is.' He glanced at the gloved hands of Howerth. 'Have you touched anything?'

'Not this one, sir. Visual inspection only. Had my gloves on the whole time in case I needed to push something aside to get a better view.'

'Good work.' Vignoles and Mellor stepped away. 'It needs checking against the wound and the blood types have to match, but we're treating this as a murder from now.'

'Right you are, sir.'

'Get a statement from the other engineer in the town, then back here. Call for reinforcements. We've a lot of people to process as fast as possible. Find who was arguing with Grimes and we've probably got our man. And find his camera...'

* ***

'Mr Mercer?' Mellor addressed the young man seated at a

table and just starting a fresh pint, and a packet of salt and vinegar crisps. Mercer sat alone. His was an unfamiliar face and it would take another pint or two for the locals to discover he was part of the crew who'd brought in the extraordinary white and silver locomotive. He could expect some lively banter and leg-pulling once they did.

'That's me.' He looked up innocently at DS Mellor and PC Howerth.

'Can I confirm you're with the gas turbine engine?'

'The GTX-001. That's correct. What's this about? She overheated, but hardly a police affair.' He laughed.

'Do you know Richard Grimes?'

'The reporter? He asked me a few questions and I've seen him around taking snaps, but that's about it.'

'Did you get along with Mr Grimes?'

'Well enough. I didn't take much notice of him, to be honest. We've enough to do without worrying about the press.'

'What time did you leave Woodford Halse engine shed this evening?'

'About seven-ish. Ellis said he'd finish up with the engine and meet me down here. I don't know what's happened to him?' Mercer started to look concerned, eyeing Howerth's uniform uneasily.

'Your friend will join you shortly.' Mellor paused a beat and lowered his voice. 'He discovered the body of Richard Grimes underneath *The Difference Engine*.'

'Good God! *Body*? You mean he's dead?'

Mellor pulled up a chair and sat opposite Mercer. He felt confident the man was going to be eliminated from a potential suspect list and didn't need two police officers looming over him. 'We're treating his death as suspicious.'

'Someone killed him?' Mercer was shocked.

'We think someone assaulted him. Whether with intent to kill is to be determined. Can you think of anyone who might wish to do that to Mr Grimes?'

'Gosh... He was a bit of a pain in the backside but that was his job, I suppose. That's no reason to kill him.' Mercer shook his head in disbelief. 'Can't say I took much notice of the fella.' He paused and drank deeply from his beer.

'Do you know if anyone argued with Grimes?'

'The boss lost his rag with him yesterday.'

'An argument?'

'It was nothing serious, just telling him where he could and could not go. Setting ground rules...'

'When did you last see Grimes?' Mellor changed tack.

'Today. We broke down approaching Woodford. There was steam everywhere and plenty of cursing, I can tell you. Then up pops Grimes with his camera. Mr Gimball - he's the assistant project manager - was not best pleased!' Mercer laughed in an edgy manner. 'We think we know what went wrong, but Gimball didn't want it caught on camera for obvious reasons.'

'Grimes was not on the train?'

'No, I think he was lineside. I was in the Dynamometer Car with more important stuff on my mind that worrying about where he was working.'

'Do you think it odd that he was exactly where the engine broke down?'

'Not given it any thought. Do you think it is?' It was a fair question to fire back.

Mellor ignored the question. 'Can you think of any reason Grimes would want to go underneath the locomotive this evening?'

'None, and he was not granted that kind of access. He was supposed to be supervised at all times when up close, but I know Miss Lessiter - she's in charge of our public relations - went back to Rugby earlier with the coaching stock.'

Mellor nodded. He needed to speak to her. 'Did you see Grimes this evening in the shed?'

'No.'

'You didn't see or hear him arguing with someone?'

'I said I didn't.'

'Thank you. The locomotive is now a crime scene and as such nobody can board nor go underneath. Detective Chief Inspector Vignoles is advising the project director of the situation.'

'For how long? We need to get her back up and running.'

'As long as it takes.' Mellor now saw Cartwright, scrubbed clean and in 'civvies' enter the bar. 'Your friend is here. We'll leave you to enjoy the rest of the evening.' Cartwright sidled over as Mellor stood up. 'Keep a lid on the chatter tonight, gents. I'm sure most in here will get to hear Grimes died, but no speculating. Grimes banged his head. Leave it at that for now.'

'But you think -.'

'Mr Mercer, no-one is *thinkin'* anything. We have unconfirmed suspicions. Nothing more, nothing less.' Mellor gave Cartwright a hard stare. 'If either of you gents remembers summat you forgot to mention, make sure you tell me first.' He handed over a card.

* * * *

David Green was stunned into momentary silence. He was standing in the signal box, his motorcycle helmet in hand whilst staring at the man he was relieving from duty. It was 6am and word had already spread like wildfire across town and railway.

'Found him face down "dead as a doornail" as Dickens said of Marley.'

'As a "coffin nail".'

'Is that right? Whichever it is, he was dead and underneath *The Difference Engine*.'

Green looked stunned. 'It was an accident?'

'That's what I heard.'

'Yesterday evening?'

'Aye. Some reckon he was nosing around and bashed himself on the head. It can be dangerous underneath engines.'

'He was very eager for a good story…'

'A bit too eager for his own good! Sorry, that was a bit flippant.'

Green was hanging the helmet up and taking a moment to compose himself and said nothing.

'You were friends?'

'School friends. A long time ago.' Green signed himself in and started to read the recent entries and the daily sheet, but his eyes were taking nothing in. *Grimes dead?* He didn't know how to process this shocking information. His palms were becoming sweaty and his pulse increasing. 'We'd drifted apart years ago…' He stood upright and strode purposefully towards the frame of levers and tried to snap back into his customary working mode, eyes flicking over the instruments. 'It was late evening he had the accident, I guess? He'd be more able to sneak in after dark…'

'No, it was more like seven. One of the engineers working on that different engine thingy found him.'

Seven? The timing hit Green like a punch. *Almost exactly the time he'd argued with Richie. How was this possible?* Green fell silent, unsure how to interpret this disturbing turn of events but was rescued from his thoughts by a series of bells. He replied and pulled levers on and off and found comfort in the action. Concentrated hard work was what he needed right now.

'Dave, if you'd like a bit of time off today, I can work on a few hours…'

'No, I'm alright!' His response sounded snappier than intended. 'Richie moved away before the war. I only saw him a couple of times after that. We never stayed in touch. It's horrid for his family though…'

'It is. But to be honest he shouldn't have been creeping about where he was not allowed.'

Green nodded agreement.

'Mind you, the police are here in force. All over the shed last night and still at it today. Makes you wonder if there's more to it. There *are* mutterings it was not an accident.'

'Get away?' Green felt an icy finger run down his spine.

'Straight up.'

Green filled in the logbook. 'Perhaps we should not read too much into that. It's what the police do in situations like this I expect. A death, even if accidental, still needs properly investigating. All the more so because *The Difference Engine* and crew are from a private company. Makes it all the more important they are thorough.'

'I reckon you're right. Well, nothing we can do to help the poor sod now. I'd best be on my way...'

Green stared out of the windows at the railway lines below. He had no idea what sort of meaningless rubbish he had just rolled out, yet it had a satisfying ring about it. But what was he going to tell the police if they questioned him? Tell them everything or try to cut Grimes out of the picture as much as possible? He didn't want to be drawn into this mess and have his role in allowing the gas turbine to overheat to become news and part of an investigation. And he certainly didn't want to have the police delve into his unproven suspicions about something that happened so many years ago. He'd threatened Grimes last night and made some unpleasant insinuations, but afterwards he found this had lanced the boil of his pent-up frustrations and resentment towards his old friend and had been surprised to find himself regretting some of his foolish words. Thankfully nobody had heard what was said and perhaps it would be better if that hair band was consigned to a bin. But this wasn't going to be that easy. Not now. Even when dead, Grimes made problems, and this looked like it was going to be the worst of all.

He was staring, sightlessly out of the window until he realised the ringing sound in his head was the telephone. He needed to calm himself down and think how best to play the ugly hand of cards he'd just been dealt.

Chapter Fifteen

Doris Lessiter was glad of the large sherry WPC Benson bought her. Benson was silently wondering if Lessiter's sudden attack of nerves was prompted more by worrying how this was going to look for the company, than genuine distress over the death of Richard Grimes.

'I can't understand why he would go there. It was off-limits.'

'That is what we need to understand. There was no remit for Mr Grimes to visit the engine?'

'Most certainly not. Once it failed, Mr Gimball made it clear he wanted Grimes to travel back to Rugby with the coaching stock. He wanted him well out of the way.'

'Why was that?'

'Not exactly good publicity, is it?'

'Grimes was on the train when it broke down?'

'No. He was not invited to travel with us. He was restricted to lineside photographs only.'

'Was he good at obeying instructions?'

'Not really.' Lessiter pursed her lips into a line then sighed impatiently. 'He had a habit of wandering off. A most annoying man.' Lessiter gave an apologetic smile and finished most of her sherry. 'I can only suppose he got off the train at Woodford Halse station when it was being prepared to return to Rugby with the crew. I gave him clear instructions to sit tight! But there were difficulties in getting a crew and a suitable engine for the run to Rugby at short notice and we ended up standing at Woodford for quite a while. In a siding at first and later in the station, so there was plenty of time for him to detrain.'

'You were not with Mr Grimes?'

'No. I had very important matters to discuss with Mr Race and then I went to an empty compartment to get on with my work away from everyone. I was busy. It was not until late that I returned to my hotel.

'Did you get along well with Mr Grimes?'

Lessiter frowned at the question. Benson waited. 'I cannot pretend I found him easy and there were a few problems.'

'What sort of problems?'

'He was rather full of himself, but in my line of work you meet many men like him and I can handle it.' The slight hesitation in her voice suggested she was holding something back.

'It would be helpful if you told me everything you can. We need to understand his character.'

'The board of directors had banned him that morning from travelling with *The Difference Engine*.'

'Why?'

'We made a discovery earlier that morning. He was not a salaried member of *The Railway Magazine* staff as he had indicated. He was a freelancer, and not even a very successful one.' Lessiter was looking uncomfortable. 'The editor denied sending Grimes to us on assignment.'

'Grimes misled you?'

She flushed. 'Perhaps one could have been more diligent... But he sounded so convincing and the company needed someone to provide a portfolio of images and a good press story.'

'How did you rumble him?'

'Mr Gimball didn't like the way Grimes was always trying to get the technicians to share restricted information. Grimes almost hounded some of the technicians, following them around. And when not doing that seemed to spend a lot of time taking frivolous pictures.'

'What sort of pictures?' Benson was puzzled.

'Informal snaps of the staff. Not the kind of thing for a serious article.' She sounded dismissive.

'Including yourself?'

She cleared her throat. 'A few times. I did not encourage him.'

Benson studied Lessiter for a moment. It was easy to see why the dead man had found her an appealing subject. But had there been more? 'Did Grimes try anything funny with you?' Benson sipped her drink. She was on duty, but a matching glass of sherry seemed appropriate to help an anxious Miss Lessiter feel at ease.

'Never! It was a strictly professional relationship.' Lessiter looked horrified but also flushed as she replied. Benson was not yet convinced and continued looking at Lessiter, waiting for her to elaborate. 'He tried to flirt, of course. A dreadful experience. I get used to that kind of attention from men like Grimes, so I could handle it...' Her face softened. It was obvious Miss Lessiter was fully aware of her good looks and the effect they might have on the opposite sex. 'I can assure you I never allowed him to overstep the mark.'

Benson smiled. 'An occupational hazard.'

'He was always ready with an inappropriate observation about what I was wearing.' She knocked back the last of her sherry. 'God, I need another.' She stood up and went to the bar without asking if Benson wished to join her and soon returned with two more schooners.

'Thank you.' *All in the line of duty*. Benson could handle the drink and felt she was making headway and now was not the time to break the flow.

'I didn't like him pointing his camera at me. I have a suspicion he used up half his film stock on me.' Lessiter fished out a cigarette and after Benson declined one, lit it and blew a stream of smoke into the air and took a moment before continuing. 'Look, it is awful he's dead. Quite horrid. But he was not someone I can pretend I liked. In truth, he repelled me.' The sherry was starting to knock the edges off her emotions. 'However, leery suggestions are no reason to kill him if that's what you think.'

'I have no such thoughts. Do you know what make of camera it was?'

'Gosh, don't ask me about technical stuff. It was just a camera slung around his neck. Neat, compact and looked expensive. The kind you expect professionals to use. He had a camera bag and a tripod he brings - brought - along sometimes. I have a Box Brownie and the pictures always turn out a disappointment with the heads cut off!'

'He had his camera with him when the engine broke down?'

'He did. I don't think I ever saw him without it.'

Benson made a note. This was important. The camera had not yet been found. 'Was there anyone on the team who had a falling out with Grimes?'

'Sufficient to kill him?'

'Or perhaps lose their temper and strike him?'

'Some got a bit shirty, but it was never serious.' She gave this more consideration. 'I suppose Ellis Cartwright ragged Grimes the hardest and poked fun at him. Just his way of getting him to go somewhere else.'

'There was animosity between them?'

'That is a strong word. I think they just rubbed each other up the wrong way. Nothing more.'

'What is Cartwright's place in the team?'

'Electronics. He is the team leader of the sparks. A dull boffin, between you and me. I can't understand anything he tells me but it sounds awfully impressive. Please don't tell anyone I said that.'

'Do you know if Mr Grimes has a family?'

'I know nothing about his private life. I tried to avoid any conversational gambits from Mr Grimes.'

'What time did you arrive back at Rugby?'

Lessiter suddenly looked unsure of herself, fiddling with her cigarette. 'I didn't take much notice of the time, actually. I was so preoccupied with other things you see and then suddenly noticed we'd stopped and hurriedly gathered up my papers and got off.'

Benson finished her drink and put her notebook away. She stood up and was about to thank Doris Lessiter for her time when she fired one last question. 'That's all right. I presume other team members will be able to confirm when you disembarked at Rugby?'

'I-I presume so. Though really, why would they take any notice? I'm sure they all had quite enough to be thinking about. Oh, but wait a moment, I sat finishing a few last notes and might have been the last off the train.'

Benson thought this answer sounded strange. The train would not have sat in Rugby Central a moment longer than strictly necessary and on the London Extension line that was usually little more than a couple of minutes at best. 'And the name of the hotel you are staying at?'

'I can't see why you need to know that?'

'It's a policewoman's lot to be pernickety,' Benson smiled, and waited.

Chapter Sixteen

It was Vignoles' duty to break the news to Grimes' only surviving parent. An elderly mother living alone in Charwelton. Mellor had managed to establish her name and address but by the time he had done so, it was far too late to knock on the door of an old lady. She would be tucked up in bed and it would do nothing to ease the pain of her loss being rudely awakened in the bleak hours of the night. He decided to delay this grim visit until morning, and it was just a short train ride from Woodford Halse to Charwelton. Vignoles elected to take WPC Lansdowne with him as Mellor had plenty to be getting on with and Lansdowne's gentle manner would be welcome during what could only be a fraught meeting. She had been given instructions to rendezvous with Vignoles at 6 am at the station.

Gladys Grimes was as frail as he feared. Painfully thin and with a tendency towards forgetfulness. Continually dipping in and out of understanding and suddenly changing the subject so it was hard to know how much she understood. They spent time on her doorstep patiently explaining who they were and why they needed to enter her house and sit and talk.

'But I don't need to sit down, I've just got up!'

'I'd prefer it if we went inside and we sat down before...'

'Are you tired?'

'No, but...'

'Then why do want to sit?'

'If we could step inside, please?'

'My house is not a station waiting room!'

They eventually coaxed her into allowing them into her compact ironstone cottage with its small windows rendering it dark and cold inside despite the warming morning sun. All three sat in her minuscule back kitchen. Vignoles was glad he had brought Lansdowne. She made a pot of tea and gave encouraging smiles that seemed to offer a measure of reassurance to a confused Gladys Grimes.

'When did you last see or speak to your son, Richard?'

'Not for a long time. No.' She looked into the distance and the silence between them expanded but suddenly she stood up and walked somewhat stiffly across to a sideboard and picked up a small framed photograph and brought this back. She handed it to Lansdowne. It was a fine image of one of the recent British Railways Britannia class locomotives, *William Shakespeare*, storming out of London Victoria station. 'He sent me this. He took the picture! He wrote to me. It's on the back, me duck.'

Lansdowne flipped the frame over and Sellotaped on to the back of the frame was a postcard with a short message from Grimes.

'One of my best. Front cover! All is going well. Love R.'

'He didn't write much.' Lansdowne handed it to Vignoles.

'He never was one for letters.' Mrs Grimes smiled.

'Mrs Grimes. I am very sorry, but I have bad news about Richard...'

'He's not able to come over? But he said he would try.'

'I regret your son had an accident last night. He died.' Vignoles thought it best to take this by stages.

'Accident? No, I don't think so. He would have telephoned Mrs Windybank in the Post Office and she would tell me if he'd been hurt.' She shook her head. 'I don't have a telephone here, you see, and Mrs Windybank is very good in passing on a message if it is important.' After more patient work Vignoles finally believed Mrs Grimes comprehended the severity of the situation. She looked pale whilst she sipped sweetened tea.

'Did your son come to see you this last week? He was taking pictures of a special white and silver locomotive that is being tested on the railway here. You might have seen it pass through.'

'I saw it. Oh, it was lovely! But he didn't come to see me. That is so like Richard; he's not very good like that. But I am sure he will! He said so he would.'

Another ten minutes of going around in circles and Vignoles felt they had done all they could. It was hard to be sure, but they had gained the impression Gladys Grimes had been unaware her son had been just a few miles away in Woodford Halse and Rugby. With the name and address of another relative, (who was hopefully slightly younger and more able), they took their leave.

'I hope Mellor and Benson have a more productive visit to Grimes' lodgings.'

'Yes, sir. It seems so sad. She's alone and he never bothered to visit.'

'As far as we can tell.'

'I wonder why not?'

Vignoles chewed on the end of his pipe as they walked the short distance to the station. 'I do know one thing; it was not because he was too busy taking photographs. That picture he sent her claiming it was a front cover image he'd bagged, was not one of his. I know that photograph and the name of the photographer who took it.'

'Lying to his mum?'

'And who else, Lucy?'

Chapter Seventeen

DS Mellor and WPC Benson wanted to look over the room Grimes had been renting. Mellor was not expecting the search to throw up much but grubbing about in the private space of a victim always held the possibility of a surprise and, as he reminded Benson, 'This is proper detecting. Looking at the everyday life of this dead geezer and trying to find that little clue amongst all his uninteresting stuff. There's usually something if you look hard enough.'

Benson was delighted. She'd been given the chance to interview Miss Lessiter and now join Mellor for the room search. The DS usually asked Lucy or herself to make tea and fetch biscuits, type reports ('Women are better at it than men'), file something away or undertake the most menial of tasks. Interviewing victims of casual pick-pocketing being typical duties. It was not that Mellor disliked them; indeed, Benson was learning to live with her Detective Sergeant voicing the opinion she had 'a fabulous figure' and 'really suited stockings and a skirt' with tedious frequency. Mellor had also been caught patting Lansdowne's bottom on more than one occasion. He just had an aversion to the idea of women making good detectives. He was not alone in this opinion. Women were being allowed into the force, but as office workers doing administrative work or paraded for the cameras whilst dolled up in their best uniforms and perfect make-up, posing with blank notebooks in hand as they offered support to victims of non-violent crime. Benson had managed to avoid becoming the pin-up girl of the British Railways Transport Police but suspected it would not be long before she was standing on a platform with a whistle close to her lipsticked mouth and obligatory notebook in a gloved hand, whilst a photographer reeled off frames of film.

As Benson walked towards the unremarkable row of terraced houses that made up Winfield Street, she was determined to give this her best shot. She knew she was a good detective and it would be a feather in her cap if she found something useful. Mrs Meldrum, the landlady, was a sour-faced creature in a garish housecoat wearing a forest of yellow plastic curlers and an indeterminate shade of lipstick that made her look ill. Her bad-tempered welcome did British landladies no favours. As Mellor started to make the introductions, she interrupted.

'You're here then? About time.' She opened the front door wider and ushered them in, glaring at their feet as they dutifully brushed the dust from their shoes on the 'WELCOME' mat. 'Sad he got himself killed, but I need to rent the room out.'

'Could see his room?' Mellor managed to ask.

'Follow me. You *are* taking everything away now? I need to get the sheets changed but was told not to touch anything and to leave the door locked.'

'We need to take a look before anything is disturbed. We have a squad car outside and will remove his gear once we are satisfied.'

'How long will all that take?'

'The sooner we start, the sooner we're out.' Mellor was losing patience.

'This is the room.' Mrs Meldrum fished a key from her housecoat and opened the door and made to step inside.

'We'll take over now.'

Meldrum gave Mellor an annoyed look and stomped back down the stairs. Mellor and Benson entered, closing the door behind.

The room was modestly sized. Curtains the same shade as Mrs Meldrum's unattractive lipstick hung at the window. There was a bed of pre-war Art Deco design with a green and brown eiderdown and fleecy woollen sheets. Mellor opened the twin doors of the wardrobe whilst Benson inspected the bedside table and the drawer beneath.

'He travelled light. A couple of shirts, a second pair of trousers and a jacket.' Mellor now surveyed the toiletries beside the small sink in the corner, then noticed a collection of bags at one side of the room. 'What's in those?'

Benson was already opening one of the bags. 'A camera tripod, but no camera.'

'Then where the devil is it?'

'A spare lens in a case. And five new boxes of film. Not much.'

'He was only here a few nights…'

Benson surveyed the room. 'He left little of his personality behind.'

'A page torn from a Loughborough telephone directory,' Mellor picked up the page where it lay on the bedspread.

'Perhaps he wanted to look for a name and address in the comfort of his room?'

Mellor looked unimpressed. 'We'd best take this back to the office and see if it reveals anything.'

Benson peered under the bed. 'Sarge!' She pulled out a cardboard box and opened the lid to reveal a scrapbook with a garish cover containing sugar paper pages. 'Lots of old press cuttings. Some photographic prints.'

'Let me see.' Mellor took the scrapbook which was made fat with the many carefully pasted cuttings, going yellow with age. 'They're old. From 1928 and a few years after. They seem to be about a missing girl.' He handed it back to Benson.

'There are some photos. A station platform. And a road… and a path. A bit boring and with nobody in them.' Benson shook her head.

Mellor glanced across. 'The kind of picture we'd take to record a crime scene?'

'There are plenty of them. It was an extensive scene.'

'Righty ho, we take it back to base and you get reading. Every page. Find out where these places are and how they relate to these clippings. No idea if it helps explain why someone did him in, but it just might.'

Benson smiled. Proper detecting!

Chapter Eighteen

Mellor was standing at the front entrance to Woodford Halse locomotive shed smoking a cigarette. He was watching as a line of big steamers were being carefully moved around the yard by the shed pilot engine. As far as Mellor could work out, the shed foreman had decided one of the O2 class freight engines was not fit to go back to work and wanted it extracted from a line of engines in light steam and for the recalcitrant engine to be pushed back into the shed on a different line for inspection. The pilot was heaving and pushing up to five locomotives at a time as it shuffled the pack to cut out the defective one. It was oddly satisfying to observe, and once Mellor understood what they were trying to achieve he found himself trying to second guess each move. He was becoming so engrossed in this shunting puzzle it took a moment for him to realise a fitter was standing close by, also watching.

'She's sprung a leak in the backhead. The fire raiser noticed when getting her up to pressure. A right pain in the backside. She's not one of ours and I reckon we could have sent her back to Darnell shed and they could fix her up. Their engine - their problem.'

'A boiler leak is dangerous.'

'It was just a weep. She'd last long enough to get home.'

'Still…' Mellor was glad he was not the crew slogging hard towards Sheffield with a heavy load behind and the boiler in danger of cracking open. That was probably why Mr Saunders was in charge and this grubby fellow was a grease monkey. 'Fag?'

'Don't mind if I do! She's got to cool down before I can get to work.'

Mellor nodded understanding and watched as the filthy black freight locomotive was pushed backwards into the stygian gloom of the shed.

'You here because of the murder?'

'Suspicious death.'

'More than suspicious.'

'Why do you say that?' Mellor looked at his smoking companion.

'Killed himself striking his nut? Come off it! A man can be crushed between wagons or get a leg or arm sliced off on the track. He can get burned or lose fingers in any number of ways. A few of the lads here have a bit of a finger lopped off. Then you cough your lungs up later in life, what with all the dust and smoke. I could go on. But drop dead because you banged your head in an inspection pit? Pull the other one!'

'And you would know?'

'Damn right I would. Worked here since I was fifteen. Never seen anybody cop more than a sore head straightening up and banging their bonce. Mebbe a small cut, but nothing iodine and aspirin won't cure.'

Mellor gave him another glance. The fitter probably knew the shed as well as anyone. He knew the risks and his assessment was fair. He and the guvnor both thought Grimes had been nobbled deliberately by someone wielding a hefty monkey wrench, so why shouldn't this man have worked out as much himself. 'Got any other reasons for thinking this death was not what it seems? You should tell me if you do.'

'I don't snitch.'

'The Honour of Thieves...' Mellor stubbed his fag end out with a decisive swivel of his size ten. 'If someone's going' round killing folk, they don't need protecting. If I find you know summat and neglected to tell me, I'll 'ave you down the nick faster than the *Mallard* down Stoke Bank!' He locked his eyes on the other. 'Cos' you're right. This *is* a murder investigation.'

The man stared back but remained silent.

'Tell me what you know, an' I'll decide if it's important or not. Mebbe it just needs a discreet enquiry and I find it has no relevance. That's it. Nobody needs to be any the wiser...'

'I don't like the idea of getting folk in trouble.'

'If they've done nuffin' wrong, they won't get into trouble. If guilty of murder, they deserve what they get.'

The fitter shuffled his feet and looked at the ashy ground, then spoke quietly. 'It's the signalman. Mr Green.'

'What about him?'

'He was here. The evening that fella was killed. I saw him. I was on a B17, fighting with sticky brake gear. Under the loco much of the time and probably out of sight to him.'

Mellor opened his pack of cigarettes and offered the man a fresh one. 'What time was this?'

'I didn't have a watch on. You just smash the dial working where I do, but I reckon it was going on seven or thereabouts.'

'Seven in the evening?'

'Yeah.'

Mellor was on high alert. 'Where was Mr Green the signalman when you saw him and what was he doing?'

'Walking right past where we're standing. He was going into the shed.'

'And then?'

'Dunno. I went back to what was doing. It was a right old fight I can tell you.' He leaned forward to accept a light from Mellor. 'All I know is it was Green and he was walking into the shed.'

'Did you see him leave?'

'I was under the engine getting on with another crappy job, but I saw him a while later going away in a hurry.'

'Running?'

'Walking fast. Like he needed to be somewhere else.'

Or get away from a crime scene. Mellor felt a tingle of excitement.

'Listen, I'm not accusing him...'

'Nobody said you were. You are sure it was David Green?'

A silence. 'It was him. We're both Woodford lads.'

114

'Your name?'

'Derek Jennings.'

'Thanks for that, Mr Jennings. As I said, it's probably nothing.' Mellor sounded deliberately off-hand. 'Most enquiries like this come to nothing. But best you keep this under your hat for now, and I'll do the same, eh?' Mellor started to walk away; the guvnor needed to know about this.

Chapter Nineteen

'A bit unconventional isn't it?' David Green could barely contain his annoyance.

'The circumstances are unconventional,' Vignoles kept his voice neutral. 'We've arranged cover for one hour. Our questions will be a brief as possible.' They were standing on the gravel approach to the signal box and well out of hearing of the relief signalman.

'I don't see why you had to get a relief in just to ask me a few questions.'

'This box is busy and crucial to the safe and efficient running of the line. I did not consider it appropriate we questioned you about the death of a friend whilst at work.'

'Can't it wait until I clock off?'

'I regret, no.'

Green lit a cigarette, making no effort to offer one to either detective. His gestures were nervy, and he drew hard and quickly on the lighted cigarette, jetting smoke into the air between them. 'The clock's ticking. You'd better fire away.' They were standing near the end of the island platform of Woodford Halse station, away from any passengers or porters.

'We need to ask you about Richard Grimes. You knew him well?'

'He was an old school friend.'

'School days were a long time ago. I presume you were still in contact?'

'We lost touch after he moved away. That was over ten years ago. I think he went abroad but I'm not sure where. He never wrote.'

Vignoles considered this a moment. 'We are treating his death as suspicious.'

'I heard he'd had an accident?'

'You shouldn't believe all you hear,' Mellor snapped back.

'I'd heard he banged his head underneath an engine...'

'Who told you that?' Mellor fired back.

'The telephone was red hot this morning. Everyone in the shed and the station are talking about it. It's a small community.'

'Can you think of anyone who might want to kill your friend?' Vignoles asked.

'Of course not. I've no idea why anyone would do such a thing.' Green stared past the two detectives towards a rapidly approaching train.

'When did you last see Mr Grimes?' Vignoles asked.

A slight hesitation as Green dragged on his cigarette. 'I'd not seen him for years. He moved away.'

'But he came back,' Mellor replied. 'Recently.'

'Yeah. He...he was here a few days ago.'

'You met him?' Vignoles continued

'He came to see me.'

'Where was this?'

'At my home. In the evening.'

'What day?' Mellor asked.

'Last Wednesday, I think.'

'Think?' Mellor snapped.

'It was Wednesday.'

'You were expecting him to call in?' Vignoles asked.

'Not in the least!' Green paused. 'It was a complete surprise.'

'A pleasant one?' Mellor's expression was hard to read.

Green didn't reply.

'Did you spend much time together on Wednesday evening?' Vignoles asked.

'Once you got over your surprise,' Mellor muttered. 'My wife was preparing the evening meal, so we sat in the front parlour.'

'An old pal you've not seen in years an' you sit in a cold, unwelcoming room?' Mellor may not have been to the Green's house, but he knew that the front room in almost every house was unused, unaired or heated for most of the year. 'I'd be taking 'im down the boozer. Relive the good times an' 'ave a right old laugh.' Mellor grinned and balanced a cigarette in the corner of his mouth, all smiles and with a twinkle in his eye.

'We had a bottle of beer each. I was at work the next day, so I need to be steady.'

'What did you talk about?' Vignoles asked.

'This and that.' Green shrugged his shoulders. 'I discovered he was working as a journalist for *The Railway Magazine*. Just catching up.'

'How did he seem? Did you sense he was worried about anything?'

Green shrugged his shoulders. 'I didn't notice, inspector.'

'Grimes was popular around here?' Mellor asked.

'He is...*was*...a gregarious character. A strong personality and I suppose as a young man he was a bit of a 'Jack the Lad'.'

'Meanin' what?' Mellor asked.

'I suppose he was not to everyone's liking, but that's not to say he made enemies. We had some good times back then. Inspector, if my friend has been killed, why are you wasting time asking me these questions? Why are you not going after the person who did this terrible thing?'

Vignoles ignored the question. 'You saw Grimes again after Wednesday evening.' He deliberately made it not sound like a question.

Green dragged on his cigarette and seemed distracted by a Western Region Hall class locomotive gently steaming behind the signal box *en route* to the station, the fireman was leaning on his shovel and the driver looking relaxed as he peered over the cab side sheet. Mellor made a point of noisily rustling the pages of his notebook as he appeared to search for something. 'See, Mr Green, I've got a few names in here that says you did...'

'Ok, he was in my signal box. It's not against regulations to invite someone in if they behave responsibly.'

'I'm not interested in regulations. I'm interested in when, where and why you saw Mr Grimes.' Vignoles replied.

'He told me he was working as a journalist for *The Railway Magazine* on a big article. He said he wanted a good vantage point to photograph that white monstrosity they now have in the shed.'

'You are referring to the TD-GTX1 gas-turbine prototype? The one he was found dead underneath?'

'Yes…' Green looked pained.

'When was he with you in the box?'

'Yesterday.' Green stubbed his cigarette out and stared at the crushed stub lying on the surface of the platform.

'He got a grandstand view when it boiled over.'

'He did.'

'Somewhat fortuitous.'

'How d'you mean, inspector?' Green met Vignoles' eye, but his jaw muscles were pulsating.

'*The Difference Engine* was halted by yourself and held until it went bang whilst Grimes was on hand to take photographs and get a good story.'

Green shrugged his shoulders. 'It was the traffic. An unloaded test train is a low priority and something had to give. He actually wanted to photograph the train passing at speed but what he got was it blowing up. How was I to know it would do that?'

'Then he was found dead a few hours later under the same engine. Do you not find that odd?'

'I had not thought of it like that.'

Mellor took up the line of questioning. 'He comes to see you right out of the blue and you arrange for him to spend time with you in the signal box the next day just as the turbine fails. Later that evening you meet your friend in Woodford shed, then he's found bludgeoned to death underneath the same locomotive.'

Green checked his watch.

'We have time enough for you to deny that you met Grimes in the engine shed sometime between half-past six and about seven-thirty yesterday evening.' Vignoles raised an eyebrow, a slight smile on his face, daring the man to deny it.

'All right so I went there. To the shed. Once I clocked off from the box I took my motorbike and swung by. I wanted a close-up view of that strange beast of an engine.'

'You didn't go there to meet your friend?' Vignoles sounded sceptical.

'I thought he was in Rugby.'

'Why d'you think that?' Mellor barked.

'They took the coaches back there and most of the crew on board and I assumed he'd gone with them.'

'You did *not* meet Mr Grimes at the shed?'

Green chewed the inside of his mouth and looked thoughtful. 'No. I didn't see him.'

Neither detective looked convinced. 'We know Grimes was there, in the vicinity of *The Difference Engine*. He was discovered underneath the gas turbine in the inspection pit, so I find it hard to believe that neither of you saw each other.'

'I didn't.' Green was now having trouble meeting Vignoles' eyes.

'Can you think of any reason why someone would wish to kill your friend?'

'Of course not.'

'Did you see anyone acting suspiciously when you were looking at *The Difference Engine*? On your own.' Mellor asked.

'No.'

'You saw *nobody* at the shed to talk to?' Mellor was caustic.

'I wasn't going there to chat. Just look.' It sounded flat and his voice lacked conviction.

'What time were you at the shed? I need to get my timings straight…' Mellor asked whilst shaking his head as if puzzling over what was written in his notebook.

'About six-thirty. I was there just a few minutes.'

'Looking at the engine, nothing else?' Mellor was sceptical

'Is your daughter at work today?' Vignoles suddenly changed tack.

'You can leave Laura out of this. She can have nothing to do with the death of Richie. She never even knew him.'

An interesting reaction, Vignoles thought. They would make a point of talking to Laura Green. They had the police car and it would not take them long to motor to Desford Junction where she worked, but they would interview his wife first. Vignoles decided he didn't want to mention his intentions incase Green telephoned and gave advance warning. Vignoles tipped his hat. 'Thank you, Mr Green. You may resume your duties. We may wish to speak with you again. I must ask you do not to leave Woodford Halse without first calling and advising us of your exact whereabouts and intentions.' He handed Green one of his cards. 'A constable will call later to take your fingerprints.'

'Why do you need those?'

'You admit to being at the crime scene, so we need these to help eliminate you from our enquiries.' Vignoles and Mellor turned and walked away, leaving the signalman looking pensive.

Chapter Twenty

Vignoles raised the heavy cast-iron knocker. The sound echoed within the hall behind the door. Mellor and he in their dark work suits were like a pair of ravens pecking at the entrance to the domestic home on a glorious sunlit afternoon.

The Green's house was the end of a terrace on Church Street in the heart of Woodford Halse. Built of red brick with a slate roof and bay window to the ground floor overlooking a square of front garden guarded with a wooden gate. Their house abutted a corner shop where Castle Road climbed up from the valley floor from which the River Cherwell meandered sluggishly below the imposing bulk of the railway embankment. This carried the mainline and access into the marshalling yards holding many wagons awaiting onward dispatch. The shunting and shuffling of this traffic was an almost continuous process that generated a bright clatter of buffers, sharp squealing of brakes and short barks from the chimneys of the shunting engines like dogs herding beasts, both day and deep into the night, and would be audible to all those living on Church Street. The life of the railway was impossible to escape. The blue painted front door was also the same shade preferred by the Eastern Region of British Railways. Vignoles had observed several other houses had chosen this same colour. In a small town (more like a large village) that almost completely relied on the railway, it was perhaps unsurprising if a few cans of paint occasionally found their way out of the stores and onto doors and window frames. Pilfering of this sort was almost a daily occurrence across the vast railway network and virtually impossible to prevent. However, this illicit paint allowed Vignoles to place a little question mark against Mr David Green at an inopportune moment for the signalman.

Mrs Green looked at them with a trusting and curious expression, clearly unaware of the dark tidings they bore.

'Mrs Green?' Vignoles touched his hat brim as he made the introductions and whilst doing so noticed Mrs Green remained unflustered, merely wiping her floury hands on her apron. 'We need to ask you a few questions concerning an on-going investigation.' This was deliberately vague but wanted to be inside before revealing the true nature of their enquiries.

'Has there been an incident on the railway? I can't imagine how I can help. I expect you want my husband, but I'm afraid he's…'

'It would be better to talk away from the doorstep.'

They were ushered into the kitchen at the rear of the house which had the back door standing open, revealing a lengthy garden with a clutch of small sheds and planting beds edged with decorative bricks neatly lined with vegetables and tall stands of pretty flowers. 'Please sit, gents. I have a kettle about to boil so can make us tea.'

'We are here in connection with a man called Richard Grimes. Do you know him?'

'Richard? Yes, we know him.' She was filing the teapot with leaf tea.

'To be quite clear,' Vignoles showed a photograph Mellor had succeeded in obtaining. 'This man.'

'Yes, that's him. Has he had an accident?'

'When did you last see Mr Grimes?' Vignoles pressed on.

'Well, now there's the funny thing…' she was pouring the boiling water into the pot as she talked, clearly a woman at ease and unflustered by their unexpected presence. 'It was only the other day. Let me think; it was Tuesday. So that would be the 29th. In the evening. He just turned up out of the blue.'

'You were not expecting him?'

'No. Neither of us were. We'd not see him for years!'

'I thought you said you were friends?'

'Yes, we are. That is, *I* hardly knew him. He was my

husband's friend from years back and there were a few times we all met up, but it was David and he who did most of the talking on those occasions. Milk, sugar?' Both detectives indicated they would have both. 'But he left Woodford such a long time ago. David and I had only just started seeing each other when I was first introduced, but then he left the village and only came back infrequently to see David, and like I said, I was busy with the young family by then....' Her brow wrinkled as she considered this fact and gently swished the hot tea around in the pot to speed up the mashing. 'He went away - but I'm not sure where. It might have been abroad? David lost contact years ago and that's why it was such a surprise when he came knocking.' She poured the tea.

'Was your husband equally surprised?'

'He seemed a bit startled!' She laughed.

'Startled?' Mellor interjected. He had been taking notes. 'Please explain.'

'Surprised.' She paused to consider. 'It was almost as though he'd seen a ghost!' She laughed with an ease suggesting she was still unconcerned by their presence despite the questioning. 'It was so unexpected you see, and David for a moment or two looked as though he was in shock. Then he invited Richie in, and they shared a beer and chatted for quite a time. Renewing old acquaintances.'

'Do you know what they talked about?'

'I left them to it. I had jobs to do in the kitchen for the evening meal and they didn't need me sitting in like a wallflower.'

'Do you think your husband was pleased to see Grimes?' Vignoles asked.

Mrs Green paused a moment. 'I think he was. But it had been such a long time. It has to be nearly ten years since they last met, and things are always a bit awkward when so much time has passed.'

'In what way awkward?' Mellor pressed the point.

'Men. You're not the best at picking up after so many years. It takes a bit of time and perhaps a beer or two to get back in tune with each other.' She smiled indulgently as she sipped her tea.

'Mrs Green, I regret to inform you that Mr Grimes is dead. It happened yesterday evening at Woodford Halse locomotive depot.'

'Oh, Heavens! How awful.' She shook her head slowly. 'In the shed? Amongst the engines?'

'He was in an inspection pit beneath one of them,' Vignoles explained.

'It is a dangerous place. I only went there once with David, and I said I would never go again. I found it too noisy and a bit chaotic and there was too much fire and steam and heavy machinery for my taste. How tragic...'

'Mrs Green, I should advise you that we are concerned about the circumstances by which he met his death.'

'What does that mean?'

'We have suspicions that it was not an accident. I must ask you where your husband was yesterday between the hours of six and eight pm.'

'David? You cannot seriously think...?' She put her tea down on the table and folded her arms across her chest in a defensive posture, the colour washed from her face. 'He was at work.'

'Are you quite sure?' Vignoles tried to sound gentle.

'He clocks off at six...'

'And after six? He works very close to home.'

'He came in not long before...eight.' Mrs Green's voice had lost its cheerful bounce.

'Was that usual? Taking nearly two hours to get from his signal box on the edge of Woodford to here. On a motorbike,' Mellor was observing her closely.

Silence. 'No. It was a bit unusual I suppose.' She finally answered, realising the two detectives were going to sit there until she did, her face now clouded with a growing sense of doubt. 'Occasionally he meets a work colleague for a glass of beer in The Gorse if he was not to be on duty the next day…'

'Your husband is at work today, is he not?' Vignoles knew the answer but wanted Mrs Green to confirm.

'Yes.'

'What reason did he give for his late return?'

'I can't recall he gave one…'

'Presumably not 'aving a beer with a mate?' Mellor added pointedly as he wrote in his notebook. 'Seeing as he is at work today.'

'I don't see why I need to explain how we live our lives,' she snapped. 'I find this is an intrusion. I'd like you both to leave.'

'Mrs Green, please think very carefully before you answer. Can you think of any reason why your husband might want to kill Richard Grimes?'

Chapter Twenty-One

Vignoles and the Detective Department team met in the biggest office in the Detective Department at Leicester Central to put their heads together and pool ideas. A blackboard on a wooden trestle was serving as a visual aid with various coloured chalks creating arrows that made connections between the crime scene and potential suspects. The name of Grimes stood bold in the centre of the board with the estimated time of his death written below together with other salient facts, the most potent of which was the monkey wrench discovered on a bench close by bearing bloody matter and a fine set of fingerprints.

'We await the lab results, but it seems probable that this heavy tool was the murder weapon.' Mellor was talking them through the case. 'It appears to have been lifted by an ungloved hand from a workbench adjacent to the locomotive and presumably close where Grimes was standing, all of which suggests an unpremeditated attack. An act of anger or frustration perhaps? That it was then discarded with little effort to conceal it with clear prints suggests the person who wielded it has little or no idea of how to cover their tracks.'

'An amateur?' PC Blencowe observed.

'As are most killers. Professional hitmen are rarer than hen's teeth. It is hard for someone to evade discovery, but even rudimentary efforts such as cleaning the weapon can significantly hamper our task. This feels impetuous and ill-conceived.'

'It was an argument gone wrong?' Benson asked. 'Tempers raised and a rash strike?'

'That seems most likely. Murder may not have been the intent, so we are looking for someone with a reason to *argue* with Grimes. The motive need not be a cut and dried desire to kill.'

Heads nodded agreement.

'We have a witness who heard voices raised and reckons one of these was Grimes. Ellis Cartwright was checking over *The Difference Engine* and was inside the locomotive and with a poor field of vision, but recognised Grimes' voice. He investigated and discovered Grimes under the engine and called for help. Cartwright also claims he saw a uniformed man. No face, but he seemed sure it was a railwayman's uniform. We also have a fitter by the name of Derek Jennings who saw signalman Green, wearing his signalman's uniform approach the entrance to the shed beside the line *The Difference Engine* was parked on, at a time estimated close to the time of Grime's death. He saw Green leave the shed not long afterwards in a hurry. When questioned, Green's reason for being on shed is that he wanted to take a close look at the damaged engine and nothing else.'

'He likes railways, so his story could be genuine, but the timing of his presence there cannot be ignored.' Vignoles took up the thread from Mellor. 'Green claims to have seen nobody, especially Grimes, whilst he went on his private inspection. This appears improbable as Grimes was heard and seen arguing beside the locomotive around the same time. Added to which, this apparently innocent reason for taking an unusual diversion into the engine shed was not explained to his wife. She was unable to give a reason for his delay in returning home that evening and admitted that Grimes had made a completely unexpected visit to the family home the evening before.'

'Green and Grimes knew each other?' Lansdowne asked.

'Grew up together in Woodford but drifted apart after Grimes moved away around 1929 or thereabouts. They met up on an off after that, but post-war there was little or no contact if his wife's memory is correct,' Mellor answered. 'I reckon there's summat between these two we don't yet understand.'

'Green has been fingerprinted, as have all those in the shed that evening and we have a team working through the whole of *The Difference Engine* project team in Rugby. We are hopeful of a match to those on the wrench.'

'Is Mr Green our number one suspect?' Howerth asked in a quiet voice. His cheeks were burning.

Vignoles understood why Howerth was asking. 'All suspects are equal until we narrow down our findings. He has to be considered a suspect until we can find good reason to eliminate him from our enquiries.'

'I don't believe he is a killer, sir. In fact, it's impossible. We'll be wasting our time...'

'Constable, I'll pretend I didn't hear that,' Mellor glared at Howerth. 'Green is in the frame and there's no ducking away - marriage bells or not. Got it?' Mellor fired back. 'You won't be interviewing Green nor have sight of that side of things. We can't have personal emotions clouding judgment.' Howerth's cheeks glowed even redder. 'However, as the DCI said, we do 'ave others to consider,' Mellor continued. 'There is Miss Lessiter, the pretty, well-dressed publicity officer for Tomkins-Dunkler. What do we think of her? And I'm not askin' for a comment on her legs.' A groan ran around the room. 'When questioned about the evening Grimes died, her story is as leaky as a sieve. She was not keen on Grimes either, so there could be motive. Benson, you questioned her the first time, where've you got to?'

'Miss Lessiter seems to be a good at her job. I've checked some of her press releases and spoken with her employer and she oozes efficiency and attention to detail, and yet, when I asked her about the evening in question, she was uncharacteristically vague. Unable to tell me exactly what time she detrained at Rugby Central and what time she returned to her hotel in Rugby. Not difficult questions for a well-organised professional who wears what looks like an expensive wristwatch. I made enquiries, and the night manager believes she did not return to her hotel until after 11 pm. That is a long gap.'

'Darn right it is. It needs explaining. Lean on her and any hesitation, we call her in for a proper grilling,' Mellor fired back.

'Two questions. Did she have sufficient time to detrain at Rugby Central and travel back to Woodford to attack Grimes then return to Rugby by 11pm?' Vignoles asked this whilst enjoying his pipe. 'The second; does she have a motive for wanting to assault or kill Grimes?'

'I heard Grimes was leering all over her and she didn't like it,' Howerth spoke up.

Vignoles nodded agreement. Mellor glared at the constable.

'If she had a car, she could get to Woodford in time but not by train, as the timetable offers nothing suitable,' Benson replied. 'I can ask if she owns a car, but I expect she and the whole crew travelled to Rugby by train from the Tomkins-Dunkler works and use the railway as their means to get about.'

'What about an accomplice with a car?' Vignoles pondered. 'This would make the attack premeditated which perhaps flies in the face of the *modus operandi*. It also hangs upon her accomplice knowing about the breakdown and the *ad hoc* arrangements to get the train and Tompkins-Dunkler staff back to Rugby.'

'That argues in her favour,' Mellor retorted.

'She told me Grimes was always taking photos of her even when asked not to. She denied that he tried anything on with her,' Benson glanced at Howerth, 'but she sensed there was some tension between them.'

'Enough for her to get someone to drive her back to Woodford and kill him?' Mellor asked.

'We have no sightings of a woman on the shed,' Vignoles added. 'The raised voices arguing were those of two men.'

'She is a striking and well-dressed lady. She would stand out a mile unless disguised,' Benson added. 'I can't see her in overalls and oily hat and work boots.'

'A jealous boyfriend?' Howerth again.

'A valid angle. I want her challenged on these points,' Vignoles replied. 'Who else are we looking at?'

'Cartwright. The electrical engineer.' Mellor continued. 'He was on site the whole time and discovered the body. He could have done the deed then reported finding the body. He claims to have heard an argument but is vague about the content and of the two men he saw, only Grimes could be identified. Sounds plausible, but vague enough that we can't trip him up easily on the details.'

'What is his motive?' Vignoles queried.

'They knew each other for years. Grew up together. Was there unfinished business?' Blencowe observed, shrugging his shoulders.

'Could be,' Mellor replied. 'We need to understand the relationships between *all* those working on the turbine and Grimes, not just Green and Grimes. There was talk of tensions amongst the team and the nosy journo.'

'Miss Lessiter said as much. Grimes was given a warning the morning of the day he died and banned from stepping onto the locomotive. She said Grimes was always trying to get the technicians to say more than they should about sensitive technical points.' Benson checked her notes. 'She mentioned Cartwright as someone who found Grimes particularly annoying.'

'Feeling annoyed is a long way from murder,' Vignoles observed, with a cautionary voice.

'You said the fight was possibly not intended to result in murder, sir. What if Grimes and Cartwright had a bit of a barney and in the fracas, Cartwright grabbed a heavy implement and the next thing he knows he's got a dead body on his hands?'

Vignoles was aware PC Howerth was smarting from the humiliation of a public put down and the awkwardness of his future father-in-law as a murder suspect. His suggestion that got Green off the hook, was well intentioned. 'Then we'll start with Cartwright. And chase the fingerprints. And find his camera! The assailant must have taken it. Where could Green, Cartwright or Lessiter have hidden it?'

'I'll keep the men on it.' Mellor replied.

'Benson. What have you found in the scrapbook recovered from Grimes' bedroom?'

'I'm still working my way through it, sir. There's a small mountain of newspaper cuttings, but also a set of photo prints taken at various locations. None include people and are a bit boring and uninformative, to my eye. A footpath, a bridge parapet, a station platform I have identified as Woodford Halse. The cuttings are about the disappearance of a young girl from Woodford Halse.'

'What was her name?'

'Rosemary Tustain, known to all as Rosie. She vanished on Saturday 23rd June 1928. Last definite sighting on Woodford Halse platform waiting for an all stations stopper going north.'

'Grimes is from Woodford?' Blencowe queried.

'Both he and Green are,' added Mellor. 'As is Cartwright.' He raised an eyebrow.

Blencowe chalked Rosie Tustain's name on the board. 'Connections...' He made more arrows from Green, Grimes and Cartwright to that of Tustain.

'A missing girl from when Grimes was in his late teens. How might this impact on the case? It is an intriguing angle,' Vignoles blew a smoke ring. He had no answer, but the investigation was taking a more interesting turn. Until now it was starting to look like an overheated argument, or a festering grudge played out in a moment of madness. Grubby, ugly and a pathetic waste of life that could well end as a manslaughter charge. It needed solving and the culprit prosecuting, but not enough to intrigue or excite an experienced detective.

However, looking at the chalked names and connecting arrows on the blackboard he sensed a deeper mystery developing. A long-lost girl and the suggestion of distant strings pulling and causing actions in the present, not unlike

like the rods and wires activated by a signalman in a distant signal box. Levers that warned of danger ahead!

'Mellor, get the case files on the Tustain case. There might be something in there that gives us a way in.'

Mellor nodded and immediately retired to his desk to place a call to the Northampton City Police records office. He felt the adrenaline flowing and a sense of anticipation that these dusty records might help them crack open this puzzling case. As he spoke with the archivist and received an assurance the files could be retrieved, he made a blunder. He pushed the scrapbook of clippings and photographs that Benson was studying out of mind and promptly forgot about it. As the investigation started to gather pace and take a dramatic twist, this oversight would come back to bite them.

Chapter Twenty-Two

'Miss Lessiter, I have a few questions more to ask.' WPC Benson had travelled to Rugby and approached the self-assured young lady in full view of her employers. It would not harm to metaphorically drag her to one side whilst others looked on. Mellor had made it clear that it was time to take the soft leather police gloves off and lean harder on everyone they questioned. This was murder enquiry and time was of the essence. It was not their problem if they put a few noses out of joint and Benson was conscious that if she made a decent fist of the tasks she'd been given, it would look good for possible promotion. Mellor was a hard taskmaster and made it clear he'd not got where he had by being 'too soft on possible crims' - as he sometimes referred to suspects. 'What you need to remember, luv, is you're not 'ere to make friends. They can curse you down the banks all they want. So what? Your job is to get results.'

Benson also had to admit a slight twinge of ill-feeling towards the strongly perfumed and perfectly manicured Miss Lessiter. Was this envy? For her wasp-narrow waist, shapely legs and perfectly coiffured hair? Was she jealous of the conspicuous cost of Lessiter's perfectly tailored twinset and a pair of heels that would not last a day working on the railway - even if Benson could afford them on a policewoman's pay? She must rein in such foolish thoughts but perhaps these feelings might help her demand the answers Mellor needed.

'I cannot imagine what more I can tell you?' Lessiter offered a quizzical smile that was frostier than Lapland in December. She fiddled with the lay of her jacket sleeve as if to suggest this was more important than anything the police could be involved with.

'You can start by telling me why you did not return to your hotel until after 11 pm?'

'I beg your pardon? I don't see why that is any business of yours!' Lessiter looked as if she'd been slapped in the face.

'In a murder investigation everything is our business.'

'You believe it to be murder?'

'We do. What did you do between leaving Rugby Central and returning to your hotel?'

'I went for a meal. It had been a long and tiring day and I needed sustenance.'

That sounded plausible, but Benson was not to be fobbed off so easily. 'Where did you go?'

'Oh, golly gosh, I cannot remember. I'm only staying here for a few days. I'm not familiar with the names of places, you know how it is? We leave today and return to base in Birmingham this evening. It will be so nice to get back to my familiar house.' Her smile had warmed up a notch.

'And familiar restaurants you know the name of,' Benson returned the smile. 'Perhaps you recall the name of the street it was on?'

'I'm absolutely hopeless with street names...'

'What did you eat? Do you remember the decor?' Benson raised an eyebrow as she poised pencil over her notebook. 'Or we could take a walk together? Rugby is not so big, and it would not take long to retrace your steps.'

'I don't have time for that.'

'Or you could tell me about your friend who waited in a car outside Rugby Central for you? It will save time, because I will find out in the end.' It was a wild punt in the dark, but it paid off.

'Oh.' Lessiter blinked a few times as she silently considered her options. 'I'm not sure quite why I am being so evasive. It's foolish and you have important work to do. I'm sorry.' Her faced softened and even her upright stance, with shoulders held back eased as she relaxed.

'Tell me the truth and don't embroider it and the apology is accepted.'

Chapter Twenty-Three

Ellis Cartwright was seated behind the deal table in the small and stuffy interview room at Leicester Central. He was fiddling with a packet of Players cigarettes, more in irritation than an attack of nerves. 'Do we need to do this here? There is pressing work to get the engine back in service and they need me.'

'Then the sooner you clear up a few details the sooner you can be back to work.' Vignoles fussed with some papers that lay before him on the desk. Finally satisfied with their order, he sat back and started to slowly fill his pipe. 'Do smoke if you wish.'

Mellor proffered a box of matches. Cartwright lit a cigarette then tossed the carton back onto the table. He sighed heavily, exhaling smoke as he did so. 'Fire away. Let's get this over.'

'Do you know David Green?'

'Green is a common name. As is David.'

'Does that mean you do know someone of that name?' Mellor made a note.

'I suppose so.'

'How about David Green, signalman at Woodford Halse?'

'I'm not sure...'

'You either do or you don't.' Mellor snarled.

'I have met many signalmen and can't be sure of their names. Many I only know by sight.' Cartwright puffed smoke in an arrogant gesture.

'When did you first meet Mr Grimes?' Vignoles took over and immediately changed the line of enquiry. Mellor and he had agreed on this plan in a technique they knew could unsettle someone with something to hide.

'He joined the project as an official photographer about two weeks ago.'

'That was not what I asked.'

'I might have met him earlier. He was a well-known railway photographer.'

'You are interested in railway photography?'

'Not really…'

Vignoles pulled an unconvinced expression and made a note. Mellor now stepped in. 'David Green is from Woodford Halse.'

'So, you said.'

'No, I said he worked in the signal box there. But you're correct, he was born in Woodford. As was Grimes.'

'Is that so?' Cartwright looked mildly bored. 'Well, that explains it.'

'Explains what?'

'They knew each other and must have argued.'

'Is that what you think?'

'Seems like it, but you're the detectives.'

'You said you overheard two men arguing when you were inside *The Difference Engine*. You identified one as Grimes but not the other?' Vignoles now took over.

'Yep.'

'It would be very helpful if you could identify the other man.'

'I wish I could help.'

'You sure you don't know David Green? The signalman from Woodford and working in Woodford box, just to make it clear,' Mellor weighed back in.

A pause. Mellor stared at Cartwright and smoked as the seconds ticked. 'Cos' the interesting thing is you were also born in Woodford Halse.'

'What of it?'

'You've not mentioned this?'

'What has that got to do with anything? I moved away when I was eighteen and went to college. I got out and improved myself. Worked my way up to where I am. I hardly ever come back except for the occasional visit to the folks and I don't intend to spend any longer there than I can.'

'I see.' Vignoles made a play of studying the papers before him. 'There's only one school in Woodford. It's quite small and you, Grimes and Green attended this at the same time,' Vignoles picked up the thread.

'Different years. I'm older.'

'You can only know that if you know who we are talking about.'

'All right, so I know who he is...'

Vignoles gave a little smile. 'You admit to knowing David Green the signalman, and both you and Green work on the railways. Are you telling us that you have had no interaction since you left school?'

Cartwright hesitated. The first hint of a crack in his veneer of confidence. 'Perhaps once or twice, I haven't kept a record.' He eyed Mellor's pencil busy scratching notes.

'Are you sayin' you cannot identify his voice?' Mellor sounded sceptical.

Cartwright fiddled with his cigarette. 'Look, gentlemen, this is a serious investigation and I fully appreciate that fact. I don't think it's appropriate to make statements I can't be sure of. That would be...immoral.'

'Wise counsel,' Mellor replied.

'It *could* have been Green arguing with Grimes, but I really cannot swear to it and don't want to point an accusing finger unless I am completely sure. That is the best I can do.'

Vignoles took over. 'What about Grimes? We've heard you and he didn't rub along well together.'

'Who told you that?'

'Never mind. Did you have a falling out with Grimes?'

Cartwright shrugged his shoulders. 'He was an annoying bugger, but that's all.' He laughed.

'Did you argue that evening? Perhaps you saw him near the locomotive sniffing around where he shouldn't?'

'I didn't.'

Chapter Twenty-Three

'Did you and Grimes get on well back in the day at Woodford?'

'He was two classes below me. We hardly met. It's too long ago to even remember, quite frankly,' Cartwright grinned. 'Come off it, even if we did have a playground tussle once or twice? So what? Do you think I would hold a grudge all these years and then kill him? Pull the other one!'

'Did you see Green and Grimes together earlier in the day? Perhaps when the engine overheated?'

'Now you mention it, I think I did. We were held at signals and everyone in the engine room and cab was getting twitchy and I saw Grimes step outside Green's signal box with his camera pointing at us.'

'Grimes was in the signal box with Green?' Mellor sat up in his chair.

'He suddenly appeared at the bottom of the steps, so I'd say he was.' Cartwright needed a fresh cigarette and Mellor obliged. 'Look, I know I said that what happened way back in school was too long ago to matter now, but there was one thing I heard from back then. A rumour, a whisper. Probably just stupid gossip, to be honest.' He shrugged his shoulders.

'Tell us.' Mellor demanded.

'Grimes and Green were thick as thieves. Went everywhere together. Proper Tweedledee and Tweedledum!' He laughed. 'But then something awful happened, and they never spoke again. Grimes left not long after and never came back to Woodford...'

'Just like you?'

Cartwright shrugged this away. 'I doubt it means anything, but that's what I know. I'm doing my best to help.'

There was a knock on the door and Blencowe put his head around the door. 'Sir? There's something you need to see.'

Vignoles nodded and terminated the interview. 'Thank you, Mr Cartwright, that was helpful. We appreciate you speaking candidly. You can return to your work now.' They all stood up to leave.

A few minutes later Vignoles and Mellor were studying the notes Blencowe had handed across.

'The blood on the wrench matches Grimes. A full set of prints has been lifted from it. From the centre section and clean and clear. The wrench is confirmed as the murder weapon and these prints probably identify the assailant,' Blencowe explained.

'How are the lads getting on finger printing everyone at the shed?'

'I think they're near done, sarge.'

'Get everything across to the lab as fast as you can. Take your motorbike. I want Cartwright and Green's prints top of the list to be cross-checked. Jump to it!'

After Blencowe had gone, Vignoles turned to Mellor. 'What do you make of Cartwright?'

'I reckon he's level-headed. Evasive at first, but most people are when put in this position. They get nervy facing us. They duck and dive and deny stuff when there's no reason. I reckon he wants to help but is cautious about gettin' involved. We've seen this behaviour time and again from witnesses. He understands the danger of saying stuff just to please us, but with some coaxing, he gave us a few good pointers.'

'Are you forming an idea whose prints are going to match those on the blood-stained wrench?'

'Same name as you, I reckon.'

'And what do you make of Miss Lessiter?'

'I don't have her down as a serious contender, but we need to be sure.'

WPC Benson was removing her coat even as they were speaking, having just arrived back at the office.

'Benson! What did you get from the PR lass?'

'She's in the clear, sarge. She was coy at first but only because she was taking the evening off to meet up with her boyfriend. She's not keen on broadcasting her romantic life to the rest of the Tompkins-Dunkler team. The man in question lives in Coventry and came over in his car to pick her up and take her out for a meal in this own city away from the eyes of her colleagues.'

'This checks out?' Mellor queried.

'Yes, sir. The staff in the pub and restaurant they visited remember them both. The night porter at her hotel admitted he might have seen them pull up in a car and didn't notice if her young man slipped up to her room when his back was turned.' She grinned.

'A bit of nookie?' Mellor failed to hide his look of envy.

'That clears the field. Thank you, Benson.' Vignoles was filling his pipe as he walked into his office indicating that Mellor should follow. They had some thinking to do about how to handle the next interview.

Chapter Twenty-Four

'Mr Green. We need your help.'

'I'll do my best, but must it be so formal?' He looked around the dingy interview room and then at the rodent-faced duty solicitor seated beside him. A man with a face too narrow and front teeth too prominent. 'Why do I need a lawyer? I've done nothing.'

'It is your legal right and we feel it appropriate that we do everything by the book,' Vignoles did not smile to put him at ease. The solicitor gave a curt nod then wrote rapidly in shorthand on his legal pad. What Vignoles did not say was that the sensitivity of the situation, with Green not only a respected member of the railway 'family' but the intended father-in-law of one of his team and brother to Mavis Green, he felt like he was walking on eggshells. This was an interview he was dreading. 'As you know, we obtained a warrant to search your house and workplace -,'

'And found nothing. Just upset my wife and got the neighbours gossiping. Thanks for that.'

More scribbling on the legal pad. Vignoles remained impassive as did Mellor. Green was correct. The searches had turned up nothing that materially added to their case and had served only to ruffle many feathers and create a tense atmosphere in the office. Mavis Green was refusing to look either Vignoles or Mellor in the eye. All part and parcel of the policeman's lot.

'You are aware we fingerprinted everyone identified in the vicinity of *The Difference Engine* from the time of her arrival on the shed and the discovery of the body of Mr Grimes.' Green said nothing, just the sound of the nib scratching the pad and the distant sound of a locomotive hissing in one of the platforms. 'Mr Green, can you explain why your fingerprints were found on a heavy metal wrench lying on a workbench adjacent to the locomotive in question? The locomotive beneath which the body of Mr Grimes was found.' The police laboratory had processed the cross checking with commendable alacrity. The accompanying note explained the match was as strong across all five digits as any example they had seen. The build-up of coal dust impregnated into the grease and oil covering the surface of the metal tool was perfect for capturing prints. Green said nothing in response to a slight shake of the head from his lawyer. 'This same wrench was used to strike Mr Grimes on the back of the skull and still bears clear traces of his blood, skin and hair. It is the murder weapon.'

Silence.

'You can see why we need your co-operation. Your prints are clearly defined and make a perfect match, so we need to understand how and when they might have been placed on this wrench.' Vignoles now laid out a pair of photographs of the tool in question on the table for all to see. 'Are you in the habit of visiting the engine shed at Woodford Halse?'

'No. I'm a signalman.'

Notes taken.

'So, you would admit it is unusual for you to be inside the shed and close to the tools used to service the engines stabled there?'

'I suppose.' Green looked nervous.

'When did you last visit the engine shed?'

'You know when that was.'

The solicitor narrowed his eyes, paused a moment then made a note. He was trying to get a sense of this investigation after only a few minutes of consultation with his new client.

'You were there on the evening Mr Grimes was found dead underneath *The Difference Engine*?'

Green shrugged his shoulders and lit a cigarette. 'Yes, but I didn't kill him.'

'I didn't say you did. I merely asked you to confirm that

you were in the vicinity that evening and explain why your prints are on the murder weapon.'

'I'm saying nothing.' Green stared at Vignoles, then blew some smoke out. The duty solicitor tapped his pen on the pad nervously, then whispered something in Green's ear.

'Mr Grimes was a friend of yours?' Vignoles continued.

'A long time ago.'

'In our first meeting you explained you were at school together and that recently you had both met up again after a long break. You stand by that statement?'

'That's what I said.'

'Did you and Grimes have an argument when you met in Woodford Halse engine shed on the night he died?'

'I never said I met him.'

'But you did meet him. Standing beside *The Difference Engine*.'

'No comment.'

'We have a witness who heard you arguing with Grimes beside the engine.'

'I know nothing about that.'

'What was the nature of the disagreement?'

'No comment.'

'We are aware that back in the days long before the war, Grimes and you were close friends. Virtually inseparable according to a witness, and yet you had a significant falling out. In the summer of 1929. Grimes then left Woodford and rarely returned, until a few days ago. He surprised you arriving at your home unannounced, and then was found dead about the same time that you were in the same engine shed as Grimes and after placing a fine set of prints on the murder weapon....'

'DCI Vignoles, the very idea that a schoolyard argument has any bearing on this matter is ludicrous. My client has already explained that he neither met Grimes nor argued with him -.'

'Mr Green, your solicitor in his round-a-bout way is actually in agreement with us on this side of the table.' The solicitor's jaw dropped. This was news. 'I agree, that holding a grudge from school days sounds somewhat implausible as a motive for murder,' Vignoles smiled, wishing to get Green to relax and talk. 'So, I ask you again to explain how your prints were on that wrench and why a witness can claim to have heard you arguing with Grimes, furthermore, why another witness saw you arrive on shed and then depart a short while later, this time walking briskly as if in a hurry. We need answers.'

'I had to get home. I was late and the food would spoil.'

'Ah yes, we spoke with your wife. She said you did not explain your late arrival home that evening and that this was unusual and out of character.'

The solicitor frowned as he wrote. This was new information.

'I can do what I like. I just took the idea of seeing that new engine up close.'

'But did not think to tell your wife about it?'

'She wouldn't be interested.'

'Why was Grimes in your signal box?' Mellor now weighed in. His voice was cold and unemotional.

'It's not against regs.'

'I asked *why* he was there?'

'He wanted a good view of the engine storming through for his magazine.'

'But it broke down?' Mellor frowned.

'It did.' Green now looked nervous. Tapping the ash from his cigarette too many times so it went out.

'That meant Grimes got a grandstand view...'

'Meaning what?'

'Havin' Grimes there in your signal box, did it put you off your stride?' Mellor leaned close to Green. 'Was he a distraction and you missed a path and ended up causing the turbine to go bang?' He winked.

'That did not happen.'

'It did. It overheated.'

'This is unsubstantiated theorising Detective Sergeant. Either level a genuine charge against my client or we shall terminate this conversation forthwith.' The lawyer was unimpressed.

'Hold yer 'orses! You don't know the half of it,' Mellor fired back. He studied Green who was now looking increasingly uncomfortable. 'You went back to the shed later because you were sure Grimes would be there as he'd not be able to resist poking about the engine. And you two had a confrontation and old arguments, new arguments, maybe a mixture of the two spilt over and in a moment of red mist you reached out, grabbed a heavy object and bashed him as he turned away. It could have been a charge of GBH, but unfortunately, you have strong arms and shoulders being a signalman, and you hit him in the worst place...'

'Idle extemporisation, gentlemen...' The lawyer made a point of capping his fountain pen and putting it in his jacket pocket. 'You should take up writing fiction, sergeant. Meanwhile, in the real world, either charge my client or we are done.' He clipped his briefcase closed. 'Though may I suggest you build a stronger case before attempting to press charges.'

Vignoles made no move. The man was right. The fingerprints were strong, and Cartwright's claims leant weight, but did they have enough? They had no motive and the missing camera remained a thorn in their side. Not finding it at Green's home or signal box had been a disappointment. But had they been looking in the wrong place? His eyes rested on the motorcycle helmet and gloves placed on a chair in the corner of the room. 'Mr Green, you travelled here on your motorbike?'

'I did.'

'Why?'

'Why not?' Silence from all in the room. 'All right, I hardly ever give her a decent run on the open road. It was a good excuse. It helps blow the cobwebs away and clear my mind...'

Green looked animated as he spoke, in contrast to the lawyer who clearly could not understand why his client was not making the fastest exit possible from the claustrophobic room.

Vignoles glanced at Mellor who needed no further prompting and stood up and left the room. 'I shall organise some tea and fresh pack of cigarettes. I feel the questioning is proving most helpful and I would crave your presence here a while longer.' He was politeness personified.

The lawyer stood up. 'Our business is concluded.'

'Sit down.' Vignoles' demeanour changed in a moment and caused the solicitor to instantly sit again. He then walked to the door and spoke with WPC Lansdowne about the tea and cigarettes. He knew better than to chance his arm with Mavis who was visibly sulking at the front desk.

It was Mellor who returned before Lansdowne, still wearing his thin black leather gloves and carrying a camera case. His face barely concealed a smirk as he sat down. 'Take note. I've not touched this with bare hands.'

'And what, pray, are you showing us?' The lawyer adopted his most disdainful voice, but his face betrayed concern.

'A camera.' Mellor carefully undid the leather case to reveal the expensive Leica inside. 'The camera was owned by Mr Grimes who used this in his work. He carried it everywhere. Never let it out of his sight. It was missing from the crime scene, but I have just found this in one of the rear panniers on Mr Green's motorbike.'

'That's impossible! No, no, this is all wrong…'

'Why is the victim's camera in your motorbike pannier?' Vignoles asked.

'This is a set-up!'

'I can assure you it is nothing of the sort,' Mellor fired back. 'PC Blencowe observed as I made the inspection.'

'Mr Green?' Vignoles enquired.

'No comment.'

'Did Mr Grimes give you this camera that evening? For

safekeeping perhaps? If there is an innocent explanation, then now is the time to tell us.'

Green said nothing, his lawyer desperately trying to assimilate this sudden turn of events.

'You need to help us out. We need to understand how and why this is in your possession.'

'I didn't put it there.'

Vignoles held Green's eyes until the signalman looked away, his face shading into red and white with emotion.

'Mr Green, possession of the victim's camera is incriminating, you must see that? I need to understand how it came to be in your motorbike pannier.'

The lawyer remained tight-lipped but gave his client a searching look. Green said nothing.

'Very well. I have sufficient evidence to charge you here and now. However, the discovery of the camera is fresh, and I need to give it further consideration before making my final decision. You will remain in custody until tomorrow when we shall reconvene,' he looked at the legal representative who was frowning and staring at the tabletop. 'We are within our rights to hold Mr Green for a further twelve hours and taking into consideration the serious nature of the crime, I shall not allow him his freedom.' He looked at Green. 'I suggest you avail yourself of a further private meeting with your lawyer and I suggest you think hard about your predicament. When we next talk I hope you make a better fist of convincing me why you should not be charged with the murder of Mr Grimes. Remember, this is a capital offence carrying the death penalty.'

The lawyer started to argue against this plan although his voice lacked conviction, and he was soon quietened. Vignoles asked PC Blencowe to escort Green to a cell and indicated that the brief could accompany him if he wished.

Chapter Twenty-Five

Simon Howerth and Laura Green were sitting on the wall outside her digs. It was a balmy evening and her side of the street of Victorian red-brick terraced houses on the north-western edge of Leicester was catching the late sunshine.

'We can split the atom, fly jet planes and send gas turbine engines along the line and yet I can't sit in my fiancée's room. I'm not sure that's progress.' Howerth sounded mildly frustrated.

'I need fresh air, and besides, it *is* nicer here than in the room.' Laura Green was trying to be upbeat, but she looked tense and distracted and her usual ebullient greeting had been muted this evening.

'That's not the point...'

'Soon enough you'll be home with me every day - then let's see how you like it.' It was perhaps intended as a joke, but something in her mood lent it a barbed quality.

Howerth gave her a funny look but decided to ignore the inflexion in her voice 'Let's hope we get some good news about a new house.'

'The waiting list is awfully long. But I heard the Corporation favour those...in the family way.' She gave him a strange look. A meaningful smile played on her lips and yet there was a sadness in her eyes.

Howerth grinned as he looked at Laura. 'Ah-ha! So that roll in the hay was all part of a cunning plan to improve our chances!' He was glad the conversation was taking a more upbeat turn but if he was hoping Laura's mood was about to lift, he was to be disappointed.

She shrugged her shoulders. 'Can't do any harm.' She muttered something under her breath he did not catch but which sounded like '*too late now...*'

'Perhaps we have to make sure?' He gave her a cheeky wink.

'Not tonight you won't.' Again, that edge to her voice.

'Oh. All right...' They fell silent. There was something about the quality of the silence that was uncomfortable and lacking the companionable warmth they usually shared. 'It looks like I shall be kissing my future wife goodnight once again on the doorstep whilst hoping that old battle-axe doesn't catch us.'

'She really is a miserable soul.'

'I wonder what happened to her husband?'

'He probably died from her nagging. Or eating too much of her boiled cabbage!' Laura tried a joke, but it fell a bit flat.

Mildred Morrison was forged in the time-honoured British tradition of flinty, unbending and demanding landladies that terrorised terraced houses and seaside villas across the land. Pale bacon and watery mushrooms served with piles of dried toast for breakfast and over-boiled veg and barely recognisable meat swimming in thin gravy were her stock in trade. Paradoxically, though, her mashed potato was delicious and provided in vast quantities which had probably kept Laura Green alive for the last two years as about the only thing she could stomach. Mrs Morrison's rules and regulations of the house were typically unforgiving, with complex arrangements for baths, insufficient heat in the bedrooms in winter and an absolute ban on male visitors. Simon had only once gained a brief glimpse of Laura's room when they seized the opportunity to dash upstairs whilst Mrs Morrison was queuing in town for something inedible for the evening meal.

'Perhaps she buried him in the backyard?'

'I'm not sure that's funny,' Laura scowled at the pavement. 'Do you like your job?'

'You know I do.'

'But don't you ever stop and think that some of the things you do are not very nice?' She glanced at Howerth and it was not encouraging.

'As police, we have to step in when things go bad. When a crime has been committed or perhaps to break up unrest and argument, so the circumstances are rarely nice but it's important work and we're needed.'

'Like a punch in the face...' Again, under her breath, but just audible.

'What do you mean by that?'

'Come off it, Simon! You know darned well what I mean. Barging in on mum and upsetting her with kinds of odd questions about dad, then badgering dad at work and even having the nerve to come to my signal box and make stupid allegations about him! It's not only pathetic but deeply upsetting.'

Howerth felt his throat constrict and his stomach turn as if he was falling from a great height. 'There is an active murder investigation on and...er...we need to speak to anyone and everyone.'

'A murder investigation in which you are accusing *dad*. Of all people! How can that be right? It's ridiculous. Your beloved DCI Vignoles and that nasty creep of a sergeant wanted to know if dad was capable of killing one of his oldest friends.' Her bitterness and pent-up anger finally spilling out.

'I heard he was questioned but know no more than that.'

'He still is! Last I knew they'd called him down to the station here for more grilling and he's not back home yet. Mum's going frantic. Trying to talk to her on the blower in the hallway with Mrs "Nosy" Morrison straining to catch every word doesn't help. I need to know what's going on. You must be able to tell me.'

'I don't sit in on interviews and I clocked off before they'd finished.'

'You left so you could be here?'

'Of course. We had an arrangement.'

'Rather than stay and make sure your detective chums don't make fools of themselves thinking dad is capable of murder?'

She gave Simon an incredulous look.

'Be reasonable Laura. I don't interview suspects—.'

'Suspect? You call dad a *murder suspect* then ask me to be reasonable!' She stood up and paced in a circle, her voice tight with emotion.

'What I mean is, I'm just a constable. I don't have any influence or any part to play in interviews. I am not a detective.'

'Evidently. But you still come here hoping for a kiss and a cuddle and never mind that your future father-in-law is banged up in a police cell!'

'He was being interviewed and was not under arrest...'

'That makes me feel better?'

'Laura, I understand why it is upsetting, but I'm sure they're just clarifying things. It will all get straightened out.'

'I thought you said you didn't know anything?'

'I don't.'

'These are just empty words.'

'Laura...' He reached for her, but she pushed him away.

'They searched the house. Did you know that? Mum and dad's place. Went everywhere. Mum said it was horrid. They poked into every drawer and opened every cupboard and were unfriendly whilst doing it.'

'I didn't know that.'

'It looks like I know more than you then.' The bitterness in her voice stung.

'That is unfair. I've been out all day on a quite different investigation out of town, up Nottingham way. I have my duties to perform.' He took a deep breath and tried to keep his voice calm and measured knowing that if he betrayed any hint of impatience this could develop into a full-blown row with consequences.

'In respect to your dad, due process is being followed. They must interview everyone so they can rule them out of being responsible. Your dad and the Grimes fellow grew up together and met up again just a few days ago. You can see how that is something any detective must ask about?' Laura Green stared at the ground. 'They're eliminating him from their enquiries, that's all. I know DCI Vignoles will gain no pleasure from this but he *has* to press the matter if a set of circumstances give the impression that someone is, um, implicated. But once these questions are answered they get a clearer picture - and it all works out...' He was grasping at straws.

'Go there now and set the record straight.' Laura Green had regained her composure and spoke quietly but with a firmness that suggested Howerth would be wise to listen. 'You have to help him. He's just not capable of such a thing. You have to believe that. This is obviously a mistake and you can help get it straightened out.' Her eyes were imploring and glassy.

'It's not that easy as a constable. What I mean is, if I go up to the sarge and question his judgment - let alone the Inspector's - I'm liable to get my head chewed off.'

'Meanwhile, dad is accused of *murder*? For God's sake, Simon, he could be hanged!' Hot tears welled then ran in tramlines down her cheeks.

'But of course, I'll try. My hands are tied by protocol and rank and...'

'A fat lot of use getting hitched to a policeman, then...' Laura wept bitter tears and again angrily shrugged away his attempts to put a consoling arm around her shoulders.

'Just get my dad out of there. Now go away! Leave me alone!'

Off The Case

Chapter Twenty-Six

'Vignoles?' Chief Superintendent Badger was on the telephone. It was early, and Vignoles was drinking a much-needed coffee whilst seated in the bay window of his office.

'Sir?'

'I've read your latest on the Grimes business. You're confident Green is your man?' Badger's voice was crisp and purposeful.

'All the evidence we've uncovered so far points towards Green and nothing directing us elsewhere.'

'So far? Then you have reservations?' Badger was startled.

'A negative does not automatically prove a positive, so whilst we have nothing directing our attentions to another, perhaps we've not looked hard and long enough?'

'You have a handful of damming positives regarding Green.'

'Indeed, we do. The camera in his motorcycle pannier is perhaps the clincher.'

'That discovery when taken together with his prints on the monkey wrench and a witness overhearing him arguing with Grimes and another seeing him practically run from the scene of crime makes it look an open and shut book.'

'Looks can be deceiving.'

'Humph. What are your misgivings?'

'I am unclear about his motivation for killing Grimes. I need to understand why he would do such a thing. He's offering us nothing and yet putting up no defence -.'

'- because he's guilty! He has no defence to offer, Vignoles. Mistakenly, he thinks by saying nothing he'll miraculously wriggle out of what looks like a pretty pickle.'

'I agree.' Vignoles spoke with a heavy heart. 'Hence the reason I suggest we move to charge him for the death of Grimes. I just harbour a nagging concern about why he did it.

Perhaps Green did not go to the shed with the intention to kill Grimes, but it escalated. Just a sorry mess in a heated moment. I feel sure that is what his defence will argue.'

'You are forgetting that he struck the man from behind and with sufficient force any reasonable person must realise could kill.'

'Manslaughter or murder?'

'The jury will decide that. Either way, he's guilty. You've got your man.' Vignoles agreed and listened as Badger continued. 'Harbouring doubts is no bad thing in a detective. It is wise to question the evidence as presented and challenge your conclusions but take courage in that you've also found no motive for anyone *else* who was in the engine shed that evening. You have however found Green's dabs all over the weapon. Now take that Cartwright fellow, for example. He found the body and that means he could have struck Grimes himself then reported it, but his prints are not on the weapon, nor was the camera about his person. Aside from those major factors weighing in his defence, have you found any reason for Cartwright wanting Grimes dead?'

'There was talk of low-level tensions between Grimes and some of the technicians including Cartwright, and then some less than welcome amorous advances by Grimes towards their pretty press lady.' Vignoles stopped and allowed his voice to lighten. 'Of them all, she probably had the strongest motive for seeing the back of Grimes, but her alibi is rock solid and whilst she might have given him a piece of her mind, she's no killer.'

'Then we are in agreement.' Badger's voice adopted the usual confident tone. 'Looking through the interviews the same applies for the local fitters and crews working the shed that evening, any of whom could have struck Grimes but all lack motive for doing so.'

'You're correct. Just those last-minute jitters that come with preparing to read someone their rights for such a serious crime.'

Badger was silent a moment. 'Quite understandable. Green is close to home. Too close to the Department, in more ways than one. I've heard he's supposed to be walking his daughter down the aisle next month to get her hitched to one of your constables?'

'PC Howerth.' Vignoles winced at the thought of the trauma and distress that must be rippling through the two households involved even as they were talking.

'That's darned bad news. Then there's Mrs Green at the front desk. She's also part of the Green clan, I understand?'

'She's Green's sister.' Mavis had mercifully gone home by the time David Green had been led away to spend a night locked up, but Vignoles had already received the coldest shoulder imaginable when he'd arrived this morning and the situation would only worsen once David Green was charged. Mavis was invaluable to the Department. Dependable and intensely loyal to his small team and yet this would feel like a betrayal in spite of the obvious fact that neither Vignoles nor any of his team had invited this turn of events. The sorry affair was going to hit her hard and Vignoles judged it inevitable she would hand in her notice - perhaps even by the close of day. His temples started to ache as the wider impact of the arrest of the signalman struck home.

'It won't do. David Green's obvious guilt won't make things easier. Your department will be ripped apart at the seams.' Vignoles reflected on Badger's perceptive words and wondered if his boss was a mind reader but remained silent. What could he say? 'People take sides, Vignoles. You have a constable compromised and I doubt the young couple will marry. It's a bloody mess and will foster divided loyalties. Mavis Green will throw in the towel and then just watch as your chaps take sides...'

'They are professionals.'

'They're human. They have feelings and personal favourites

and this could destroy friendships and working relationships. What is needed is an independent team to take over. Mellor and you must be seen to have no further involvement.'

'We're close to solving a major crime.'

'But at what cost to the Detective Department?'

Vignoles knew Badger was right. He was aware tensions were running high. Only last night, Mellor and PC Howerth had crossed words and it had been heated. Most of what was said was better left unrepeated and unreported.

Howerth had been angry and stuck his neck out questioning Mellor's judgement in arresting Green and got a 'carpeting' in return. Mellor had given him both barrels and it had been an ugly scene. Howerth had been out of line and needed putting straight as insubordination could not be tolerated, but both Mellor and he understood why Howerth had made a stand. They understood why he felt he *had* to make a stand. His fiancée's father was about to be charged with a serious crime which carried the death penalty and Howerth could be forgiven for wanting to vent his frustration. Once Howerth had been set straight and sent packing, Vignoles told Mellor that as long as Howerth returned to the office contrite and willing to obey orders they would forget the incident and cut him some slack. Vignoles now gave a weary sigh and answered Badger. 'The charge should be delivered by someone at arm's length from the Green family.'

'My thoughts entirely. The case is now going over to County. DCI Thornbury will be with you shortly and I want all case files handed across forthwith. I expect Thornbury will take the prisoner to Northampton and press charges there. It won't do any harm to ensure your chaps are aware that *all* matters pertaining to this case are, as of now, being handled by the Northants Constabulary. It won't prevent sore feelings and upset back at base, but at least you won't be seen as the villain of the piece.'

'Understood.' Vignoles suspected it would not be that easy

and the next few weeks were going to be tricky.

'Expect Thornbury and his men within the hour.'

The line went dead.

Chapter Twenty-Seven

It had been easier to get an interview with her father than she'd imagined, and Laura Green was now being led into a small interview room inside the impressive setting of Wootton Hall, the grandiose home of the Northamptonshire Constabulary. The young constable given the job looked at her with puppy dog eyes filled with curiosity about this pretty woman who was the daughter of a man claimed to be a merciless killer. A man who was awaiting formal processing and his time in court before the judge placed the black cap on his head and pronounced the dreadful sentence that surely was the prisoner's due.

Green sat in the hard upright wooden chair in front of the interview table, which she noticed was bolted to the floor. A weak light filtered through a small opaque glass window high in one wall. It didn't open and the air in the room was stale with the tang of sweat, cigarette smoke and cheap disinfectant. It was a dispiriting room and every bit as bad as she'd feared on the train journey across to Northampton. The cell her father was held in was probably worse. If anything, this realisation steeled her resolve to get to the bottom of what was going on. It was going to be an awkward and uncomfortable conversation, the like of which she had never dared have before, let alone dream would be necessary, but it couldn't be avoided. She felt slightly nauseous. It was becoming a more frequent occurrence and she was finding it hard to eat breakfast. The lack of food made her feel lightheaded. Laura closed her eyes and took a few deep breaths to compose herself and quell the queasy sensation. She really had to tell Simon. He deserved to know, he *needed* to know and yet…somehow, it felt like an unwelcome distraction now. An awful thing to even think, but the unwelcome truth was a baby was the last thing either needed to be thinking about right now. The sound of footsteps and the door opening jolted her out of this muddling reverie, and she watched as her father entered the room. He looked older and tired, but he smiled warmly on seeing his daughter.

'Laura? You came all this way to see me?'

She bit her lip, suddenly unable to answer without breaking into tears. She made to stand up but the officer who'd brought her father from the cell told her to stay seated. 'You've got 20 minutes. Stay seated facing each other. No touching hands or passing anything over.' His voice was emotionless and curt. 'I'll keep the door ajar and will be standing right outside. By rights, I should sit and watch, so be thankful.'

David Green raised an eyebrow and winked at Laura. 'You get used to their ways...'

'It must be awful...'

'I've had better food and the bed is hard.' He gave a lopsided smile. 'But we're used to the long silences and time alone in our signal boxes so I can handle it.'

'That is not the same.'

'But similar. You can no more leave your signal box than I can a cell.'

'I suppose.'

'What brings you here?'

'To see you of course. Do you need to ask?'

'Your mum couldn't face it. How is she taking it?'

'Not well...' David Green fell silent and stared at the battered wooden tabletop. 'How is she supposed to take it, dad? This is a terrible shock.'

'I can believe that.'

'Is that all you can say? They're accusing you of... of you know.'

He looked Laura straight in the eye. 'I didn't do it. I never laid a finger on Richie.'

'I know that.' She wiped a tear from her eye. 'If I thought you'd really done it. Hit your old friend and killed him...I...I'm not sure I'd be here now.'

David Green nodded and even gave a slight smile. 'Then that's good.'

'No dad, it's not good. It's terrible. Quite awful, actually. You're not saying anything, not defending yourself. Do you not see how bad that looks?'

He shrugged his shoulders. 'I'm innocent.'

'But that's not enough!' Laura felt impatience make her pulse rate increase and something like anger well up. Her dad was always quiet and reserved but now this cool, almost casual belief in his innocence was making her irritated. Could he not see these dreadful surroundings and what they meant? The guard listening at the door? The dreadful murderous charge against his name? 'It won't do.' She gulped air, telling herself to stay calm. 'You've got to fight to clear your name. I can help. We all can. But you have to give us something to work with.'

'You're not a detective.'

'Simon is. A constable, anyway.'

He shook his head. 'There's nothing else to say. I went to see Richie, we talked for a few minutes, then I left. It appears someone else attacked him shortly afterwards, but I have no idea who that was. None at all. But it was not me.'

'Then why are your prints on the murder weapon?' She spoke in an urgent whisper hoping the guard would not hear. 'You have to tell me, whatever the truth of it is. You've got to explain how and why they're there.'

'Oh Laura...' He took a breath. 'I stepped backwards and knocked it off the workbench. The bench was piled with tools and I guess I nudged the handle. I picked it up and put it back. You don't leave things on the floor for others to trip over.'

'It fell when you were talking to your friend?'

'That's right.'

'What were you talking about?'

'This and that.' He shrugged his shoulders, but he looked away from his daughter.

'That's not good enough. They're claiming you argued. A falling out. That you hit him in anger then ran off.'

Green said nothing.

'I need to know.'

'I told him I didn't want him calling around again.'

'So, you *did* argue?'

'A few heated words.'

'Why? After all these years you felt so strongly you didn't want him around. After sharing a drink of beer in the house the night before? What really happened?' Laura felt the queasiness return but this time driven by a nagging sense that something was not right. Simon had warned her this interview could be painful, that there was something her father was not admitting. Simon had upset her, but she was starting to appreciate that her policeman fiancé might have been right. 'We need to know, dad. We want to understand.'

'We?'

'Me and Simon.' Her urgent whisper was almost a hiss.

'It's better you don't.'

She felt a sensation as though she was suddenly falling from a great height. Oh God, there *was* something bad... 'Whatever it is dad, please tell me. I know you didn't kill your friend, but you need to explain what is going on because at the moment the situation is making you appear guilty.'

David Green looked away.

'What about the camera? Did Richie give it to you?'

He shook his head. 'He had it around his body when I saw him in the engine shed. I have no interest in his camera nor his pictures.'

'Then how did it get in your bike pannier?'

'I have no idea. Someone must have put it there.'

'Who?'

'I wish I knew.'

'But why would they do that?'

'To implicate me. And they've done a fine job.'

Laura glanced at her watch. At any moment they were going to be asked to part. Why was her father taking this so calmly? Why was he not raging at the injustice of it? 'What is it you and Richie fell out about?'

David Green grimaced as he wrestled with some internal dilemma. 'In my tool shed, on the top shelf tucked away behind the paint tins you will find a little tin box. It once had toffee inside.'

Laura held her breath and willed the guard to stay out of the room as the minute hand crept around.

'Retrieve it, Laura. Inside the tin -.' He stopped. 'I showed what is inside to Richie that evening as we stood beside the gas turbine. It was given to him by a girl in what they thought was a secret tryst. But I saw them…together. And…' He shook his head. 'It was such a long time ago. It was foolish, utterly childish jealousy I suppose that made me steal it. I should have chucked it away years ago.'

'But you didn't. Why was that?' Laura was frowning. A youthful act of petty jealousy hardly seemed a matter of life and death.

'We argued that evening in the shed over this. He tried to snatch the tin off me but I wasn't letting go. Not after keeping it so long. I stepped backwards and knocked the monkey wrench off the bench. I picked up the tool - my worst luck - and put it back, then I told him to go and see the police and make his confession.'

'Confession?' Laura was confused.

'I've long suspected he did something. Something very bad…'

'Is it about the girl?'

David Green did not get to answer. The guard strode into the room and demanded the interview be terminated. 'Time's up. Back to the cell for you Mr Green.'

Laura stared at her father, desperate to hear his reply. Instead, they had to say hurried goodbyes.

Later, as she sat in the buffet on Northampton Castle station waiting for her train back to Rugby, she stirred sugar into her tea and replayed what she'd learned. Simon had been right. There was more to all this than either she or mum wanted to admit – or hear. Dad was keeping something back, but at least she had got him to admit this. It was step forward, of sorts. A girl, two young men and an argument. A falling out. But surely neither man could still be burning any kind of a candle for this woman now, after so many years? It was ridiculous. Was her father an adulterer? This just wasn't credible. He was as loyal and devoted to his wife as anyone could be. He'd never show any hint of straying, added to which he was either in work in his signal box which he could not leave or pottering about the house and garden. It could not be true. However, her father was now accused of murder and banged up in a cell facing the sheer horror of execution whilst the family argued over bail money they were struggling to gather together.

Perhaps this explained why he was refusing to speak out in his defence? He *had* gone to see Grimes to make an accusation, one that sounded ominous. He'd even brought something along which she was now entrusted with retrieving. Evidence of wrongdoing. Something that must have upset Grimes. It was hard to understand what it all meant, but it didn't look good and in spite of her reluctance to admit it, all this could be interpreted as a motive for killing Grimes. And then there was the camera. His explanation was useless. With a heavy heart she had to admit she wasn't convinced - so why would the police be? Why would someone else take it and put it where it would incriminate her father if he'd done nothing wrong? She needed to get to Woodford as quickly as possible and retrieve that tin and see what lay inside.

Her mind was whirring with ideas and images, some quite disturbing and they were all making her headache. She walked onto the platform where the sun was warm and comforting and she took solace in listening to the block bells in the nearby signal box and interpreting what signals and points were about to be set, imagining she was back in her signal box, far removed from all the troubles crowding in around her.

Chapter Twenty-Eight

Jane? There's a young lady to see you.'

'Send her through, please.'

'She says she'd rather speak somewhere more private,' Mavis Green lowered her voice and gave WPC Benson a long look. 'Outside the office.'

'Righty ho,' WPC Benson looked up from the report she was writing and raised a quizzical eyebrow but then stood up and straightened her uniform. There was something about Mavis Green's manner that intrigued Benson.

'Did she say anything more?'

'I'd rather leave her to explain.'

Benson had been working on a report for DS Mellor, but it was dull stuff and was glad to have an excuse to leave the office and so followed Mavis Green to the entrance, only to discover that her niece was standing there. '*Miss* Green?'

'Please, call me Laura.'

Benson gave Mavis Green a swift glance, aware of the close family relationship between the two, and gently ushered the younger woman outside and back into the sunlight streaming through the station canopy. 'It's a lovely day so we can get some tea and sit on a bench outside.' Laura Green willingly accepted the invitation.

A few minutes later and they sat overlooking the turntable at the southern end of Leicester Central, both with mugs of steaming tea. 'What brings you here?' Benson was certain it must have something to do with the arrest of Laura's father and braced herself for a difficult conversation.

'WPC Benson, I think you worked on the David Green case?'

'Please call me Jane.' A momentary pause as she noted the formal manner by which Miss Green referred to her father. 'I was on the case for a short while but none of us is working on it now. The case is in the hands of Northamptonshire Constabulary -.'

'I know it is. But there are things about the investigation I still don't understand, and I'd like your help.'

'As with any serious case there are puzzles, contradictions and things that take a lot of work to understand especially for someone on the outside looking in.' Benson instantly regretted how she'd phrased that.

'He's my dad. I am not an outsider. I didn't come here to be fobbed off with empty words. I need to understand what happened and I want to find answers to questions worrying me. I thought you might be able to help.' Laura Green looked away and hastily wiped away the suggestion of a tear.

'I'm sorry, I didn't mean to sound unfeeling.' Benson made as if to sip some tea but found she had lost the taste for it. 'It must be very hard for you.'

'That does not even come close.'

'I was only on the case for a day or so. I am not sure what I can tell you.'

'You worked alongside the detectives investigating. You have a far deeper insight into how my father came to be accused of something he didn't do, than I.'

Benson considered how to handle this. It was natural that Miss Green was going to defend the innocence of her father. It was impossible to imagine otherwise, but was it also possible she knew something the detectives were unaware of? 'Do you have any information you believe might prove your father's innocence?'

'I don't think so. But I hope I soon will.' She looked back at Benson with a steely resolve in her eyes. 'Simon thinks you are a good policewoman. He claims you are a detective in the making.'

'Does he now?' Benson smiled and decided she needed some tea after all.

'I feel as though I can trust you to tell me honestly about things which are worrying me.'

'You should be speaking with those now running the case...'

Laura Green ignored the attempt to deflect her questions. 'The dead man's camera. What do you know about this?'

'It was not with the body and the DCI demanded it was found...'

'In dad's motorcycle panniers. I heard.'

'I can reassure you the discovery was observed by a fellow officer...'

'I am not suggesting the police did anything underhand, but have you stopped to think this through? It was found in the panniers of the very same motorbike my dad chose to ride when called in for questioning with the threat of a murder charge hanging over his head.'

'Go on.' Benson observed the young woman.

'For argument's sake, let's say dad *is* the killer - and for the record I want you to understand that is not possible - why would he put it in such an obvious place instead of throwing it in the Great Ouse or burying it or putting it somewhere impossibly hard to find? Why would he bring an incriminating object here of all places? You've met him. He's not simple. He's a thoughtful man. Everything he does is considered and careful. He's a signalman controlling a busy line section and as such cannot make mistakes in his job, so why should such a man make such an obvious gaff?'

'Well...' Benson was searching for an answer. She too had wondered about the camera. Vignoles had been eager to find it, knowing it was vital, and suddenly, there it was. Easily discovered and about as damming a piece of evidence as they could have asked for. She remembered at the time it felt too convenient. She looked up and watched as a big green Western Region Hall class locomotive slowly backed onto the turntable having recently drawn its train into the station. 'You think this is out of character?'

'I would stake my life on it. It would be an idiotic and foolish action. It has to have been planted. The camera, or perhaps more pertinently the film inside, is presumably central to the case. Perhaps the reason Grimes was killed?'

'The film was inside but exposed to light and destroyed.'

Green nodded. This was unsurprising. 'I've been to see dad and tried to get him to open up.'

Benson leaned closer. This was interesting.

'He had no interest at all in the camera, and I believe him. He wasn't even that interested in Grimes' photographs of the gas turbine.'

'Is he going to say otherwise?'

'Were his prints in the camera?'

'I think not...'

'But he left clear ones on the murder weapon?'

'I can't disclose this information, Laura.' Benson looked at the fiery young woman seated opposite then along the empty platform. After a pause she spoke. 'There were none on the camera, as far as I am aware.'

'Does that not seem odd? Prints on the weapon and no attempt to rub them off, but great care to do the same with the camera before putting it somewhere any policeman could find with their eyes closed?' Benson winced at the dig at their competence. Her mind was whirring. Laura Green continued. 'The film was destroyed but the camera was dumped where it could lead the investigation astray.'

'Are you implying a set-up?'

'Dad didn't put it there, so someone else did! And from where I am sitting, as *an outsider*, it seems to be working.'

They both silently drank tea and considered this scenario as *Albert Hall* slowly turned about on the turntable, the huge weight of the engine perfectly balanced on the central pivot so it could be set into motion by the driver and fireman giving the table's handle a short shove. Benson felt her jumble of thoughts also trying to find some balance and order as she watched the graceful engine spin about, its brass and copper metalwork glinting in the sun.

'Laura, did your father tell you anything that helps convince you of his innocence?'

'My father *is* innocent. I don't require convincing.'

'Let me reword the question. Did he tell you anything that would help convince the Director of Public Prosecutions and the investigating team in Northampton of his innocence? Feelings and emotions won't wash. They need solid facts.'

'I understand. There *is* something,' Laura Green reached for her handbag and opened it. 'Dad told me to retrieve this. Hidden on a top shelf in his shed. A place full of tins of screws, pots of paint and goodness knows what. Somewhere no one goes except dad. I doubt the police even noticed it, let alone realised it had any relevance in their search.' She pulled out the rusting toffee tin.

Benson felt her pulse quicken.

'Have you heard the name Rosie Tustain?'

Benson blinked. 'Rosie Tustain?'

'A young woman who went missing. Years ago. In 1928 I think it was. She was never found.'

'Way before my time so I don't know the details, but the strange thing is I read that name for the first time just days ago.'

'Where?'

'Show me what you have. I can decide if I think there is a connection. Tustain is a common family name around these parts.'

Green nodded in agreement. 'Dad said he's had this since he was a teenager. He took it to show Richie the evening he died.'

'To be clear, the evening Grimes was killed?'

'The same. They argued over it beside *The Difference Engine*.'

'He admits they had crossed words?'

'He does, but no more than that.'

'What was the argument about?'

'We were pressed for time, but he made it clear there is something about what is inside this box that remained a sore point between them. Grimes was angry when he saw dad had this, they had a tussle and dad knocked the spanner thing onto the floor and then picked it up. Hence his prints being on it. More argument followed and then still clutching this tin, dad left.' She now opened the lid.

'A hairband?' Benson looked mildly disappointed.

'I think it belonged to Rosie Tustain. Dad didn't get to say much before a thug of a guard entered the room and I had to leave.'

Benson asked if she could take a closer look. She carefully removed everything inside the tin. 'This note. It was written by your father?'

'No. Look at the name, 'Richie'. Richard Grimes was always Richie back then.'

'Why has your father kept a lover's note and what I presume is a token of affection from a young girl? It seems bizarre.'

'I don't know.' Laura Green looked as frustrated as Benson about this. 'But it seems to me all this belonged to Grimes way back when they were teenagers and for some reason, dad took it and felt it important enough to keep for all these years.'

'How odd? And even odder for the two of them to argue over it so many years later?'

Green looked away, her thoughts elsewhere as she watched a heavy coal train rumble through the station.

'Laura. I don't know what this means, but I have to warn you that this could be taken as a motive for…you know what.'

Green nodded almost imperceptibly and bit her lower lip. 'I think that's why he didn't want the police to know about it. He knows his behaviour is out of character and this could be seen as a reason for them to fight and…' Her words were barely audible above the terrific sound of a panting steam engine and the heavy trucks it was pulling grumbling over the elevated railway, the arches below amplifying the sound.

'You still believe your father is innocent?'

'Yes. I can see why others might say otherwise, but he did not strike and kill Richie Grimes. There is a mystery here and the things in this tin might explain it.'

I'm not sure. Benson was sceptical but drained her tea. 'I need to get back. The sarge will be furious if we sit here any longer. But I have something I'd like you to see.'

'What is it?'

'There is a book. A scrapbook album of photographs and press cuttings, to be exact. It seems to be about a girl who disappeared back in 1928. Her name was Rosie Tustain. You can see why I am interested in that name. We found it in Grimes' rented bedroom. The assumption is that Grimes made the scrapbook.'

'Why did he do that?' Green's voice barely concealed her excitement.

'He seemed to be collecting everything and anything he could on the subject. He had some kind of fascination with her disappearance.'

'And then dad turns up with her headband? It has to be the same girl.'

'Steady on. There could be a connection, but jumping to conclusions is unwise. My sergeant asked me to study the scrapbook and report back.' Benson looked guilty. 'For God's sake don't tell anyone, but I took the book home to study in the evening as I was run off my feet all day. Then the case dramatically accelerated and the next thing I knew we were handing everything over to an inspector from Northampton. He was none too friendly either. I was too embarrassed to admit I had the book at home. It is strictly against regulations to take evidence from the office.' Benson looked embarrassed.

'I found the time to rush back to get it without telling

anyone what I was doing but by the time I returned to the office the county police were gone. Off in their police van with your father and all the files. Except for one. I should have spoken up and arranged to get it across to them, but...'

'You still have it?' Laura Green was excited.

'In my desk drawer. I want you to take it, but just for tonight. Make of it what you can, then bring it back tomorrow. Do not forget. I will then send it across to Wootton Hall and take what flak comes back. I will say nothing about you seeing it and you must deny all knowledge about my *faux pas*.'

'Thank you. But what does it all mean? Was Grimes obsessed with this woman?'

'I think Grimes was doing his own amateur reinvestigation. Taking pictures of locations he considered significant. I think he was trying to create a trail of the route this young woman took on what might have been her last journey. Perhaps he got close to the truth?'

Laura Green felt an unpleasant lurch inside her tummy. 'I don't like the sound of all this when taken together with that Alice band and letter.'

'There's more.' Benson gave one last careful study of the contents of the tin, determined to memorise everything and write it down as soon as she could.

'There are photographs of some individuals in the book. A grainy image of the missing girl cut from a newspaper and a school photograph of her. She was very pretty. What intrigues me more, however, is a pair of photographs, one of a young man simple titled 'E.C' who I believe to be Ellis Cartwright. It was he who found Grimes' body.'

'Oh!'

'The other shows two young men larking about in the sun near a railway embankment. One of them is Richard Grimes.'

'And the other?'

'Your father.'

Chapter Twenty-Nine

Eddie Earnshaw had been at work since 6 am. He was now back in Leicester North shed topping up the water tanks of his engine for the day. Once done, he and his driver could then enjoy their cold lunch from their metal 'snap' tins. This was one benefit of their unglamorous roster all week that would see them working a succession of mundane short 'trip' journeys that involved shuffling a motley collection of wagons between one station yard and another in and around the local area. They rarely went faster than twenty-five miles an hour, were usually rostered a less than perfect six-wheeled goods engine that wheezed and rattled alarmingly and spent a lot of time idling away the day whilst waiting for wagons to be loaded or unloaded. This relaxed schedule also gave them time occasionally to nip back on shed and have a natter with whoever else was in and around the loco crew 'bothy'. In fine weather such as they were enjoying, nobody of sound mind wished to be inside this unpleasantly dirty construction and most lounged outside seated on oil drums, a rickety chair or packing case.

Earnshaw however, now left his driver leaning against the windowsill of the bothy deep in conversation with a chum about the finer points of runner bean cultivation and walked away, searching for his friend PC Simon Howerth. They'd checked their respective work timetables last night and the two young men realised they could find a way to meet at Leicester North at lunchtime. After their curious and intriguing 'council of war' with Laura Green the evening before, the two friends reckoned they should meet every evening or during the day if possible to exchange any discoveries. Time was of the essence.

* * * *

Laura Green and Simon Howerth had chosen to meet in a pub they rarely visited close to the little-used West Wharf station. It was convenient for Laura once she'd closed her signal box further down the line. The pub served mediocre beer and lukewarm gin and tonic but was at least cheap, the lighting dim and the saloon usually empty. It was also unlikely any of the detective team would step inside. Neither wanted to meet Howerth's colleagues right now.

'We have twenty minutes until Eddie joins us, just as you requested.' Howerth was puzzled. His relations with Laura needed repair and so he'd gratefully accepted the invitation to meet for a quiet drink but was unsure he wanted Eddie sitting in on it. It had been a surprising request from Laura, but when they'd spoken on the telephone she had been insistent about Eddie joining them. Something in the tone of her voice intrigued him. She sounded more excited than angry, so he arrived with hope in his heart.

'Most of what I want to say, I want to say to you both.'

Simon supped some ale. 'About what in particular?' Not their lover's tiff, he hoped.

'About your future father-in-law being wrongly accused of murder and banged up in a cell and what we're going to do about it.'

'Ah…'

Laura drank deeply and then stared at the slice of lemon in her almost empty glass. She was still fighting with her emotions. The ancient steam locomotive working the West Wharf yard could be heard giving short toots on its whistle as it shunted the last few wagons into order before being quietened down for the night. 'A man was killed that night, but not by my dad. I struggled to believe that you - the police, I mean, not you - could have thought he capable of doing such a thing. I was furious, angry, upset. The full works.' Simon tactfully remained silent. 'Of course, the police have to investigate everyone and respond to what they find. I can understand that.' A sad little smile, but it was enough to encourage Howerth. 'I went to Wootton Hall and talked to dad. He didn't strike Mr Grimes and he did not kill him. I don't believe dad had any interest in the camera let alone taking it from the body and stuffing it into his panniers for the police to find.'

'I don't understand that part. It makes no sense.'

'I'm glad you agree.' She paused to take a breath. 'You warned me the truth can be hard to uncover and once in the open can be even harder to accept, but I'm going to face whatever I have to and prove dad to be innocent of murder.'

'What did your dad tell you?' Howerth realised he was gripping his pint very hard.

'Not a lot, but it was vital.' She emptied her glass. Howerth moved to stand up to get a refill but Laura put a hand on his arm to keep him seated, then kept it there. 'Dad suspected Mr Grimes of doing something bad a long time ago. I think their relationship soured after that and whatever it was it has haunted dad ever since. I will tell you more when Eddie joins us. Dad took something from Grimes back then and kept it, believing it to be evidence of wrong doing. I'm not so sure to be honest, and it could even look bad for dad. It could be seen as a motive for hitting Grimes.'

'But we know he didn't.'

She smiled at Simon. 'No, he didn't. But someone *did*.'

'Someone with a strong motive to see Grimes dead.'

'And seek to retrieve items dad has kept secret since 1928. Simon, I really think dad is in the safest place for now. Locked away in a cell. It sounds crazy, but I think we must stall getting him out on bail until we identify and trap the real killer!'

'We?'

'Ah! Here's Ed. Right on cue!'

With greetings over, fresh drinks bought and cigarettes lit Laura Green faced the two men. 'I need your help. Both of you. Help me untangle the horrid, knotted mess that has dad facing a murder charge. I need your help to prove his innocence.'

'Sounds like a deal. What did your dad say happened when he met Grimes at the engine shed? Tell us exactly what he believes happened,' Earnshaw asked.

'They met that evening, although dad did himself no favour by denying it at first. They had heated words.' Laura Green looked pained as she spoke.

Howerth didn't much like what he was hearing. 'The lack of motive is considered the only weakness in the case against your dad. Finding a motive is exactly what the prosecution wants.' He could see Laura looking downcast as he was speaking. She was able to appreciate the situation without him needing to spell it out further. 'We need to understand what were they arguing over.'

'A woman.'

Howerth and Earnshaw looked shocked.

'Someone from before dad met mum, so it's not what you think. But it has to be serious to matter after so many years.' She composed herself for a moment. 'Dad didn't say much, be he did lead me to a discovery. It was hidden in his garden shed. He's kept it since he and Grimes were about eighteen.' She now placed the toffee tin on the table. 'What's inside relates to the girl in question. She also lived in Woodford, and I guess one or both of the young men as they were back then were interested in her.'

'Interested?'

'Simon, don't be slow!' Earnshaw replied. 'They fancied her. Love rivals.'

Green opened the tin. 'I'm not sure about that, but even if so, I cannot believe their feelings for her back then are the motivation for the disagreement now.'

'Unless she suddenly reappeared?' Earnshaw queried.

'No, Eddie. The girl went missing and was never seen again. Presumed dead. Probably abducted and not a trace of her since June 1928.'

'Oh…' Earnshaw was shocked.

'The young woman was called Rosie Tustain and she wrote this note.' Laura Green took it from the tin and unfolded it. 'She's asking Grimes to meet her at what I suppose is a special place they reserved for their assignations.'

'All very Romeo and Juliette. Why did Grimes and this girl need to keep their relationship secret?' Howerth was puzzled.

'I don't know, but perhaps we need to find out. Dad might have the answer but I'm not sure if he'll tell me.'

Howerth was inspecting the note and hairband. 'Whatever their reasons this hairband was given to Grimes as a keepsake...'

'Or did he keep after doing something awful to her? A kind of trophy.' Howerth felt his blood run cold even as he spoke.

'Ugh!' Green shivered.

'Is that why your dad has it and kept it secret? It could be incriminating?'

'Whatever the story behind the band, your dad must have nicked this from Grimes,' Earnshaw added. 'It looks so innocent. Like nothing, and yet...'

Laura Green sighed deeply. 'I don't know why dad did what he did, but when he showed this tin to Grimes that evening they argued.'

'He took this to show Grimes in Woodford shed?'

'Yes, Eddie.'

'If this is to do with why that young woman disappeared then it's solid grounds for a heated argument.'

'But despite an exchange of words, dad did not kill Grimes. So how does this fit in with someone else killing him?' Laura bit her lip. 'There has to be someone else involved.'

The three inspected the note and hair band once again in the vain hope the secrets held would be revealed. 'She's asking to meet Grimes, but it says little else. Hardly a romantic love letter or the sort of note one might keep,' Howerth observed.

'But you might if the date was never kept?' Earnshaw pondered. 'Did something happen to stop them meeting?'

'Yes, she vanished!' Howerth was not liking the direction

this was taking.

'There's more.' Green now dug the scrapbook out of her shoulder bag. 'WPC Benson had this. She recovered it from the rented bedroom Grimes was staying in. He made it. I promised not to show it to anyone and feel bad breaking my word, but in all honesty all I care about is getting dad out of jail. You must promise not let on you ever saw this.'

'Is that Police evidence?'

'It is, Simon. She took it home to study and forgot to hand it back.'

He whistled long and low. 'She's in for a severe reprimand if this gets out.'

'I don't want to get her into trouble.'

'You won't hear it from me!' Earnshaw was itching to take a look.

'Me neither. She's put her neck on the line to help you. We must do our best to protect her.'

Half an hour later and they all sat back in their chairs. A stunned silence fell. 'I'll refill our glasses and then we can discuss this.' Howerth was soon back. 'This strikes me as an amateur version of what we call a 'Murder Book'. A page by page account of the most serious kind of investigation.'

'There's not a lot of detail though, and what there is comes mainly from press cuttings,' Earnshaw observed.

'Press cuttings placed in careful date order; a train timetable with a number of connections between Woodford and Loughborough highlighted and a series of photographs that look to be taken more recently. They follow a walk from Loughborough Central to a remote place by a canal bank and some other locations outside Woodford Halse.'

'We know these places...' Earnshaw agreed. 'But this photograph looks older than the others. It's smaller and grainier. Taken on a different camera I would say.' He was closely inspecting the print in question. 'A stretch of canal on a summery day. There's also a narrowboat moored on the far bank. That interests me.'

'Why, Eddie?'

'I can't say what it means, but it feels significant. I think the photographer was interested in the composition and the boat on the far bank served to make it more interesting.'

'The style of the photograph and the age of the print and the paper are all different,' Green observed.

'Taken by someone other than Grimes?' Green asked.

'Yes, yet Grimes thought the picture important enough to put it in his file, and I don't think he cared about the composition.' Howerth was now inspecting the tiny print. 'Is the boat and whoever lived on it connected to the mystery?'

'Have you noticed Grimes has pencilled the word 'Blackbird' underneath. Could that be the name of the boat?' Earnshaw suggested.

'I reckon so.' Howerth agreed. 'We need to trace the boat. But does it still exist?'

Eddie nodded his head in agreement. 'If this was photo was taken before the war it could be wreck by now.'

Green flipped the pages over until she came to a page that had given them all pause for thought the first time they had looked at it. WPC Benson had given her forewarning, but it still sent an unpleasant shiver down her spine seeing the photograph of her father as a young man with his arm around the shoulders of Richie Grimes. She knew they had been friends and Grimes had only recently revisited her parents' house, but this previously unseen photograph unsettled her. However, what she wanted them all to think about now was the pair of photographs of a bespectacled man, one of which showed him in a white lab coat. 'What about this Ellis Cartwright? WPC Benson told me that he was -.'

'- the man who found the body of Richard Grimes.' Howerth completed the sentence.

'Suspect number one?'

'I reckon so, Eddie.'

Chapter Twenty-Nine

'Surely the detectives must have interviewed Cartwright?'

'They did.'

'And presumably ruled him out.' Earnshaw didn't want to dampen enthusiasm, but this fact was staring them in the face.

'They didn't have sight of this book or the tin of artefacts and the story of the missing girl,' Howerth countered. 'If he is in any way implicated, and Grimes seems to think he is, that could change everything.'

'But *is* there anything?' Green was looking worried. 'I think Eddie is right. Your DCI must have challenged Cartwright but let him go having been convinced he had no motive and a plausible explanation of his innocence.' She stopped and took a deep drink. 'I can see why dad is reluctant to speak about this. It looks awkward.'

'Steady on, Laura. An investigation can lurch one way then the other. Good news, bad news, back to good news again as layers are peeled back and revealed. We have a lot to work with here. A girl that Grimes had a romantic involvement with vanishes and is presumed dead. Does her disappearance have anything to do with Grimes?'

'Or Cartwright?'

'Or dad...'

'No, Laura. You cannot seriously believe that,' Howerth was taken aback.

'No. I'm being foolish. My mood is swinging wildly from one emotion to another at the moment, the silly goose that I am!' She angrily wiped away a tear.

'Rosie Tustain lies at the heart of this and we need to find out all we can about her and about this Cartwright.' Howerth was feeling more convinced by the moment that his future father-in-law was innocent and that they were on the edge of what was shaping up to be a fascinating story.

'We have a murder book compiled by the dead man. It looks like he was retracing the last journey of Miss Tustain in order to uncover the truth. It also looks like he was killed

for his efforts. That makes this a double murder investigation.'
Earnshaw drank some beer. 'The man who found the body of
Grimes is best placed to cover his tracks and divert attention
away.'

'I agree.' Howerth replied.

'What do you mean?'

'He could falsify evidence. Tell the police he saw and heard
something he didn't...'

'Then we go after Cartwright!' Laura Green's voice had
regained its vigor.

'We need to be careful, darling.'

'He needs to be careful. He hasn't faced me...' Her eyes
flashed with a fire inside. 'Right. Then we gather all we can
about Cartwright, about Grimes and especially his time in
Woodford before the war and about this Rosie Tustain.' Both
men nodded, slightly in awe of the dynamic manner in which
she was barking the orders. 'We put it together and then
Simon, you go to your DS and demand he makes an official
reinvestigation. I have to work my last week in the box next
week, so time is pressing. Drink up boys!'

Chapter Thirty

Eddie Earnshaw had learned that *The Difference Engine* was due back on shed at 4 pm when they would shut the locomotive down for the night. He was due to clock off about the same time and could easily find a way to start a conversation with some of the crew of white-coated boffins. The gas turbine was attracting attention and much discussion - not all favourable - and so one more curious footplate man eager to talk about their 'big white beast' was hardly going to arouse suspicion. However, before that, he wanted to talk to Simon about something he'd been thinking over during the morning and was pleased to see the constable strolling in through the entrance and giving a friendly greeting to the gateman. Howerth was scanning the lines of engines parked up on the shed apron checking out what was on shed.

'Not here?'

'*The Difference Engine* is in Marylebone, but due back mid-afternoon and I'll have a sniff about.'

'Nothing to report then?'

'There's something I want to show you. I want your opinion.'

'Sounds intriguing.'

Earnshaw led his friend into the shed and to one of the many workbenches that lined the walls. 'Grimes was clobbered with a wrench.'

'That's right.'

'Do you know the size and make?'

'Yep, I was the one who found it. I told you that last night. The fingerprints were clear as anything due to the oily muck along the centre of the shaft.' He made a face. 'And they matched David's - worst luck.'

'Can you find one like it here?'

185

Howerth inspected an array of spanners and wrenches that hung from a wooden board behind the workbench, each with a painted outline on the backboard that mirrored the tool in question. 'These are the same.'

'Now drop it on the floor.'

'Eh?'

'Go on Si. Close the jaws tight so they won't bend and drop it from a low height to be sure you don't damage it.'

Howerth did as asked and dropped the heavy tool from a height of a few inches. It still made a loud clatter as it hit the concrete floor. 'Now what?'

'Stand and face me as if you were David Green and I was Grimes. You've just knocked it to the floor, now quickly pick it up and put it on the bench.'

Howerth did as his friend instructed. He was slow and wooden in his movements.

'Do it more naturally. Almost without thinking. Imagine you're arguing with me about something, and you just grab it.'

He dropped the tool again then quickly grabbed for it and held it up. 'OK, Ed. I've chucked valuable tools around and made a horrid racket. To what end?'

* * * *

'Sir?' Howerth approached DS Mellor who was seated behind his desk in the tiny cubby hole of an office the station maintenance team had built for him. It was barely larger than an airing cupboard but at least had part of a window revealed high up on the back wall and most of the ceiling was taken up by filthy toughened glass that formed one of several light wells in the building. Two metal filing cabinets, a desk and two chairs were more than enough to fill the space. Mellor had his feet up on the desk and was reading the sports pages of the paper, a cigarette burned as it dangled from the corner of his mouth. 'What's up?'

'Sarge, I've been thinking…'

'Never a good idea, constable. Your job is not to think but to do what I tell yer.' Mellor lowered the paper and frowned as he saw the monkey wrench. 'Mending summat?'

'No sarge. This is the same as the one I found. You know, the murder weapon.'

'Must be thousands just like it in every engine shed in the land, but since it ain't the actual murder weapon or bloody better not be, what you doin' bringing it 'ere?'

'It's the fingerprints. They're really clear and fresh and there's no doubt who's they are, but they worry me.'

DS Mellor stared at Howerth. 'You angling for a job with the forensic boys, or do you fancy yerself as a detective?' His voice and expression were unsympathetic.

'Of course not, sir.'

'Glad to hear it, constable. After our little conversation the other night I thought you'd know better than to come in 'ere and start actin' like some smart alec know-it-all.' He shook his newspaper in a manner that suggested Howerth beat a hasty retreat.

'I'm not trying to be clever, sir. It's just that something struck me as not quite right. You always tell us we've got to be alert to anything that doesn't look right and report it.' It would be dangerous to mention his friend Eddie's part in this and he was trying to flatter Mellor's ego. He got a cold, blank stare in return, which was unnerving, but ploughed on. 'Mr Green claims he bumped into a wrench overhanging a bench.' Howerth now placed the heavy tool on the corner of Mellor's desk. 'Like so. It fell to the floor.' He placed it on the floor knowing that the strident crash of dropping it was not going to lighten Mellor's mood. 'He bends down and picks it up…' Howerth held the wrench at a point slightly higher than midway down the long handle where it was perfectly balanced. 'This is the place where his fingers wrapped around the shaft as we know.'

'Clearest prints I've seen. Case closed. Sorry, lad, I know he's family an' all, but...' Mellor blew smoke into the air. He shrugged his shoulders.

'If I asked you or anyone else, they'd all pick it up in the same place. It's heavy, and the natural thing to do is grab it just above the middle point so it's not unbalanced in the hand.'

'Is that all?' Mellor was unimpressed.

Howerth gulped. 'Now, if I wanted to use this as a weapon, I'd want as much force as I could get. I'd hold it near the end of the handle, like this.' He now wielded it as if it were a tennis racquet. 'Much more force and more control to ensure I killed the man I hit. I couldn't afford to make a mistake or he'd cry out, perhaps twist around and fight back...' He tailed off.

'Put that bloody thing down!' Mellor snapped as he watched Howerth mime bringing the hefty tool down on an imaginary head. 'Your point?'

'I think Green's prints suggest he picked the wrench up from the floor, exactly as he claimed. He did it by holding it along the shaft where it balances - and where it makes it a poor weapon. Do you see?' He demonstrated once again. 'What if the killer came along later, having seen Green place fresh prints on the shaft, but this time held it at the far end where he could direct a powerful and accurate blow whilst avoiding smudging Green's prints and leaving none of their own if he was wearing gloves? The forensic team said the end of the handle was rubbed smooth.' He braced himself for the stinging rebuke that was surely about to follow.

'You suggesting we made a mistake?'

'Just another way of looking at the evidence. Sir.'

Mellor stared at the constable until the young man's ears burned. 'Well, thank you kindly for that little instructional episode, constable. Now, there's been a break-in at a storeroom at Bulwell Green.' Mellor picked up a note lying on his desk. 'Get over there. When yer done, straight back here and collect this lump,' Mellor waved his fag towards the wrench. 'Get it back to the shed before they accuse you of stealin'.'

'Righty ho, sir.'

'Scram!'

Earnshaw spun about the heel and hurried out.

Mellor lit another fag and smoked for a minute or two whilst staring at the lump of forged steel lying on the corner of his desk. He dropped his feet to the floor and snatched up the wrench then unceremoniously dropped it to the ground. He reached down and felt for it. Instinctively clasping it where it would best balance in his hand. He looked closely at how his fingers lay curled around the handle. The cigarette bobbed on his lip as he now raised his arm and made as if to strike an imaginary person. It felt all wrong. The weight was so evenly balanced that despite the heft of the tool, it was almost light in his hand. It was a poor weapon. He shifted his grip to the end of the handle and raised his arm and described a perfect sweeping move that would deliver a powerful and potentially lethal blow. He swung again. Mellor was getting annoyed. That whippersnapper of a constable might have a point.

'Remind me never to cross you whilst playing tennis,' Vignoles appeared at the door.

'Guv?' Mellor was startled, but soon recovered. 'We might 'ave a problem.'

Chapter Thirty-One

Laura Green might have done better to curb her desire to tackle the problem head-on. A wiser course might have been to take the so-called 'Murder Book' and toffee tin straight to DCI Vignoles and let the professionals make of it what they would. At the very least it would have been sensible to share her ideas with WPC Benson when they met for a few brief moments outside Leicester Central to hand back the scrapbook. Benson had been eager to hear what Green had made of the contents but was also mindful she should not be caught red-handed with police evidence. This eagerness to get the book back to her office combined with Green's impatience to be away on her own investigative journey ensured the meeting was brief and almost nothing was said between them.

For his part, PC Simon Howerth had been made to promise to say nothing within the Detective Department until they were ready to deliver the case as a *fait accompli* to the senior detectives. As it transpired, he was immediately sent off to investigate a possible theft from a goods yard near Nottingham and spent the day not only away from Leicester Central, but too far away to be able to make any inroads into uncovering information about the Grimes case let alone get close to Ellis Cartwright.

Unbeknown to the 'Three Musketeers' engaged in their private investigation, WPC Benson's confession that she still had the scrapbook Grimes had compiled was received by DS Mellor in a more positive light than she had dared imagine. He glared at her, clicked his fingers with impatience as he demanded she handed it over, then made her stand almost to attention as he slowly turned the pages. His cigarette burning in the ashtray was ignored. He remained stonily silent as he studied the book and silently chastised himself for the heinous sin of having let it slip from his mind. Out of sight, out of mind was the excuse rolling around in his head, but he was mightily dissatisfied with this excuse. He finally slammed the covers closed and looked at Benson who was keeping her eyes focused on the wall behind his head.

'You forgot to bring this in?'

'I apologise, sir.'

'You didn't remember something that holds what looks like significant information in a murder enquiry?' His voice was cold and level.

'The case moved so swiftly and then transferred to Northampton before I had time.'

Mellor gave a shake of his head. 'It could be vital to the prosecution of the case.'

'I appreciate that, sir.'

Mellor looked out of his office window whilst drumming his fingers on the cover of the book. Benson awaited her punishment. Mellor stood up and noticing his cigarette which had now created a long line of burned ash, picked it up and in so doing dropped ash down his smart suit. 'Bloody 'ell.' He dragged angrily on the cigarette, glaring at Benson as if it was her fault, then stubbed the cigarette out and with the same hand attempted to brush the ash off with no success. 'Out! I need to speak to the DCI about this.'

Benson hurried off, with Mellor following close behind. Mellor pointedly closed the door to Vignoles' office behind him. Benson noticed the sergeant had taken the book with him. Perhaps he was not going in to discuss her failings but the contents of the book?

'You need to see this, guv.'

Mellor was already trying to turn the situation into something advantageous to them both. Mellor was to blame every bit as much as Benson, and he knew it. He'd given her the book after the most cursory of glances and promptly forgotten about it. 'Grimes was investigating the disappearance of a young woman from Woodford Halse.'

He handed the book across the desk.

Vignoles raised an eyebrow and waved his DS to take a seat. 'Rosie Tustain? Her name was brought up in the group meeting.'

'She is a name we were interested in, but the case was taken away before we made any significant progress. Take a look at the back page. Lift up the press cutting Sellotaped in and you'll see what was missed...at first.' Mellor was sounding contrite.

Vignoles did as instructed and was immediately interested in the small photographic prints pasted to the backboard, showing David Green, Richard Grimes, an extremely attractive young woman and what looked like another familiar young man. 'We know this man?'

'Ellis Cartwright.'

'Well, well, well...' Vignoles reached for his pipe and tin of Red Breast tobacco and started filling his pipe. This was going to take a while and he always thought about knotty problems better with a lit pipe. 'Remind me. where did you get this?'

'From beneath Grimes's bed.'

'In his London digs?' This had only just been searched after some delay finding the address.

'Rugby.'

'You missed it when you undertook the initial search, but it was found when uniform came to collect everything?' He gave Mellor an arch look as he lit his pipe.

'Not exactly...' A pause. 'We had it from the start, but it got overlooked. We didn't give it the detailed attention it deserved as it appeared to be mainly second-hand source material. Press clippings...' Mellor tried to disguise his awkwardness by lighting a cigarette.

Vignoles turned more pages. 'Could this hold a motive for the attack on Grimes?'

'It might.'

Vignoles read on quietly for a few minutes. 'Did Grimes take these pictures?' He was inspecting the unremarkable series of scenes that had previously failed to interest Benson.

'I reckon so.'

'Was he conducting some kind of investigation?'

'I believe he was. The young woman in the photo is Rosemary Tustain of Woodford Halse. She vanished off the face of the earth. Last seen in June 1928 boarding a train going north from Woodford. A partial sighting at the time suggested she alighted at Loughborough Central, but as the press reported over the next few weeks the public sent in observations from almost everywhere in the UK. You know how it is with these appeals. It ended up she was seen here, there and everywhere and it just confused the investigation rather than aiding it. They never found her, dead or alive.'

'Why was Grimes so interested? After such a long time, and whilst travelling light he still had this with him whilst doing a story for *The Railway Magazine*.'

'Under false pretences.'

'Indeed. Was this his attempt at working undercover?' Vignoles smoked a while as he studied more pages, then placed the book on his desk and spun his chair around so he could watch the station concourse. The Manchester to Marylebone express was due at any moment, and he wanted to see what was on the front. 'You've already raised a question over the use of the monkey wrench as an effective weapon when perfectly balanced in the hand. Now, this appears out of the blue...' He smiled, knowing his bluff and tough DS was inwardly squirming. 'I'd almost say you were fighting David Green's corner. Mavis been bending your ear?'

'She doesn't speak to me.'

'To me neither. Can't say I blame her...' Vignoles allowed himself a moment of satisfaction as *Royal Lancer,* one of Leicester Central's favourite Gresley A3 pacifics steamed gently to a halt outside, the rake of clean maroon liveried coaches gleaming in the sunlight. The railway was starting to look more cared for than it had for years, with stock and locomotives brighter and shinier than since the outbreak of war. The station, however, was a different story. It still had glass in the roof but was in need of repair and a deep clean and the whole station could benefit from the attention of a small army of painters, cleaners and handymen.

He ended this short reverie and turned back to face Mellor. 'I shall ignore the startling fact this clearly belongs in Northampton along with the case files and privately cheer we have a moment to study this and consider how we feel about the David Green conviction. New information affords us good reason to have a fresh look.'

'You think the case is unsound?'

'Is that not what you were demonstrating to me yesterday?'

'I s'pose it was.'

'You have at least studied this thoroughly?' He tapped the closed cover of the scrapbook.

'Not as thoroughly as WPC Benson.' Mellor knew it was time for a tactical withdrawal.

'Then we'd better bring her in and hear her expert appraisal.' His look made it clear he understood the situation and would expect Mellor to accept his failings with good grace or expect repercussions. Vignoles knew Mellor adopted a tough and somewhat dismissive approach to the two WPCs and was reticent about acknowledging their contribution to the team. Vignoles was therefore both annoyed at this serious gaffe in investigative procedure and quietly pleased. Mellor was going to eat a large slice of what the Americans liked to call 'humble pie'.

'At ease Benson.' The WPC had feared the worst when Mellor had asked her to enter the DCI's office, his face blank and impossible to read. 'The DCI requires a summary of the content of this book and your assessment of what it means.'

'Yes, sir,' Benson felt her career was still in the balance, but perhaps a good performance now might at least see her demoted for just a few weeks to menial duties and nothing worse. After giving as accurate a summary as possible at short notice, she moved on to the crucial part. 'I assess that Richard Grimes was conducting his own private investigation into the unexplained disappearance of Miss Rosemary Tustain in the summer of 1928.'

'Do the contents offer any indication as to why Grimes was doing this some twenty-eight or so years after the event?' Vignoles asked.

'He does not offer any running commentary or resumé. The scrapbook is a personal repository of his findings. A catch-all for any scrap of information or evidence he could collect and not for presentation to a third party.'

Vignoles nodded that he considered this to be a reasonable assessment. He was quietly turning the pages as Benson spoke. 'Have you found any information within that would explain these photographs on the back page? The girl is the one who went missing?'

'It is. Miss Tustain. Aged 17-years at the time of her disappearance. Her image repeats in nearly all of the newspaper clippings.'

'And the other three?' Vignoles knew who they were but wanted to press Benson.

'David Green and Richard Grimes. I have not had time to identify the location but as they both hail from Woodford, it is not unreasonable to think the photograph was taken there when they were young men, possibly around the time Tustain vanished. The other is Mr Ellis Cartwright.'

'The same Cartwright who works for Tomkins-Dunkler?'

'Correct.'

'And the same man who found Grimes under the engine,' Mellor added. He was feeling left out.

'Thank you, sergeant, I have made that connection.' Vignoles was not letting him off the hook yet. 'Benson. This series of photographs. What is your assessment of these?'

'As Mr Grimes was a photographer and they are of decent quality, I am of the opinion he took them. They look as if he was recording a sequence of locations that perhaps imply more than can be seen.'

'Explain.'

'I think he might be trying to recreate a journey and record the places where key events took place.'

'Places where Tustain might have gone?'

'That is my interpretation.'

'Does the material within the book offer a motive for Mr Green to attack Mr Grimes?'

Benson paused. It was time for her to declare further evidence existed that she had sight of it. But it was evidence of *what*? Even as she was organising her thoughts she was getting a sense that Laura Green might be mistaken. A hair band, a funny shaped stone and a scrawled note hardly added up to very much now she was standing here in the gaze of these two powerful detectives. If Benson declared knowledge of the toffee tin and its contents, then she would have to explain her meeting with Laura Green, which had gone unrecorded, despite being materially important to a murder enquiry. This was a serious breach of protocol. Benson decided she would have to find a way to convince Laura Green to come to the station as soon as possible and let Vignoles see the tin. For now, she must pretend she knew nothing about it.

Benson tried to think how to answer as the seconds ticked by. If this book really was evidence of an amateur murder investigation and Grimes had reached the conclusion it was Green who had abducted the young girl, then Green had motive to kill Grimes. 'It could suggest a motive. However, the book in itself offers no insight into Grimes' conclusion as to who was involved in Miss Tustain's disappearance.'

'Grimes had suspicions?'

'I cannot say if he did or not based only on the evidence in the book.' It was a guarded reply, but factually correct.

'But if Grimes reckoned his evidence pointed to Green?' Mellor weighed in.

'Then Green would have a reason to stop Grimes.' Benson felt her cheeks burning.

Vignoles nodded. 'Has anyone else seen this?'

'No. Of course not.' The slight catch in her voice warned Vignoles this might not be the case.

'Very well. Dismissed.'

Benson saluted and briskly left the office. Vignoles decided to let Mellor have a moment to quell his obvious annoyance at a WPC getting centre stage, by watching as the magnificent A3 class engine whistled, then in a cloud of pale steam smoothly eased into motion as it resumed the journey up to London.

'What do you make of that?'

'Several valid points. But key questions remain unanswered.'

'Explain.'

'Why's this Cartwright feller included in the picture gallery? I'd say he was a suspect in Grimes' eyes.'

'Hmm. Putting Cartwright aside for the moment, what else was lacking in WPC Benson's considered summary?' Mellor did not miss the gentle dig.

'The blasted camera. Why did Green take it and keep it?'

'The last roll of film held something that Green believed might prove his guilt?'

'But it was so amateurish it was almost a joke. Why not chuck the camera away or better still, just rip the back off the camera where it lay beside the body as if it sprung open when he fell? Green has actually incriminated himself by keeping the camera, film or no film.'

'I agree. This detail worries me. There is no logic to Green retaining the camera. He's reticent and stubborn and sticking to a silent defence, but he's no fool. It feels like a plant.' Vignoles again faced Mellor. 'Right, we need to review everything we know about Green, Grimes and especially Cartwright. Dig further back into their lives and focus especially on Cartwright. We're talking about three young men and an attractive woman all in Woodford. Old rivalries? Was one of these three responsible for something terrible happening to the Tustain girl? Were all three involved in whatever happened to her and now one of them - Grimes - was threatening to break ranks and needed to be silenced? We really need to go through the case files on Miss Tustain again and with a fine toothcomb. Newspaper reports only skim the surface.'

'We're reopening the case?'

'It's not ours to reopen...and I doubt we'll be allowed to get the Tustain case files back. Dammit!'

'No, sir, they dragged their feet digging them out and getting them sent over. They only arrived late yesterday afternoon and are still unopened and lying on my desk.'

Vignoles grinned. 'You don't say? Fate is dealing us a good hand. I want to pull together a strong argument to take to DCI Thornbury. He's no lover of our department, so we get just one crack at this. We work fast. All hands to the pumps. Find out all we can, organise our thinking and see where it leads. We work over the weekend as I don't think we can wait much longer than Monday to make our move – and he'll soon get wind we have the Tustain files.'

'So quick?'

'We are holding material evidence,' Vignoles looked at the book on the desk. 'Badger will bawl us out and let's not even think what the Northants constabulary are going to say. It won't be pretty. I can fudge something about this slipping behind a filing cabinet until Monday, but no longer.' Before Mellor had time to reply Vignoles tossed the scrapbook at him. 'You'd better get cracking. And if you know what's good for you, you'll use the WPCs wisely. They're brighter than you give them credit.'

Chapter Thirty-Two

DS Mellor was shown into the office of the Assistant Director of the Brush Electrical Engineering Falcon Works in Loughborough. Malcolm Bryant's office was elegant, and the carpet, varnished wood panelling and book-laden shelves all helped deaden the noise of the massive engineering works busy assembling steam and new-fangled diesel locomotives in the great construction sheds.

'You have an office about the size of our department!'

They both laughed. They had lit cigarettes and exchanged a few pleasantries as Mellor eased the conversation around to the reason he was there. 'Back in the late '20s you were in charge of personnel?'

'That is correct. I was fortunate to step up the ladder in 1935, but until then I had over four hundred employees to keep a watchful eye over.'

'One of those employees was a man called Ellis Cartwright. I appreciate this was a long time ago and it might be hard to remember him.'

Bryant took a moment in silence to consider the name. 'We had a man by that name, and I do remember him. Some people stick in the mind. Mostly for good reasons, occasionally for less, um, positive reasons.'

'Cartwright was in the latter category?'

Another pause whilst Bryant considered his reply. 'There was a complaint.'

'What was the nature of the complaint?' Mellor's ears pricked up. He'd come there that morning in an attempt to build a more complete picture of Cartwright, but expected to come away virtually empty-handed.

Bryant looked uncomfortable. 'As you said, this was an awfully long time ago, sergeant. So much water under the bridge and everyone has long since moved on...'

'Mr Bryant, this could be important. I need to learn all I can about Mr Cartwright. Anything you can tell me may prove valuable.'

'Is he in trouble?'

'He's not under arrest. It is however important we learn all we can about his character to help our enquiries.' It was the usual vague answer.

'Very well. From memory, Cartwright was one of those intense young men you sometimes encounter in this business. Especially in the fast-emerging specialisms around electronics and the such like. These chaps can be so very blinkered in their focus on their work. This makes them superb technicians, but I sometimes wonder at what cost on a personal level.'

'Can you explain?' Mellor was not sure where this was leading.

'I'm no analyst of human psychology you understand? We design and build engines and aircraft and such, but if you're going to develop and maintain a good workforce it pays to learn how to read people. Observe how they interact. How men bond as a team and to keep an eye out for those who might prove to be troublemakers.'

'Agitators?'

'Yes, those of course... Nobody wants union unrest in their factory, but I'm talking here about the slightly odd ones. The loners.'

'Cartwright was a loner?'

'I would say he was.' Bryant exhaled an extravagant plume of smoke. 'He was studious and hardworking and had no interest in in shop floor politics or anything in that line. He was an excellent engineer, as I recall.' Bryant stubbed his cigarette as he considered his next words. 'Don't get me wrong, a man can live his private life as he pleases, and we should be careful not to judge others by our own way of life. He rarely socialised and seemed to lack friends. His work colleagues said the same and he often made excuses not to join them for a drink after work.' Mellor was making notes but his expression made it clear he was yet to hear anything that was going to turn the murder case. 'He rarely talked about football or cricket or even showed any particular interest in railway locomotives for that matter.' Bryant frowned. 'I realise none of this constitutes a crime.'

'No, but it marked him out as different enough for you to remember?'

'It did.' Bryant fiddled with the lid on the box of cigarettes on his desk, perhaps feeling the need to smoke another. 'Then he was accused of following one of our office girls after work and making inappropriate advances.'

Mellor sat up straight. 'Tell me all you know about this.'

'She always walked home along the canal path. It lies close to the works entrance and makes a quick shortcut back to her part of town, although after the unfortunate incident we advised her this was perhaps an unwise route.'

'What was Cartwright accused of?'

'Nothing very much in the end, if I remember correctly. It was her word against his. However, Miss Lambton was a sensible girl with no hint of flightiness about her and I was more inclined to believe her side of the story. Not that anything really *happened*, but she was frightened and I don't see why one of our girls should accept that behaviour from a fellow employee.'

Mellor nodded. 'Is there anything more specific you can tell me?'

'It was dusk, and she believed she was alone on the canal path, which in itself is not surprising as it is infrequently used, but she then became aware of a figure who seemed to just appear from nowhere close behind her.'

'As if he had been waiting?'

'Perhaps. He claimed he'd stopped in a doorway to light up. We walked the path with Miss Lambton and she was adamant he appeared from out of a bricked-up doorway with a deep recess. There was no access path or road within fifteen yards or more, so it would appear he was lying in wait, but there again, his explanation was plausible. She became alarmed by his sudden appearance and walked more quickly, but he caught up.'

'She recognised him?'

'Not by name, but his face was familiar. He acted as though they were colleagues and was very familiar. A bit fresh. Miss Lambton said she thought he knew where she was headed. He told her how dangerous it was to be out walking alone and how he would chaperone her home.'

'Was he just being overly protective?'

'That was the root of the problem. Miss Lambton told us he linked arms with her in spite of asking him not to. He kept her pulled close to his side and his manner became more overbearing whilst claiming only to be protecting her.'

Mellor agreed he could see how Cartwright might argue she misread his intentions. 'Did he try anything on?'

Bryant made a wave with his hands to suggest it was a finely balanced matter. 'The girl said he started telling her how he'd seen her every day going to and from the works and how pretty he thought she was and couldn't take his eyes off her. She became alarmed at this point but was too scared to tell him to stop talking in that way.'

'How did it end?'

'She was close to the footpath that would take her away from the canal towards her home and with some effort got him to release her arm. She claimed he was reluctant to let her go and then lunged forward to grab a kiss and put his arms around her, but she dodged free and ran and to her immense relief he did not chase after.'

Mellor made more notes. 'Something or nothing?' He spoke the words softly. Was this the breakthrough he was hoping for? 'Did he have sinister intentions or just a foolish lad who was inexperienced with women?'

'Quite...' Bryant looked unhappy. 'I find these matters so tricky.'

'What did you do?'

'We gave Cartwright a stern reprimand and let him stay on. He was a very skilful young man.'

'I thought you said he was dismissed?'

Bryant said nothing, drumming his fingers on his desk. 'Yes. He was. But that was for the second offence.'

'He did it again?' Mellor stared at Bryant.

'The constabulary came to us about eight weeks later asking if we employed Cartwright and they interviewed him. The girl in question was not an employee, but a local shop girl. He met her near the railway station and somehow convinced her to take a walk with him along the towpath.'

'She did so willingly?'

'He'd spoken to her several times over a week or so and I suppose won her confidence and she agreed.'

'Not knowing that he had a previous reprimand for inappropriate behaviour on the same towpath?'

'But how could we know he would do this again? We can't chaperone every young lady and neither can we completely discredit his character in public and put him out of work.'

'What was he accused of?'

'He lured her - as the investigating constable said - to his place and invited her in and then things got unpleasant. She at least escaped with just her blouse and hair in disarray but in a frantic state and made her escape before matters went too far, finding refuge with two anglers who accompanied her to the town to make a formal complaint.'

'He tried to rape her?'

'That was the accusation. Once again, it was a case of who to believe and how to interpret the facts as given by each party...' Bryant tailed off. 'An unhappy mess. We had no choice but to summarily dismiss him. I was not prepared to give him any further benefit of the doubt.'

'Where was Cartwright living at that time? You said this young lady escaped onto the towpath?'

'Yes, that's correct. He was living in a rotten old houseboat for Heaven's sake. A former coal barge back in the days when the Grand Union still had such traders on the canal. It was a sorry old thing.' Bryant made it clear he disapproved of the idea.

'Do you know where it was moored?'

'I think I can remember. Not precisely, but I could give you an indication. Not that there would anything there now.'

'Can you show me on a map?' Mellor stood up, feeling adrenaline starting to pump. 'Do you have a map of Loughborough?'

'I have one in my draw somewhere…'

Chapter Thirty-Three

'Mr Green, we would like to ask you some more questions.'

'Why bother? I thought you lot had made your minds up.'

'Contrary to what you might think, I like to keep an open mind on any case I have been involved with.' Vignoles was conscious he had to be respectful of DCI Thornbury seated beside him. He had only been allowed this interview after lengthy persuasive talks on the telephone and agreement that Thornbury would sit in.

For his part, Thornbury was doing his best to be professional but quietly fuming inside. Vignoles could appreciate his predicament. Knocking a great hole in the case against Green would leave the Northants Constabulary with the embarrassment of seeing the case dropped and having to explain how they had got it so wrong. This was bad enough, but when it was a case handed across as 'done and dusted' by Vignoles and the Transport Police, it would be doubly humiliating. Tensions were now running high between the two forces and so it was an awkward situation for all gathered in the claustrophobic interview room. 'I want to look again at that meeting between yourself and Mr Grimes in Woodford shed because it seems to me there is something you're not telling us.'

Green shrugged his shoulders. 'I didn't kill him.'

'As things stand based on the evidence and information we have, a case is going to court that says you did.'

Thornbury butted in. 'What Vignoles is saying and being too bloody polite about it, is it's not too late to alter the charge. Come on, Green, you and this Grimes feller had a falling out. You argued. He was a right pain in the backside and he needled you. I can understand that. Both of us on this side of the table can. A jury can. Maybe he said some nasty things that got right under your skin? The blood started pumping and you're angry and next thing you know you've got a lump of steel in your hand and threatening him.' Thornbury lifted his right arm as if miming the action but in so doing made an intimidating gesture towards Green. 'You didn't even hold it like a weapon. Remember? We know where your prints were on the shaft.'

Thornbury had accepted Vignoles' argument about how Green had most probably held the monkey wrench and he wanted to try this revelation out on the prisoner. Greens' eyes widened for a moment as he considered what he was hearing. 'But that bugger Grimes wouldn't shut up, would he? You take a swing, just to put the frighteners on him but the daft bugger turns away and...well. There you go. The wrench hits his bonce and the next thing you know he's on the floor. You're looking at manslaughter. You could be out in eight, maybe less.'

'I never hit him with it. I just knocked it to the floor.'

'You told us that in the first interview,' Vignoles took over. 'We've had our forensic team on to this and we think we know how you clasped the handle of the wrench. Do you remember?'

A moment of silence. 'It was like you just said. I picked it off the floor and replaced it on the bench, handling it where it was best balanced in the hand.'

'You knocked it off the bench because you were arguing with Grimes. It makes sense. The more you explain your actions, the better your chances.' Vignoles was not going to let this stubborn, obstinate man duck the facts any longer. 'We know you were arguing. You were overheard. Tell us what the argument was about.'

'You'd do well to answer the DCI's question. We've given you the perfect way out of dodging a rope around your neck, so take it.'

'It was stupid.' Green replied. 'Sitting here now, I'm not sure what I thought I was doing. Raking old stuff up...'

Vignoles opened the fresh pack of cigarettes he'd brought along. They were Green's preferred brand. He offered one whilst willing Thornbury to stay quiet. Green accepted a smoke and the light.

'I accused my old friend of something. Something very bad. But I have no proof he did anything. Nothing. Perhaps I just imagined it all and ended up making him mad for no reason? I dunno now. What good did it do? What have I achieved except venting years of resentment and frustration against a man who was once my best mate?' He smoked. The two DCI's joined him, both knowing now was not the time to interrupt. 'I did not kill him, but I can see how telling you this will only convince you that I did, and that's why I tried to stay silent until now,' Green looked Vignoles in the eye. 'Perhaps I should have killed him? But that would make me as bad as him. My last words to Richie were to tell him to come to you and confess his crime.'

Silence. The sound of tobacco burning as the air was sucked in.

'You see, he and I fought all those years back. Back in '28. It was over a girl. The prettiest girl you could ever imagine. Richie was always the confident one, the one with the swagger and the words that got the girls laughing and smiling and I was always the one hanging around next to him. Hoping for one of them to notice me. Fat chance of that! And I was the one who always found himself dragged into things I never wanted to do. Stupid stuff. Unimportant stuff that neither of you would care about now. Filching a bottle of beer or a packet of fags from the corner shop.' He exhaled deeply. 'And then one hot day when we'd got a bit tipsy drinking stolen beer, along came Rosie.'

'Rosie who?' Vignoles wanted Green to say her name.

'Rosie Tustain. Everyone fancied her. All the lads in the village, but of course Richie wanted her the most...' Green wrinkled his nose as if smelling something unpleasant. 'Trouble is, the drink had gone to his head and he didn't know how to handle it. He made a complete ass of himself. Went for her. Grabbed her and tried to kiss her and...handle her. Know what I mean? She was so angry and fought back and next thing her dress was ripped apart and there she was almost naked.'

'How do you know all this?' Thornbury queried.

'I was there.'

'Watching as he tried to rape her?' Thornbury was unsympathetic.

'I never thought it was going to go that far. It looks bad on me, I know. I feel ashamed even now. I didn't do enough to protect her.'

'Too busy enjoying watching,' Thornbury sneered. 'Or did you join in? Is that why you're so reluctant to speak out?'

'No! No. At first, I was just stunned. Shocked. But then I hit Richie. Almost laid him out. She got away. That's the truth.'

Vignoles stared at his pipe bowl for a moment. 'A foolish drunken episode many moons ago. You did the right thing in the end, but what has this to do with Grimes lying dead beneath the experimental turbine locomotive in 1956?'

'We argued about the girl that evening.'

Vignoles took a deep breath before speaking. 'David. We know that Rosie Tustain disappeared in the summer of 1928. She has never been seen since and is presumed dead. Are you implying there is a link between Grimes' assault on Tustain and her disappearance?'

'Maybe.' A long silence. 'I thought he did it. Took her away and...'

'And finished what he tried that day?' Thornbury added.

'It's possible.'

'That is what you accused him of that night in Woodford shed? You accused him of abducting and murdering Rosie Tustain?' Vignoles was feeling a cold shiver down his spine. He had argued for this interview in the hope he would help secure Green's release and restore harmony to his department. It was now taking an even darker turn.

'Yes.' Green stared at the table. 'He denied it.'

'Just as you are denying killing Grimes.'

'Yes.' Green's voice was quiet. Defeated.

'What evidence do you have to support your theory that Grimes is behind the Tustain disappearance?'

'I saw them together. Kissing and everything. How could she "go all the way" with Richie after what he'd done? It was crazy, it was just plain wrong. I watched them doing it in the open...'

'Christ, you're a right little pervert! First you watch him trying to rape her, then you spy on them at their most intimate time. I've heard it all now. The only thing I don't understand is why Grimes didn't go for you. Or perhaps he was going to, but you got in first? Is that it?' Thornbury was feeling more confident. Whatever doubts DCI Vignoles might have harboured, this interview was reaping rewards and he was sure they were going to secure a strong conviction.

Vignoles had to try and rescue something from this. 'Mr Green, can you explain why your friend Grimes had a scrapbook in his lodgings that tracked the story of Rosie Tustain's disappearance and the subsequent police investigation in newspaper cuttings and why he was taking photographs of a route perhaps taken by Miss Tustain on her fateful last journey?'

'I know nothing about this.'

'He seems to have spent years compiling it.'

'He never said a word to me.'

'Not when he called at your home the day before he died?'

'No...'

'You sound unsure.'

'He said something about knowing who did it. I ignored him. I didn't want to hear his excuses. I closed my ears...'

'Can you explain why this same book has a photograph of Ellis Cartwright inside alongside a photo of yourself with Grimes and one of Miss Tustain?'

'Cartwright? Do you mean the kid with glasses no-one liked?'

'He was the technician who found Grimes' body in the inspection pit.'

Green looked confused. 'I don't understand? *Speccy* Cartwright? Jesus. I've not seen him since schooldays.'

Thornbury butted in. 'You thought Grimes did it and so you killed him. Trouble is, Mr Green, why would Grimes spend hours investigating a crime he committed? That makes no sense.' He shook his head sadly. 'It looks like you killed the wrong man, old boy...'

Chapter Thirty-Four

'Do you like her? We always call engines 'she'.'

Laura Green read his name badge and took a moment to reply. Ellis Cartwright was one of a number of the technical team on duty at the one-day exhibition of *The Difference Engine* that Sunday in Leicester Central station. He was dressed in dark trousers and shoes, a white shirt and tie and an especially pristine lab coat with the Tomkins-Dunkler logo sewn on a breast pocket that displayed an impressive line of pens and pencils. However, this was a day for the company to show off their pride and joy and allow small children to step inside either of the cabs or peek into the engine room, rather than serious work.

Their engine presented a dazzling spectacle thanks to the cloudless sky above Leicester and in stark contrast to a filthy B1 class engine standing at the head of an all stations 'stopper'. The crew of the 'steamer' leaned on the side of their grime encrusted cab and watched the small crowd milling around the TD-GTX1. The fireman seemed to be delighting in observing how the pall of dark grey smoke curling from their locomotive chimney ducked under the station canopy and thence around the almost mirror finish of the futuristic engine. Laura Green blinked as the pungent smoke tickled her eyes and noted the annoyed looks being cast at the hissing B1 by the white-coated figures manning the small display stand the Tomkins-Dunkler team had set up.

'I think so,' Green replied. 'It intrigues me.' Here was the man she had come to the station on the off-chance of meeting and he was speaking to her. She had no great expectation that any of the technical staff would be present at this one-day event but was restless and unable to concentrate on anything other than trying to push forward with her single-minded plan to prove her father's innocence. Perhaps just standing beside the locomotive that was somehow implicated in this awful mess, might offer her some solace, and besides, it was Sunday and there was little else meaningful she could think to do. However, now she was standing next to Ellis Cartwright with a chattering crowd milling around, she was uncertain what to do next. 'It is like something from a space film.'

'I am glad you think so.' He gave her an ingratiating smile. 'We at Tomkins-Dunkler are eager to capture the futuristic mood of the times. Such a contrast to that smelly thing over there…' He nodded his head towards the steam engine which was continuing with its noxious display of sickly-coloured smoke, now turning sooty black. The fireman was probably throwing oily rags on his fire in a piece of mischief that would see him get a stern rebuke from the station master. Laura Green could hear the signal wires twang and the starting signal drop, so the naughty fireman might just get away with it.

'I like a steam engine…'

Cartwright looked disappointed. 'They have no future. They'll be sent to the knacker's yard in the next few years, just you wait and see. Now, look how clean and bright *our* machine is…'

Green was thinking the same about Cartwright. He had to be about the same age as her father and yet there was something almost boyish about his face. He was impeccably cleanshaven and his skin scrubbed so vigorously it looked blotchily pink, an effect exaggerated by the blinding white of his lab coat. The black-framed glasses he wore had strong lenses that made his eyes with their pale grey irises appear too big, whilst his lips were surprisingly full and girlishly pink. Green liked a well-presented man, but on Cartwright, it looked obsessive and unappealing. His skin was baby-like if such a description could be used to describe a mature man. As the B1 locomotive started its train into motion with twin jets of steam erupting from the drain cocks and a tower of smoke colouring the sky, her nostrils were filled with the familiar scent of combusted coal and hot machine oil vaporising in scalding steam; scents she spent every working hour surrounded by and which she had grown to love, but in spite of these strong smells she thought she caught a hint of sickly floral talcum powder emanating from Cartwright. She shuddered with revulsion.

'Is your fiancé here with you today?'

'No.' His big eyes must have spotted the little diamond on her left hand and she felt oddly annoyed about this.

'You came specially to see *The Difference Engine?*'

'I did.' Green forced herself to look back at Cartwright without betraying any of her suspicions about his character.

'Then I'm impressed.' He broke the gaze and handed her a flyer extolling the virtues of the engine. 'I like a pretty woman who finds engineering enticing.'

It was a curious choice of word and the way his bug-eyes gazed at her, made Green feel grubby. She glanced at the flyer but didn't read the over-excited words composed by Miss Lessiter and instead, tried to gather her thoughts. She had to steer this around to the real reason for being there. The chance was too good to allow to go to waste. She felt a nagging regret that Simon was in Woodford today trying to follow another line of enquiry. Never mind. She was in a public space where nothing untoward could happen and it was time to grasp the nettle and accept whatever sting she got in return. Green looked at Cartwright. 'I was rather intrigued. This *is* the engine they found a dead man underneath?'

Cartwright blinked. 'We don't broadcast that. Unfortunate though the incident was, it has nothing to do with Tomkins-Dunkler.' His voice had dropped lower, further masked by the noisy departure of the steam train.

'You sound very sure of that?'

He gave her a hard stare. 'The police have the man responsible and he was not part of our set up.' He gave her a half-smile that could almost have been a smirk. Green found his face even more repellent. 'But *you* would know more about that than I.' It was barely a whisper.

Green felt an unpleasant icy tingling ripple down her spine. The noise and hum of voices all around seemed to grow louder as she became lightheaded. 'What do you mean by that?' It was with great effort she kept her voice steady.

'Miss Green? Laura Green.' He smiled broadly. If anyone was observing the exchange it would look as though he was enthusiastically extolling the performance characteristics of the engine. 'Am I right?'

'How do you know my name?'

'I like to be prepared for all eventualities. In my line, it pays to allow nothing to escape notice.' He kept his voice light and loud. '...and the driving cabs are even heated with carpet underfoot and swivel chairs with armrests for the crew!' He instantly switched tack as an elderly gent with a handlebar moustache drew close, then grabbed a handful of flyers. 'I can show you inside if you wish...' His voice dropped as Mr Handlebar backed away. 'I have a break in ten minutes. Far end of the station.'

'Thank you, Mr Cartwright, that was most interesting.' Adopting a breezy tone Green waved her flyer, smiled sweetly and turned away. Her mind was racing. He knew who she was! How? And why? What did this mean? She walked along the length of the platform, stopping to buy a mug of sweet tea along the way after promising the bring the mug back later. She now stood staring blankly along the twin tracks of the elevated railway line and at the shimmering image of a distant train held at a signal. It looked like a desert mirage trapped in glassy waves of heat.

She suppressed her rising panic and confusion inside and tried to gather together all she knew about Cartwright. She'd come here to meet him - and do what? Now it came down to it, she had no idea what her plan had been or even if she had a plan. It was a spur of the moment idea that was proving ill-conceived and she had not even taken the time to tell Simon where she was.

Well, here she was, and she'd better not make a hash of it. She blinked away welling tears and desperately wished Simon was beside her or at least in his office just across the tracks. Why had she not asked him to come along? The station was busy near the gleaming locomotive but elsewhere it was Sunday-silent and slumbering in the early afternoon heat.

'I was not sure you would wait.'

'I needed some tea.' The liquid was almost untouched and cooling.

'Why are you here Miss Green?'

'Why are you standing at the opposite end of the station to your precious engine?' she briskly retorted.

'Because the death of that man beneath our engine has nothing to do with Tompkins-Dunkler and I felt that standing amidst a crowd was not the place to discuss such an unsavoury matter.'

'Who said I wanted to discuss it?'

'You brought the matter up, not I.'

'The company may not be responsible, but perhaps one of its employees was?'

'I cannot imagine whom.'

'Someone who was present at the time Mr Grimes met his death.'

Rather than rage at the implied accusation, Cartwright laughed. 'Miss Green. Or should I say, the future Mrs Laura Howerth?' He watched as Green tried to make her dry mouth swallow. 'You would do better consoling your father in his cell than wasting time here making foolish accusations. The police have made their investigations and reached their decision. The weeks until the trial will pass all too quickly.'

Green replied as calmly as she was able. 'You are in the scrapbook. Your photograph. I've seen it for myself.'

'What scrapbook?' He snapped back.

'You've not seen it?' She smiled. 'I also do my research.'

'How do I know if I've seen it or not if I don't know what you're talking about?'

'Mr Grimes' scrapbook about the Tustain girl. You're included.'

His Adam's apple bobbed once. 'I have no idea what that is, but you have made a false assumption. Yes, I'm from Woodford, just like Grimes and your poor dad. It is a small place, as you know.' He shrugged. 'Anyone of about the same age stands a chance of getting a mention I'd have thought.'

'Perhaps, but just this same three back in Woodford engine shed after so many years. Curious, do you not think?'

'Drink your tea, Miss Green, you look in need of some liquid refreshment. It is a hot day and you should be careful...'

'What do you mean?' She shot him a glance but drank deeply of her tea. The sugar was comforting.

'A woman in your condition.' His look was arch as his buggy eyes raked her body.

'Excuse me?'

'Nothing escapes me, I can assure you.' He fished out a pack of Players and popped one between his fleshy lips. 'Smoke?'

Green hesitated but relented. Even if she barely touched it, the cigarette would give her something to focus on as she tried to remain calm. This man knew too much. She had to tread very carefully. He held out his lighter so she could light up.

'You think I killed Grimes.' He sounded oddly matter-of-fact.

She concentrated on getting her cigarette lit, seeing her hand tremble and hoping he didn't notice. She made no reply.

'I'm not offended. I should be, of course. You see, your father did the world a service. Take comfort from that. Terminating that unpleasant man's miserable life was a social service, believe me. I'm sorry that the court of law won't see it that way, but he actually did us all a favour. Oh, you look shocked?'

Green didn't know what to say and hid behind a cloak of cigarette smoke.

'I'll come clean. I'd have gladly seen the end of Grimes but I'm too much of a softie to go around clubbing him or doing anything messy. Too squeamish about blood.' His pathetic baby face screwed up for a moment in disgust. 'I take my hat off to your father.'

Green stared into the dregs of her tea, unable to think straight. Her world was starting to unravel and she no longer knew how to prevent it from doing so. *Why was this man saying these things? Was he applauding her dad for killing Richie Grimes? Oh, God...* She could feel her legs turning to jelly.

'Miss Green, I understand your wish to help your father at this difficult time and I can help you. I have access to information that could significantly improve his situation.'

'You do? What information?' Like a drowning woman, she gleefully grabbed for this unexpected lifeline.

He paused and smoked in a measured manner that oozed self-confidence and calm. 'Do not misunderstand me, he is in trouble. Clouting a man from behind does not look good, especially if the man then goes and dies, but juries can be swayed by circumstance. When the victim is a black-hearted devil of a man with no conscience or moral compass, capable of the most heinous of crimes towards a beautiful young and innocent girl, few in a jury will feel much sorrow or remorse for his passing. Some, like myself, might feel that justice, albeit rough, was meted out.'

'Please tell me! What do you know?'

He flipped his arm forward to reveal an expensive wristwatch and glanced at the dial. 'A train north is due in five minutes. It stops at Loughborough Central. There and back in less than two hours. You can be back and home in time for tea. How about that?' He smiled gently, his face still ugly, but Green was past caring. He could offer hope for her father and that was all that mattered.

'Loughborough? Why do we need to go there?'

'Because of the young lady. That poor pretty young thing.... She was last seen there. If this book you talked about was worth anything, then it must have mentioned that?'

'Yes, yes it did! I'm sorry, I was not thinking straight.

'Look, our train approaches.'

Green felt another twitch of unease as she heard him speak as if it were a foregone conclusion she would board the train with this man. She tried to clear her thoughts. *Don't do this! He could be dangerous!* But was she going to refuse, and forever wracked by guilt knowing she ignored the chance to save her father? How could she possibly turn down the chance to discover something that might help rescue her innocent father from death row?

Chapter Thirty-Five

Whilst Laura Green was at Leicester Central, PC Simon Howerth was back in Woodford Halse, stepping off the train onto the familiar platform of the station where he'd spent so many hours of his youth watching trains.

Something had changed. It no longer felt like the comforting place of his birth and upbringing. The tangle of roads, the ironstone cottages or red brick terraces bisected by the massive presence of the railway that dominated everything seemed altered today. He returned regularly and his face was familiar to all and in such a small close-knit community there was little they didn't know about him, his job and his relations to the Green family. Whereas just a few days ago this was pleasingly reassuring, affirming his sense of place in the world, it now felt as though everything had shifted and as he walked down the approach road that dropped from the station on to Church Street he was feeling as though he was entering an alternate version of this funny little place he still called home.

It looked the same on the sun-drenched surface, but he felt like a stranger walking into an unfamiliar wild west town just like he'd seen in Saturday matinee cowboy films. Faces stared, people stopped what they were doing, conversations stilled as the heat rippled the air. No cars disturbed the silence today and even the giant freight yards and engine shed were somewhat quietened by the Sunday pace of life. Some smiled, but their eyes betrayed unease, one of two even gave a greeting but were hesitant, but most just watched. Watched him walk like a new sheriff into town, unsure if they wished him to succeed or to fail, but making no effort to offer support.

He could see the tower of St Mary's and felt a wave of sadness wash over him, a shiver of clammy cold despite the blazing sun. The banns had been read for the first time and his intended marriage to Laura was in the church diary whilst weeks of preparation had already taken place in the Green household. Now, with David Green's arrest, what had once been a subject of excited anticipation was a source of urgent debate within Woodford as to whether this could, or should, take place. How could a man accused of murder give his daughter away? It was impossible! The *shame* of it! The scandal! The ripples of rumour and counter-rumour spread to the farthest edges of the modest sprawl of Woodford-cum-Menbris. Some were so horrified at the turn of events they were stunned into silence, others more disbelieving and steadfastly defended Green's innocence, but there were plenty who appeared to revel in the thrilling excitement and shocking scandal of a real-life murderer in their midst.

'He seemed so normal...'

'The quiet ones are always the worst...'

'I always thought he was too good to be true...'

'To think I saw him only last week and we talked for a few minutes and never guessed he was a cold-blooded killer!'

'I sold him a pack of fags. He handed over his money and there was me never once suspecting those same hands took a man's life!'

'I even bought the murdering so-and-so a glass of beer...'

But perhaps even more insidious and corrosive were the growing numbers of theories, each more lurid than the one they replaced as to why David Green would kill his old school friend. Dark mutterings of terrible deeds were spreading and it took little imagination for the name of Rosie Tustain to be recalled and her unexplained disappearance soon woven into the fabric of these tales and rapidly becoming the most powerful, and credible reason for Grimes' death. Howerth was glad he'd told Laura to stay away. He'd suspect the worst and Mrs Green had gone to stay with her eldest son in Banbury to evade the whispers, staring faces and stony silences.

The two families were working to find the substantial bail

money, no easy task for poorly paid working families with few savings to call upon, but even if they bought temporary freedom for Mr Green, his would be an unhappy homecoming unless they could prove his innocence. Laura believed they should stall his release anyway, harbouring fears for her father's safety. The killer was still out there and if the person responsible suspected David Green knew his identity, then his life was in jeopardy.

This was why Simon Howerth set his jaw in a determined fixed expression, steeled himself for an uncomfortable afternoon and set about encouraging some of the older inhabitants who might have memories of Ellis Cartwright back in the late 1920s to talk. Whatever the rumour mill might be weaving, there were three men and a girl identified in that scrapbook Grimes had taken to his rented room in Rugby. One man was murdered, the girl presumably met a similar end and one banged up in a cell. The other was walking free. His part in this horrid mess needed explaining. He'd been present at the moment Grimes died and yet claimed innocence. Howerth agreed with Laura and Eddie. The man was their chief suspect, before they could even consider confronting him, Howerth knew they needed more information. That's what his sergeant would demand and what DCI Vignoles spent so many hours seeking out before tackling a suspect. When Howerth came to face Cartwright, he needed far more than suspicion and a photograph in a scrapbook. It was time to do some digging. Someone in Woodford might talk, perhaps after a pint or two to help loosen their tongue.

A round of the pubs was in order. It sounded like a pleasant afternoon's work, but Howerth already knew it would be a tense and difficult task to break down the walls of suspicion and distrust within the community. He would need to keep his wits about him and not let the drink cloud his judgment.

Howerth was also doing his best not to worry about what Laura was doing back in Leicester. She'd agreed her presence in Woodford could be counter-productive and may even cause a sensation as the local gossips flocked to look and stare and had decided to go to the open day at Leicester to see if she could get close to the team working on *The Difference Engine*.

'Don't worry, Simon, there will be hordes of people there. I'll just be in a crowd of trainspotters, train boffins and grammar school boys in all probability and that's about it. Perhaps Cartwright will show up, but I doubt it. I just want to see him, nothing more.'

'What good will that do?' Howerth had tried to persuade her to stay away.

'Probably none, but I need to do *something*. I need to see this man for real. I want to get a measure of who he is before we confront him.'

'We? No, Laura. When the time comes I'm the policeman and I'll handle that.'

'A policeman not on the case and with no authority to question Cartwright!' She'd fired back, eyes flashing.

'Touché. But seriously, do not confront him!'

'Go and gather all you can and we can all talk about how to handle Cartwright after…'

Howerth knew when to step back and let his wife-to-be get her way but was quite clear in his mind that if Laura, Eddie and he did find something that gave them a lead on Cartwright he'd rope his fellow coppers in. The man was starting to look like a double killer and he wanted to keep Laura as far away from him as he could.

Chapter Thirty-Six

They sat facing each other in the empty coach. As it was a Sunday service it was poorly loaded, with fewer than a dozen persons on the train. They could speak freely, but Laura Green would have felt more at ease if there had been someone else in the open saloon. The train gently puffed northwards and the sun slanted into the carriage as the pretty Leicestershire countryside rolled past the opened window, the embankments rich with wildflowers as the telegraph wires looped through the blue sky. It was a truly glorious day and it was hard to imagine anything terrible could happen on such a lovely day.

'Miss Green. Or should we drop the formalities?'

'I prefer we don't.'

'I am too presumptuous.' He winked. 'As you wish, Miss Green.' Cartwright made an apologetic gesture. 'This book. The one Grimes compiled. May I see it?'

'I do not have it.'

'Is it easy to retrieve?'

'It is not. I saw it only once.' She was starting to gather her wits again and realised she must not be too free with the information she gave out. It would be better Cartwright did not realise she was actively investigating him or that she had contact with WPC Benson.

'Never mind.' He threw his arms out as if it was of no consequence. 'And did it tell you anything useful?'

'I'm not sure. I'm no detective.'

'Yes, best leave that kind of work to the professionals.' Those buggy eyes were studying her. 'But it must have contained something that suggested Grimey was getting close to solving the mystery? Whatever it was, it got him killed.'

'It was hard to know what it all meant. It followed the course of an old investigation into the disappearance of a young girl. She was from Woodford. I suppose you must have known her?' She smiled knowingly.

He shook his head slowly and sighed. 'Poor Rosie.' He looked at the carriage floor for a moment as if trying to decide how to proceed. 'It is as bad as I feared. The book. The obsession. It all fits. He was a dark and twisted soul.'

'Who was?'

'Grimey. That's what we called him back then. Richard Grimes. Even as a lad I could see there was something not quite right about him. Oh, nothing serious at first, but little signals that made me want to keep away from him. It didn't surprise me when...when it happened.'

'When what happened?' Green could feel her stomach churn and her hands were in danger of shaking. She twisted them together.

'He assaulted her. You didn't know? Practically stripped her naked and then tried to...' He stopped. 'It would be indelicate of me to say more to a young lady when alone with her in a railway carriage.'

'Please, Mr Cartwright -.'

'Ellis.'

'I want to know. I need to know what happened.'

'The thing is, I believe your dear father also suspected Grimey was not quite right in the head. That's why my sympathies lie with him in his dire predicament. The two fell out in 1929. It was a bad argument.'

'I think I know that. Dad hardly spoke of him.'

'Understandable. He was right to harbour suspicions. It reflects well upon his character I must say, even if he didn't know, none of us *knew,* at the time.'

'Knew what?'

'They argued about the same time the poor girl vanished. I am guessing your dad thought Grimey had abducted the girl and did what he did to her. Even the most optimistic person would have to concede she lost her life as a result. Perhaps it is best she didn't live...'

Laura Green groaned. She knew this must be the case, but hearing it spoken aloud made it seem worse.

'The police did their best, but they found nothing. The trail went ice cold, so how could a young man about to commence training to be a signalman do better? Of course, he couldn't. Neither could I, nor anyone else for that matter.'

'Yes, I see...' Green felt her spirits plunge. Her father had suspected Grimes of a heinous crime for all these years and when he reappeared the long-repressed anger spilt over. If what she was hearing was true, then it was understandable. It was easy to see why he might in a moment of rage strike Grimes. She fought back tears.

'Until now, this terrible crime has remained unsolved. Your father should be admired for striking out as he did. A selfless act of righteous retribution. Few will have sympathy for Grimes.'

'You said you know something that proves Grimes did all this?' Her voice was flat. This was looking desperate now. She'd hoped he had proof that someone else committing the deed, but now it looked as though he could only offer a means to ameliorate what was a very serious crime. Offer her a means to justify and accept a violent and terrible act committed by her dear father.

He nodded sagely. 'That is why we are going to Loughborough. The last authenticated sighting of Miss Tustain was there.'

'I saw something about that in the newspaper cuttings in the book.'

'Is that so? It took me years to piece together what I think happened. But we are approaching. Let me explain more as we walk. Please do not be afraid or alarmed Miss Green.'

'Laura...'

He lowered the droplight in the carriage door, feeling his pulse increase as he stepped gallantly onto the platform and offered his hand as she stepped out. He'd won two little battles so far. He'd got her alone and they were on first-name terms. 'Just a short stroll along the pretty canal path in lovely sunshine and then back. It will be worth it.'

Chapter Thirty-Seven

Vignoles and Mellor were seated around the desk in Vignoles' office with Grimes' scrapbook of cuttings and photographs opened between them. A blackboard stood on an easel close to hand upon which PC Blencowe had previously been chalking out names, dates, alibis and possible reasons for Grimes' death. They had taken turns rubbing out and added notations as the morning progressed. Both detectives were now smoking and working their way through a bottle of beer each. As it was Sunday and neither of them was technically on duty the beer needed no justification. Vignoles had taken the Grimes scrapbook home to give it closer inspection the night before. 'We'll get it to Northampton on Monday. Nobody of any rank will be in work today so I can't see a day more will hurt.' It was a wise decision, as Vignoles found the contents of the book so compelling he'd telephoned Mellor to tell him to meet him in the office that morning. The crate of Tiger ale and the promise of fish and chips later was compensation for a spoiled day of rest. Both men were finding the quiet office, the leisurely pace of the station and the influence of the hops were aiding their thinking and they were making progress.

In spite of believing they were close to resolving the once and for all case and potentially allowing the welcome release of David Green, the day was about to be turned upon its head suddenly and dramatically. Their sense of quiet confidence at finally untying a knotty problem was soon to be shattered by alarming news. The first gentle ripples of trouble ahead were starting to wash over the sun-bathed station as the sound of the crowd gathering for the open day swelled, although almost no one was as yet aware anything was wrong.

It all looked so innocent and could have worked out so very differently if only Vignoles and Mellor had not decided to take a stroll across the station to take a quick look at *The Difference Engine* before the crowds gathered and Laura Green arrived. This was a chance to smoke and run their eyes over the white and chrome of the machine once again before settling down to the important work in hand. Ellis Cartwright had also been conspicuous by his absence at the time Vignoles and Mellor stood beside the engine, otherwise, he might have found himself called into their office for an uncomfortable session that would have seen him charged and safely locked away in a holding cell. Fate sometimes has a strange way of dealing its hand of cards.

The senior detectives were also unaware that PC Howerth, who was also off duty, had taken himself down to Woodford Halse on his own investigative operation. An ill-conceived plan to coax older citizens to open up about their memories of Ellis Cartwright. In spite of the increasing haze of alcohol, it was unfortunate that Howerth had chosen to go it alone, as he was starting to form a similarly bleak opinion of the electrical engineer as his commanding officers back in the Detective Department.

'We need another go at Cartwright. There's something about this guy not sittin' right wiv' me.'

Vignoles agreed. 'He heard the argument between Green and Grimes, but denies hearing what it was about...'

'Do we believe him?'

'It makes an easier lie keeping things vague. He claims to just have heard 'raised voices' but can tell us no more. Less for us to trap him with. Cartwright is clever.'

'What if 'e was part of the argument? The three of 'em - not just the two?' Mellor asked.

'Why did Green not mention this? If Green is innocent, then the three having a ding-dong plays out better for him. He claims he's the first to leave the scene thereby leaving Cartwright as the assailant.'

'Ok. So, what if Cartwright can make out what the argument

is about and doesn't much like what he hears?'

'And realises he needs to take care of Grimes?' Vignoles replied.

'It could work.'

'Cartwright claimed he couldn't see either man, but I looked through the windows in the engine compartment and whilst there's a narrow field of view, the glass was spotless.'

'He could have seen two old mates from way back when?'

'Maybe not mates, but he knew them both, of that, I'm now sure.' Vignoles was feeling annoyed with himself. He'd been too lax in his investigative work. 'I took too much of what Cartwright said at face value. He ran to alert the shed master about discovering a body but we were too quick to accept him as the innocent bystander. We didn't attempt to recreate the exact location of the argument and the view from the locomotive nor if it was possible to hear raised voices from inside.'

'Who's to say he was inside the engine?' Mellor exhaled smoke in an angry puff.

'Yes, and don't forget he sent his colleague on into town, ostensibly to secure a bunk for the night and some food.'

'Perfectly reasonable and plausible.'

'But it left him operating alone.'

Both men winced. It was too obvious. Too simple, and yet they'd walked right in and bought the lie.

'He pulled the wool right over our eyes...' Mellor drank some beer. 'I reckon he saw Green knock the monkey wrench to the floor and watched how he picked it up again. Cartwright realised that with gloves on he could reuse this same wrench to clobber Grimes, thereby implicating Green. It was clever.'

'It took a raw constable to see through that.' Vignoles blew a smoke ring into the air. 'He took the camera and planted it in Green's motorbike panniers. He had plenty of opportunities as he was in Woodford for a few days. A crude act, but it helped point the finger at Green.'

'I'm the ass who bought that as well.' Mellor growled. 'It didn't make sense but was 'appy to take it at face value.'

'I was just as fallible.' Vignoles was annoyed with himself, but for all their failings they were at least making headway. It was the nature of police work to go down blind alleys and make wrong connections, incorrect conclusions and false accusations. It was frustrating, but he could feel the tingle of adrenaline and his mind was now bright and clear. It was not too late to nail the real culprit and Green could walk free.

Mellor was feeling something similar to Vignoles, knowing they were close to making a decisive breakthrough.

'Grimes and Cartwright worked together for the last couple of weeks. Grimes blagged his way into the project on a lie. He was a failing freelancer in need of a story and yet for all that I don't think that was his motivation.' Vignoles waved the stem of his pipe towards the opened book. 'Adding to this book of his seems to be his main concern.'

'Getting close to Cartwright?'

'Closing in on his quarry. Keeping him in his sights until he had proof of his guilt.'

'Grimes thought he had something on Cartwright. Maybe he did? He must have kept the important stuff in his head, as the scrapbook offers us nothing.' Mellor gave this some thought. 'I wonder if he met up with Green to discuss this? I'm still not sure why they argued.'

'Perhaps they didn't?' Vignoles added. 'We only have Cartwright's word about that. It could have been a meeting to agree on a strategy to tackle Cartwright.'

'Then why does Green not tell us that?'

'Because he's scared. He's just a signalman minding his own business until Grimes shows up out of the blue. He might share their suspicions but had little command of the facts. He is starting to realise now, when it's too late, that Grimes was playing with fire'

Mellor agreed. 'So, Green left the shed after their strategic meeting. Then Grimes saw Cartwright approach, but whatever his private suspicions, he'd have no immediate cause to be alarmed. It would be normal to see the technician working near his engine. I can imagine Grimes turned away to leave as they didn't rub along well together. That made it easy for Cartwright to clout him on the back of the head then pull the body under the locomotive.'

'Why did he do that?' Vignoles queried.

'There were fitters still working in the shed and a chance someone would see the body if left in the open.'

'Plus Cartwright wanted the camera. He needed to buy himself a few minutes to squirrel the camera away to collect later and plant in Green's bike panniers. Only then did he go to raise the alarm.'

Mellor started chalking their thoughts onto the board. 'So, what was the flashpoint between these three men?'

'It has to be the young Tustain woman.'

'A love triangle?'

'Rivalry, jealousy... I think we can safely assume something bad happened to that girl and one of the three was responsible.' Vignoles turned the pages of the book. 'If this the route of her last walk, presumably accompanied by her killer, then what is the significance of this boat with the smoking chimney?'

'Cartwright worked at the Falcon Works before Tomkins-Dunkler.'

'In Loughborough and close to the canal.'

Mellor grinned. 'We need to find out where he lived back then...'

'I think we can guess.'

They both looked at the tiny image of the old houseboat.

'Right, we haul Cartwright in. Get over to the engine and find out where he is!'

Mellor was out the door without bothering to put his jacket on. Vignoles, now feeling the surge of energy that came when a case was drawing to a healthy conclusion, stood at the open bay window of his office. The lazy blue haze of exhaust from a departing local train was creating just the faintest smudge against the skyline of mills buildings and tall chimneys, the gentle beats of the engine pistons softly echoing in the hot noonday air. There was a gentle murmur and chatter of people milling around *The Difference Engine* and he watched as a gaggle of schoolboys lead by a tall, bearded teacher appear at the top of the stairs leading from the subterranean booking hall. Vignoles could see Miss Lessiter in something fitting and flattering talking in an animated manner to DS Mellor. It was perhaps uncharitable, but Vignoles was surprised that Mellor seemed oblivious to her charms and instead his body language was that of someone impatient for a response. Mellor span about on his heel, clearly scanning the almost empty platforms before barging unceremoniously through the school party on his way back.

'He's gone! Twenty minutes ago.'

'Did Miss Lessiter say where?'

'Lunch break. She thinks he and someone matching the description of Laura Green were talking near the trade stand.'

'What? Laura Green?' Vignoles felt a cold shiver down his spine. 'Is Lessiter sure about that?'

'She seems confident. Laura's a pretty girl and the gutter press found a picture of her and her dad and they've been plastered everywhere to add spice to the arrest story. Lessiter keeps clippings for the company, and as their locomotive is mentioned she is familiar with the coverage.'

'But why was Green talking with Cartwright?' mused Vignoles. 'Could Lessiter shed any light?'

'No. It was busy and they were some distance apart. She said Green left first.'

Vignoles stood and stared out the window. 'It could just be a coincidence. There is no reason to suppose Cartwright has followed her.'

'He was going for his lunch.' Mellor sounded as though he

didn't think Cartwright had any interest in buying a sandwich.

'Damn!' Vignoles was putting his jacket on. 'Benson has hinted she was worried Laura Green was trying to make her own private enquiries. She warned Laura off, but now I'm wondering. I don't want to think what Howerth might have told her about the case.'

'I'll strangle that lad...'

'But why was she here today otherwise? I can't see her wanting to see the engine bearing in mind its part in her dad's predicament.'

'Silly mare. That idiot Howeth's behind this!' Mellor looked horrified. 'If she reached the same conclusions as we just 'ave and let Cartwright know, who knows how he might react?'

'We need to find her and get her to safety. That comes first. Cartwright can wait.'

'Find one and we find the other.'

'That's my fear.' Vignoles was staring at the large wall map of the former Great Central Railway London Extension that hung on his wall since the offices opened in 1899. 'Where do we start? Did she go into town and he followed? Or to Woodford?'

'Everyone in the case comes from Woodford.' Mellor lit another cigarette.

'A local left ten minutes ago heading north. Stopping at Loughborough Central.'

'She's gone there?'

'If Benson showed this book to her it is full of Loughborough locations.'

'Then Loughborough it is.'

'What if he jumped the train as well?' Vignoles picked up the keys to the police Rover and tossed them to Mellor. 'You're the better driver. Get us there as fast as you can!'

Mellor sprinted out of the office as Vignoles hastily scribbled a note which he left on WPC Benson's desk. She was the duty officer today but had been called out to a minor incident along the line although she was expected back shortly. She needed to know where they were, but more importantly, he needed her to put out an all stations alert for Cartwright and ask the constabulary in Loughborough to put extra patrols along the canal. As many men as were on duty on a Sunday needed to be out and looking for Green and Cartwright. It was far from a perfect situation and Vignoles was torn between staying in the office and placing these calls and issuing instructions, or and acting decisively and driving straight there with Mellor.

Add indent) Something told him that speed was of the essence and no amount of considered policing and following procedure sitting at his desk was going to protect Laura Green. As he sprinted after Mellor he was praying the snap decision he was making was the right one...

Chapter Thirty-Eight

'I want to make a telephone call.' To her relief Laura Green had spotted the red kiosk outside the station.

'This won't take long,' Cartwright was eager to hurry her along.

'You have reassured me of that, but I would feel better if I let...' Green stopped. Whom should she say? She must not make him suspicious. 'I always like to let mum know where I am.'

Her nerves were starting to jangle, and she was silently berating herself for agreeing to accompany this odd man on what was surely a wild goose chase. Why on earth had she agreed to this? He'd made oblique references and hinted he could show her something that would improve her father's situation, but as she'd walked out of the booking hall doors, she knew she must alert someone to her situation. Not waiting to hear Cartwright put forward any more objections, she closed the kiosk door and opened her purse only then, to her dismay, realising she had just a ten-shilling note and meagre a handful of coins. She might get a minute to speak – if that.

But whom should she call? Simon was walking around Woodford. He could be in a pub with a telephone, but which one? Despite telling Cartwright she was calling her mother she was the last person Laura wished to call now. Her mum's nerves were shot to pieces and the last thing she needed was to hear her only daughter was with a strange man walking along a lonely canal towpath on the trail of a missing woman...

She held the handset and felt it become clammy. Her tummy moved in a strange and unfamiliar way. Was that the first sign of that other life inside? Was this a warning to get out of this situation? Or urging her on? Her head was spinning. Too many mixed emotions and the kiosk was over-heated and smelt disgustingly of urine, sour cigarette smoke and perfume. What about Eddie? No, Eddie was working today.

Damn!

'You alright in there?' A toothy, smile and those big eyes peering through the scratched and stained-glass panes like a demented owl, perhaps focusing on its innocent prey.

'Just a moment please...' Green glanced nervously at the man smoking impatiently outside. She would have almost no time and had to make the few words she spoke sound innocent as she was sure he would be trying to listen in. 'Operator...the Detective Department, Leicester Central, please...'

She'd almost mumbled the words, but thankfully the operator had heard her correctly. 'Do you wish to place an emergency call?'

'No, thank you. I just need to speak.'

'To whom do you need to be connected?'

'Um...just the office number. Whoever answers...'

A quick glance outside. The sound of their train whistling as it pulled away perhaps helped mask her words. She made an effort to smile and stand tall. 'Connecting you now...'

It was WPC Benson who picked up. She had entered the office almost the same moment the phone rang and had yet to see the important note left by Vignoles.

'Is that Jane?'

'WPC Jane Benson, that is correct. Who's speaking please?'

'It's me, Laura. I have almost no money so this will cut off. Just listen. I am in Loughborough walking along the canal with someone we are interested in. I need you to know where I am, but I'm Ok.'

'Sorry? Who is this?' Benson was struggling to make sense of what was being said and to put a face to the voice, which was hushed and barely audible.

The phone started to issue warning beeps. 'I have to go.' The line went dead and Cartwright opened the kiosk door at the same moment.

'Your mother did not recognise your voice?' He smirked.

'It was a poor line. Awfully crackly. She's a bit deaf.' Her voice came out sounding odd.

'Then you should speak louder. Now come along, we don't have a lot of time.'

'I hope you are not wasting my time, Mr Cartwright?'

'Ellis, please.' Cartwright strode away down the far side of the bridge that spanned the railway tracks towards the clutch of light industry buildings at the far end of Great Central Road. 'Just wait and you'll see!' There was a strange glint in his eye, but it could have been the bright light reflecting in his glasses. 'It was Richard Grimes who walked this way all those years go with a girl on his arm. Just imagine? Why on earth would that pretty young thing agree to do something like that?'

Green was struggling to keep up and wondering why she had agreed. 'Are you talking about the Tustain girl?'

'Rosie. Such beauty…' His brow creased. 'Pretty, but rather foolish. Putting her trust in such a man.' He suddenly stopped and faced Green. 'You do trust me, Laura? I don't want anyone thinking I coerced you. You really can turn about and go back if you have doubts.'

Green had many doubts and part of her wanted to run back to the relative safety of the station. Was this foolhardy or was it vital and necessary? She wanted to find out the truth. A man had been murdered and a young woman too. Solving such heinous crimes was never going to be easy or safe. She had to follow this through. Maybe this unappealing and intense electrical engineer was barking up the wrong tree and whatever it was he claimed to know would prove worthless, but could she afford to take the easy option and walk away? Would he be so willing if she came back another day with PC Simon Howerth and with the Detective Department on high alert? She was darned sure he would not. Green gave a wan smile. 'Can we get this over with?'

Chapter Thirty-Nine

WPC Jane Benson put the receiver down and walked over to her desk. *What on earth was that about?* They were used to the odd crank calls and had learned to ignore most of them, although some warranted writing down and giving further consideration. Benson thought this call fell into the latter category.

Was that Laura Green, the signal woman? It could have been, although her voice sounded rather odd. The message was short and could be summed up as 'I am in Loughborough beside the canal and all is fine'. What was that supposed to mean? Why was she calling the department if she had nothing to report?

Whilst she was mulling this over, Benson saw the note. Equally brief, but in moments her eyes read the name Laura Green and that DCI Vignoles and DS Mellor were driving to Loughborough and it all fell into place. They were going after Miss Green, sensing she was in danger just as the young lady in question had called in with a peculiar message.

And what was that about being with someone they were interested in? A suspect? Benson needed to think. Everything about the call felt wrong, and in the light of the urgent note from the DCI, it seemed possible Green had been sending a coded message. Benson now suspected that it implied she was anything *but* all right.

She jumped into action. As Benson was placing the telephone calls Vignoles had instructed her to make, she saw mental images of the various points along the canal in Loughborough as depicted in the scrapbook she'd found in Grimes' lodgings. Heavens, Green was retreading that fateful journey...with a possible suspect in the murder enquiry! This was alarming. How had the young signalwoman got herself in such a situation?

It took an age to get the constabulary in Loughborough to grasp the urgency of her request. The desk sergeant repeatedly asked if this was a missing person enquiry and how long the young woman had been missing? He needed to know if a circular had been sent around advising the local forces about this unfortunate disappearance. The desk sergeant saw no reason why he should rouse his two constables on a Sunday afternoon and send them out looking for a woman who was not as yet reported missing, and who had telephoned only recently to say she was 'all right'. Yes, Benson could appreciate his point of view, but...

After a wearisome ten minutes, Benson had to settle on accepting that they would send a bobby out to walk the length of the towpath where it bisected the town. It was unsatisfactory, but the best she was going to get.

Her next calls were to Loughborough Central and then Woodford Halse station. She would work her way through the other major stations straight after, but these two stations seemed the most relevant. Vignoles had named Loughborough as the most likely place Laura Green had gone with Ellis Cartwright and Laura's telephone call had also named Loughborough, but Benson reckoned Woodford Halse was a reasonable second choice. What was to stop Green and her 'man of interest' from doubling back on themselves and leading everyone astray? Perhaps Green had been made to place that call under duress to create a diversion?

Benson felt disappointed she was not part of the team chasing Green and Cartwright, but appreciated the trust the DCI had placed on her shoulders. She was manning the department alone and it was up to her to place vital calls, rouse others to action and collate any information sent in and then respond appropriately. She sat more upright at her desk and adjusted the lie of her uniform even though there was nobody there, then lined up her notepad and freshly sharpened pencils on the desk. She was ready.

* * * *

As fate would have it, Eddie Earnshaw and his driver were parked up in the yard at Loughborough Central. Theirs was a lazy day of short trips between a clutch of stations where they would do some lethargic shunting to assemble a motley collection of wagons of all sizes and shapes. The timetable was forgiving, and the hot sun unforgiving on their metal cab which was already overheated by the fire. Flopping into each corner as far from the fire and with a canvas side sheet pulled across to cut out some of the sunlight was the order of the day. Discussing yesterday's cricket results or idly considering which beach they were dreaming of sitting on was about the limit of their conversation, although between these desultory exchanges, Earnshaw was trying to give time and energy to chewing over what he knew about the David Green case.

His little notebook was thin on detail, and no amount of staring at what he'd written there was helping him find a solution to the problem. He had too little information, but one word kept leaping out at him - Loughborough.

And here he was. He'd seen the photographs in the scrapbook and had agreed that whatever this book meant, it was the key to the crime and those pictures were of Loughborough station and around the canal that snaked past close by. He stared out of the cab across to the island platform which stood empty in the baking sunlight and felt disappointed that no amount of looking at the place in question unlocked the mystery. The heat was sapping his energy. Across the soporific stillness of the yard, he could just hear the ringing of bells in the signal box and a louder jangle of the telephone in the stationmaster's office. Calls being made, trains signalled. Wires would soon be twanged and thrummed. Heavy linkages clunked and clattered as signals and points set. His driver grunted as the little disc signal on a short stubby pole set in the compacted ash of the yard rotated to give them the all-clear.

'We're off.'

Earnshaw leaned out and looked forwards then backwards to check all was clear and swung the handle of the hand brake to release it. 'All clear...'

The telephone had been ringing with that insistent manner which suggested it urgently needed answering. From their position close to the goods shed, Earnshaw had a clear view across to the Stationmaster's Office and could see the man himself standing with the receiver to his ear, nodding occasionally, but saying little. The call ended and the station master strode purposefully out of his office onto the platform just as his driver was opening the drain cocks in preparation for them to moving off. He called across to Earnshaw.

'Fireman! Driver! There's an emergency.'

'What is it?' The driver shut the drain cocks and Eddie instinctively gave the handbrake a quick turn as they both leaned from the cab.

'A man and a woman. The police want them. It's urgent. They got off the local just now but left the station.'

'What d'you want us to do about it?' The driver was puzzled.

'They're headed down the canal. Two detectives are motoring here but need us to keep our eyes peeled. They want sight of the couple. As you cross the canal slow down and take a look. You've permission to block the line if you get a sighting. Inform the signalman if you have anything to report.'

'Right you are, duck,' the driver was still looking confused, but it was Sunday and there was next to nothing expected along the line for the next hour and if the stationmaster was happy they messed about looking for a couple of lovers taking a walk, so be it.

'Who are they?'

'An older man and a young lass.' The stationmaster answered Earnshaw's call across the tracks. 'She's one of us. A signal woman.'

'Laura Green?'

'Yes! Do you know her?'

'You bet I do! Driver, come on...' Earnshaw was releasing the handbrake. 'Get her to the canal bridge...'

His driver gave him a cross look, not appreciating the insubordinate command, yet something about his fireman's urgent appeal made him respond. Their grubby freight engine had not made such a standing start in years and rattled their train of loose coupled wagons alarmingly whilst wheezing and panting from every joint. Fortunately, their goods guard had witnessed the exchange and anticipated their restart and made sure he was holding on tight.

Their engine threw a series of dark clouds into the air, the exhaust making the distinctive 'pom pom' sound of a military artillery piece that gave this class of engine their nickname as they lurched forward. 'She's my best mate's fiancée. God knows what's happened but I've got to help her!'

They scurried out of the station and it was not long before the driver shut off the regulator and applied the brakes, slowing the train rapidly as it approached the latticework of the short bridge spanning the canal. 'Jump off. The guard can protect the train and tell the signalman we're here for the duration,' barked the driver.

'Eh?'

'Get out and get down there! We'll take care of things up here. And take your shovel! You might need it to clout him!'

Eddie Earnshaw needed no further urging and before the train came to a stand, he was off and running to the bridge parapet looking for a place to scale the fence and scramble down the steep sides to the towpath.

In the distance, a faint ringing of bells could be heard. The tiny tinkle from within the signal box as urgent messages were communicated, the clatter of telephones ringing and the more solemn clang of an approaching police car.

* * * *

'Not far now, guv.'

'Step on it.'

'I'm pushing it as fast as I dare.'

Vignoles grimaced. Mellor was driving like his Formula One hero Mike Hawthorn, but time was passing and his sense of dread increasing with each minute. Their highly polished police car flashed down the road, the silver Winkworth gong clanging incessantly beside the radiator grille, turning heads and making motorcyclists wobble as they veered close to the gutter. As Mellor swung the powerful car around a stationary lorry into the path of oncoming traffic, they held their breath, but Mellor was able to hurl the car back on the road in the nick of time. Mellor was a confident driver, but he was on the edge of what was safe and wise. 'Probably best you get us there alive…'

Mellor grinned, but there was a bead of sweat on his brow. 'Station, sir?'

'Central. Correction.' Vignoles was attempting to read the town map in the road atlas, but the swaying movement made it hard to focus. 'Up past the station then down towards the canal. I have a hunch they might be on the towpath.'

'Following the trail in the photos?'

'Yes.'

'Can we head them off? If they're going to the location where that old boat was moored, we'd be better going in at the northwestern end?'

Vignoles stared at the map and tried to trace the course of the Grand Union Canal. 'Good thinking! Follow my directions…'

It now felt like they really were in a rally with Vignoles the navigator shouting instructions and not always in time whilst Mellor hurled the car on squealing tyres around the corners.

'It's hard to get to…the middle of nowhere.'

'That's why he chose it.'

'There's a narrow track called Swingbridge Road, we'll have to take our chances on that. We should be ahead of them as it's a decent walk on the towpath from central.'

Mellor gritted his teeth and urged more power from the engine. 'Is *that* the road?'

'Afraid so…'

'Bloody 'ell!' Mellor slammed the brakes and changed down a gear as the car kicked up clouds of dust whilst bouncing along what was barely wider than a footpath then clattered over the splintering wooden boards of the narrow bridge spanning the canal. 'Hold on! This don't look safe…'

They both breathed a sigh of relief as they made it to the other side.

'Take it easy. We need to spot them and stay out of the canal!' Vignoles was eyeing the foetid water that lay oily and filthy, just a foot or so from the side of the car.

* * * *

'This is a long walk. I thought you said I'd be back on the train within a couple of hours. I didn't agree to a full-scale ramble.'

'We've only been walking twenty minutes. We're nearly there. I used to work here and know the walk.'

'You lived here?'

'See that dirty great building over there? That's the Falcon Works. I started my apprenticeship in there and got my first taste of electrical engineering.'

Laura Green was trying to process this information. 'You lived around here? When was this?'

'I used part of this towpath every day to get to and from work. That's how I saw them.' He gave her a sideways look. His eyes were bright and his face flushed. 'I saw them clear as day. He'd not reckoned on me being here.' Cartwright sniggered. It was not a pleasant sound and Green felt repelled. She was fit and healthy and used to long hours heaving the heavy signal levers, but even so, she was starting to tire. She was sick of this canal and the litter-strewn towpath and even more so by the proximity with this man.

'Who do you mean?' She needed him to spell this out.

'Grimey and Miss Tustain.' He shook his head as if still disbelieving.

'They were lovers?'

'Impossible! The very idea she would want *him*!' Cartwright seemed angry, almost offended at the idea.

Green bit her lip and remained silent. She was trying to untangle the story, make sense of what she was hearing and all the time trying - and failing - to understand where her father fitted in.

'Laura, you must understand this. Grimes attacked her. No one else. He assaulted her. I'm sorry to speak so bluntly, but he stripped her completely naked before...' His tongue licked his pink lips as he spoke the words and Green felt bile rise in her throat.

'Grimes didn't know I worked around here. He thought he'd lured her to a quiet stretch of canal where nobody would see them and even if someone did, they would not know either of them. He had his arm around her. Holding her tight as if he didn't want to let her escape. Let me show you.' He suddenly put an arm around Green's waist and held her tightly to his side. 'Like so!'

'No, let me go!'

'Of course. I was just demonstrating.'

'Sorry...' Green took a breath. 'Was she struggling?'

Cartwright fell silent for a while. 'He was a charmer. A manipulator. He'd charmed her down here. She was under his spell. She had to be to have even agreed to meet him here.'

Green was not convinced. There was something that didn't quite ring true about this story, although she couldn't put her finger on what that was. The only encouraging aspect was that her dad had not been mentioned once. He seemed far away and out of the picture. This had to be a good thing and she needed to hold firm to that. She really must remain calm and get Cartwright to tell her all. The ending was going to be bad, but she needed to hear it. 'Where are we going?'

'Your patience will be rewarded soon. Just down here.' Cartwright steered her down a spur of the canal leading into a particularly overgrown and abandoned quayside lined with locked and abandoned warehouses and the water filled with sunken or slowly disintegrating barges. It was a dismal and uninviting place and Green recoiled. 'Down there?'

'See that?' Cartwright pointed to an especially ugly, derelict-looking craft that lay with its bows under the still water, the stern barely clearing the surface. Boards had sprung loose in places and a heavy tarpaulin, now green with moss, had been tied over the cabin roof and sides. A wonky chimney poked through a hole. 'I once lived in her. My home whilst I was working here. She was a fine craft back then. Long in the tooth perhaps, but nothing like she is now.'

They walked closer. A sense of dread falling over Green with each step and yet she seemed unable to break away. 'I moored her elsewhere in those days. Down where the river meets the canal in a lovely quiet spot. I can show you if you like?'

'Why would I want to? Look, Mr Cartwright, I appreciate you want to help, but I can't see why we are standing here.'

'Ellis.' He paused a beat. 'I just want you to know how it happened. To understand. It will all make sense, I promise.' They were beside the half-sunken wreck. 'There I was, working away all hours in the Falcon Works getting on with my life and trying to make something of myself. I wanted to be the best in my field, show the world that I could make it, not idling about drinking and getting up to trouble like Grimey and Green. What a pair of layabouts they were back then!' A strange smile as he studied Laura Green's face. 'I know, your father also made something of his life and became a respected signalman, so don't go jumping on your high horse.'

Cartwright stepped aboard the tilting deck. 'It's safe. The water is shallow, so she has nowhere further to go down...'

'I'd rather not.'

'Come on. Hop aboard. This is why we're here. There's something I need to show you inside...' He surprised Green by pulling a key from his pocket and unlocking a padlock that held the cabin door fast. It was oiled and opened freely.

'You own this?'

'Not exactly. She'd cost too much to re-float and repair and besides, the canal is going to wrack and ruin and will silt up before long. There's no point. A few years back, I found her lying here abandoned and unloved and decided I'd reclaim what was once mine.'

'Why? And what's this to do with Dad and that poor girl? I don't understand why you brought me here.'

'Please...' He held out a hand. 'Trust me, Laura.' His eyes were intense behind the lenses, his outstretched hand steady. His grip was firm and oddly reassuring as she accepted. Green knew she should not trust him and yet the desire to discover what secret lay inside was too strong to resist. She'd come this far already. It was no good turning around and walking away. He might get angry and follow her and she was sure she could not outrun him, and it was a long way back to the station. If she tried to make a break for it into the town that lay behind the warehouses the streets would be deathly quiet and her chances of finding somewhere to seek sanctuary, minimal. *In for a penny, in for a pound, eh, Laura?* She stepped off the reassuring solidity of the wharf onto the waterlogged wreck, getting her balance in the cramped cockpit whilst staring into a pitch-black cabin.

'It stinks!'

'She is past her best, I admit.' Cartwright laughed, then stamped his foot on a loose board. 'That'll scare off the rats and there is no water in the cabin.' He ducked inside and moments later an oil lamp flared, and Green heard a scrabbling sound and watched as one corner of the tarpaulin was pulled away from a side window, allowing a rectangle of sunlight to flood into the narrow cabin. It instantly appeared more inviting and she saw the floor was indeed dry. 'No glass in the window but it lets fresher air in. Come inside...'

'We don't have much time. I must catch my train. Please now explain yourself - and it had better be worth this long trek. You promised me proof of dad's innocence...' Laura Green ducked through the doorway and she was speaking, but then started, instinctively bringing a hand to her mouth. 'Oh!'

The wooden planked walls of the tiny cabin were plastered with newspaper cuttings and photographs. Some were the colour of old tea, others spotted and foxed with mould and curling at the corners where the paste had failed to hold. Headlines and smudged type almost covered every square inch, but what instantly held Laura's attention and caused her to gasp in surprise was the row of little prints, each showing the young and smiling face of Rosie Tustain. At least three of the prints were of the same image, but in different sizes. The effect was startling and in the claustrophobic confines of the narrowboat cabin it was impossible to escape the reproach of her youthful gaze staring back across the years.

'Take a seat.'

'What is this?'

'Let's call it my research lab. Grimey had a book. I used these cabin walls.'

Her eyes started to recognise many of the often lurid headlines from the local papers of the time, the same she'd seen and read in the scrapbook. 'This is weird...'

Cartwright shrugged his shoulders. 'Enticing a young girl out on a sunny afternoon for a gentle stroll beside a canal then raping and killing her is weirder.'

Green suddenly found her mouth was parched and could

not swallow.

'Sit down.'

'I'd rather get this over. Just tell me. Show me what it is you have here that will prove my dad is innocent.'

'Innocent?'

'You promised me you had information.'

'I recall saying I could prove to you who killed this pretty young woman. I can do that, but I cannot offer you anyone else responsible for the manslaughter of Mr Grimes. Or was it murder? Either way, not quite the same thing. Sorry.'

'You cannot prove dad is innocent?'

'If you remember, I thought your dad deserved a medal for ending that miserable man's life. He truly did society a favour.' He paused, that irritating smirk on his face yet again. 'I can help ameliorate the situation, if you will just shut up and listen. Now sit.' His voice had taken on a hard note that shocked Green. She sank onto one of the hard benches lining the edge of the cabin.

'You have a choice. You can remain in ignorance and watch as your dear old dad dangles from a rope.' A pause. 'Or...' He closed the cabin door. 'Or you can be a good girl and do as I say...'

*   *   *   *

'We can't drive any further.' Mellor slapped the steering wheel in frustration.

Vignoles was already clambering out and trying not to fall into the water in doing so. 'Which way?'

'They could be anywhere. And where are they going?'

'To the mooring site of that boat is my hunch.'

'But why?'

'We'd better find out. Grimes had two pictures of that location. One was recent. He considered it significant.'

'I reckon it's this way!' Mellor was already racing along the towpath, Vignoles, taking a moment to double-check Mellor's orientation, followed.

Unbeknown to the detectives and still some distance behind, fireman Earnshaw was trying to get his legs to run faster, hampered by his heavy work boots, cotton overalls and the cumbersome shovel. He was sweating and breathing hard, the whites of his eyes bright as he frantically scanned the deserted canal for signs of Laura. Thud, thud, thud, his boots pounded the hard earth. He was young and working on the footplate ensured he had more than enough energy for the run, but was he in time?

* * * *

Simon Howerth was seated on the platform at Woodford Halse. His head was muggy from too many pints, too little food and the oppressive heat of the afternoon. He was feeling groggy. It had been a tense and trying few hours. The beer would have been welcome under pleasanter circumstances but when consumed whilst pressing people he knew, if only by sight, to talk about another villager, he'd found even the best bitter had tasted sour in his mouth. He'd rattled a few cages, had some crossed words, received distrustful looks and even heard a few ugly mutterings behind his back. One man had hurled a vile insult about his future father-in-law. It was fair to say Woodford was divided into those who considered David Green innocent and the victim of police incompetence and misdirection, and those who felt he deserved all he got.

Howerth rubbed his temples and fought against a blinding headache that was developing. He needed an aspirin and some water. All jokes aside about the drink, he knew what was causing the constricting pain in his head. He'd finally struck a rich vein of long unspoken information about none other than Ellis Cartwright.

How much was true he couldn't judge. The passing of

time allowed resentment to develop and skewed people's memories. The police constable in him knew he should not take everything as fact, but there seemed to be more than a grain of truth in what he'd learned. Stories about Cartwright's strange relationship with girls and hints at disturbing episodes with young girls. His failure to settle down and marry was also cited as proof of his inability to forge a meaningful relationship with a woman. There was the story about how he left his first job at the Brush Falcon Works because he'd followed a girl down a dark alley and tried to molest her. Another odd tale about being caught loitering around a girl's school in later years, and all manner of salacious rumours of his antics during the wartime blackout. There was a good chance some of these anecdotes did not relate to Cartwright and even if they did, had been suitably enhanced for the telling, but if only half he'd heard were true, it reflected badly on the engineer. A man who seemed to prey on young women. A man who had been known to carry a candle for that missing Tustain girl. He'd left the town not many months before she vanished to start work in Loughborough, but had been visible joining in with the searches across the fields and down the winding course of the Great Ouse, as locals and police formed lines with long thin sticks beating their way across the countryside vainly searching for clues or her body.

Cartwright had claimed whilst making a show of searching for the girl that he cared about Rosie Tustain, that he liked the girl, though not one person was aware they had any kind of social contact. He'd been interviewed by the police but cleared of suspicion, but so had all the men of Woodford, with the same result. It was not exactly conclusive, but Howerth felt sure this mass of rumour and suspicion spelt trouble.

However, he had also to admit there was a counter-argument causing him consternation. He'd learned of another titillating story concerning this young woman doing the rounds, telling of how Grimes and Green - yes, the same David Green

251

- had been involved in something salacious with her and the two lads had received a dose of brotherly retribution for their efforts. This didn't look good, but the local bobbies had grilled both young men and their alibis were deemed strong. That was a crumb of comfort.

Howerth was glad he'd persuaded Laura to stay away. It would have been distressing for her to hear this. Worse still, sitting alone on the platform he could not help but feel a deepening sense of foreboding. Hearing the gossip of Grimes and Green getting up to no good with Tustain was not encouraging, but what these rumour mongers did not seem to know was that Green had kept hold of her Alice band and a love note. It really did look as though Green had argued with and struck Grimes. There was a link, a powerful and ugly connection and whatever the local bobbies made of it at the time it was hard for Howerth not to fear the worst. Had Grimes suspected David Green of the crime? Was that the conclusion he'd reached? Had Grimes found a reason to stand in the privacy of the signal box with Green so he could make his accusation? Was this behind the reason they had met that evening in the engine shed? Could this be why David Green was choosing a defence of silence?

He groaned and held his head in his hands. This was awful… A telephone started ringing in the station building. Jangling like the synapses in his brain.

Howerth could not bear to imagine the quiet and kindly signalman as abductor, rapist and double killer. It just could *not* be possible. He had to hold on to the fact that Grimes had included Cartwright in his scrapbook and the rumour mill spat out far more unpleasant scraps about Cartwright than Green. Cartwright was there that night and could have delivered that killer blow. Perhaps he intended to do the same to his future father-in-law? If Green and Grimes had spoken and Grimes had started to confess to Green he had proof of Cartwright's guilt, then the danger was real. Howerth needed to get back to Leicester and tell Laura. He needed to keep her away from Cartwright and then he needed to speak to DS Mellor. To the DCI, if necessary.

He impatiently looked along the tracks for a sight of his train. Howerth had made up his mind. Cartwright was dangerous and no more so when alone with a young woman.

The telephone stopped ringing at last. A porter called his attention. 'Constable Howerth! You need to get up to Loughborough as quick as you can!'

* * * *

'They both came aboard *Blackbird*. On to my boat, uninvited. They broke the etiquette. Nobody steps aboard unless invited to do so.' Cartwright was filled with self-righteous indignation. 'I saw them!'

'You were following them?'

'I wanted to see what they were doing…going to do.'

'Holding hands and walking into the countryside. I think I can imagine…' Laura Green gave him a strange look, but in her mind had a momentary memory of that afternoon on the railway embankment with Simon. How much had happened since then? She longed to be back there, free of all this emotional and mental torment. 'But why would you do that? It's…'

'What?'

'A bit strange.'

'Be as sniffy as you like, Laura, but I knew Grimey and knew his intentions were not honourable. They were in here. Doing you-know-what. I waited. But that was my mistake. I should never have let him go so far. I shall always regret my hesitancy. I should have called out and demanded they get off my boat, but instead…'

Green found her throat had constricted.

'See this?' He pulled a threadbare mattress off the bench

opposite the one Green was seated on. 'See that?' He showed a hideous brown stain. 'Blood. Her blood.' The stains were extensive and unappealing.

'How can you be sure? After so many years this cannot be the same mattress. An overturned coffee pot could cause the same kind of stain.'

'Coffee?' He laughed. 'Denial won't help. He slit her throat as she lay there stripped naked.' Cartwright leered at Laura Green. 'Before or perhaps after he had his way with her. I don't know for sure.'

Laura thought she might be sick.

'He carried her. Holding her like she was a sleepy lover in his arms, lifted her over the fence and into the trees on the little hill not far from the river's edge. He laid her down so gently…'

'And you watched all this? You did nothing?'

'It was too late to save her…'

'But what about the police? You must have run off to raise the alarm?' She was shocked. 'How did you know it was too late? Who were you to decide? Oh God, that means you are almost as bad… Let me out, I've heard enough!'

Cartwright moved to block the narrow doorway. 'But I've not finished, Laura.' Suddenly, he froze. 'What's that sound? Are those Police car bells? Did you hear them?'

Laura Green had not heard anything. There was a terrible roaring of blood in her ears and she knew was going to be sick. He head was swimming with red and silver stars behind her eyes and her nostrils filled with the stinking wet smell of this wretched boat. 'I need air…'

Cartwright ignored her plea. 'This a crime scene. I preserved it all these years. I've always kept *Blackbird*. I moved her from the original mooring to deflect suspicion but kept everything just as it was as best I could. I have other things here… things I took from her. Afterwards.'

'W-what? I-I don't understand…'

'She was not buried deep. It was easy. I come back once a year and pay my respects. It's the least I can do. Today is the anniversary of her demise.'

'Oh, God...' Laura Green fainted.

* * * *

'Smoke!'

'Something's burning.' Vignoles immediately sensed trouble.

'Could be kids...'

'I can't see any.'

Mellor speeded up as Vignoles fought a stitch in his side. They came to the canal spur leading to the abandoned wharf and immediately saw the plume of sickly smoke rising from the battered chimney and curling around the rumpled tarpaulin.

'There's someone on that boat.'

'Surely it can't be...'

Both men made the connection instantly and a mixture of fear and adrenaline gave them extra speed to reach *Blackbird* in moments. The cabin door was locked from the inside. Mellor kicked it repeatedly. 'Bolted!'

Vignoles frantically tore at the heavy tarpaulin, but it was awkward and roped in place and he made little headway.

Mellor was back on the wharf searching in the tall weeds for something to use to attack the cabin door. He found a steel bar and whilst shouting for Vignoles to stand back, laid into the little door with all his strength, urged on by the increasing plume of smoke and the sound of retching and coughing from inside. Vignoles meanwhile was trying to untie the securing ropes on the burning tarpaulin. A running man now closed in on them, face red and sooty black. 'Is she safe?'

Eddie Earnshaw didn't wait for an answer and practically launched himself onto the cockpit just as the door splintered. 'Let me through. I know about fire!' He dived inside as angry red and orange flames licked around the door. Shouts, a thump and a wracking cough followed. Mellor peered inside the narrow opening and tossing the metal bar aside, hauled the spluttering form of Cartwright into the cockpit, manhandling him by his jacket and shirt, ripping both in the process.

Mellor's furious face loomed over him. 'If you've hurt her...'

Realising there was too little space in the cramped cockpit and with Cartwright doubling over with his violent coughing, Mellor unceremoniously tipped the man overboard into the rank, dirty brown water.

'Sink or swim! Your choice!'

'Quickly!' Earnshaw was now at the door, weighed down by the shape of Laura Green in his arms. He was trying to hold his breath, eyes streaming whilst furiously stamping with one booted foot at flames licking around his ankle and catching on his overalls. Mellor grabbed the unconscious woman and hauled her to safety. Her clothes were stained with soot and a strong smell of burnt hair, yet she looked otherwise untouched, her eyelids fluttering. 'Get her some air...'

Earnshaw scrambled out, wincing at the pain from his burned ankles, one hand already showing itself bright red and raw. 'Get off this thing...' He could barely speak. 'There's oil down there!'

Vignoles carefully took Green from Mellor and carried her to the cleanest stretch of wharf he could find and even as he did so she opened her eyes and started to cough. 'She's alive!'

Mellor and Earnshaw grinned at each other in spite of the pain both were feeling, then hearing flailing and splashing in the stagnant water, nodded in agreement. They now stood close to the stern of the *Blackbird* and looked down at Cartwright who was gasping for air, arms uncoordinated and useless. He was frantically struggling, his glasses lost and a look of fear in his eyes.

'Know how it feels?' Mellor looked down at him. 'Calling for help, calling for mercy and no-one offering it?'

Chapter Thirty-Nine

'Help me!'

Mellor shrugged his shoulders. 'Why?'

Earnshaw gave a nervous look at Mellor. 'We should get him out.'

'No rush.' He glared back at Cartwright. 'We'd be better letting you drown like the filthy rat you are.'

Cartwright went under the water but bobbed back up, face going a strange colour. Mellor cursed angrily then reached down. 'Ah well, I gotta follow rules. It's my job to protect life. Worst luck, sometimes.'

He and Earnshaw found an arm each and hauled the soggy creature out of the water and onto the wharf. They rolled him onto his front and let him splutter and wheeze. 'Lie there and kiss the last bit of freedom you'll ever know. Miss Green needs urgent medical attention, so don't mind us if we look after her first. Don't even think about leaving or we'll toss you back in the water and say you were resisting arrest.' Mellor gave the pathetic figure of Cartwright a last withering look.

Vignoles was trying his best to make Laura comfortable. 'You need to be checked over, but I think you'll be fine...'

'We need an ambulance.'

'I'll go! Earnshaw darted a look at Laura Green to reassure himself that she was not in immediate danger and with his skin crying out in pain, ran off as quickly as his injured legs would carry him.

Chapter Forty

Laura Green made a swift recovery. She had inhaled smoke, but it was fortunate that she had fainted before Cartwright had tossed the oil lamp at the locked cabin door. Her breathing had been shallow and minimised the damage to her lungs, aided by her proximity to the window with no glass. The minor burns would heal and with a judicious trim and an artfully placed veil her singed hair would be more than acceptable in time for the wedding.

Other than that, she seemed to have come through the ordeal remarkably well, expressing her gratitude for being saved but perhaps more than anything, taking strength from the realisation that her father was soon to be exonerated and free to walk her down the aisle.

Ironically, it was Simon Howerth who was suffering perhaps the worst out of the two of them. His pride had taken a dent in that he had been stuck, in a somewhat inebriated state, on a slow all-stations stopper chuffing northward whilst this dramatic rescue unfolded with none other than his best friend as the hero of the hour. Whilst grateful, he knew he would spend the rest of his life having to live down the fact he'd spent the afternoon in a succession of pubs whilst Eddie had rescued his future wife from almost certainly being burnt to death. He was already calculating what might be the appropriate number of pints he should stand Eddie in gratitude before calling 'time' and asking Ed to get a round in…

However, that was not the end of Howerth's 'trauma'.

'But Laura, you never said a word! Talk about a shock to the system! It was the doctor who checked you over who took me to one side and reassured me that both expectant mother and unborn child were doing fine. I nearly had a heart-attack.'

'Ah…'

'When *were* you going to tell me?'

Laura Green was seated in a comfy armchair in the back kitchen of the family home in Woodford Halse. Her face was radiant, despite a bandaged wrist and ankle, plus hair trimmed shorter than she usually wore it. This gave her an almost elfish look and the unexpected bonus of making her look far younger than her years. In fact, mused Howerth, it created a rather fetchingly fashionable look in the style of the gamine film stars Audrey Hepburn and Leslie Caron.

'I'm sorry Simon,' she then giggled, which somewhat undermined her apology. 'No, truly. I was waiting for the right moment and then everything went a bit crazy.'

'You can say that again.'

'But you do understand? Everything happened so fast, and it just didn't feel right once dad was under arrest. It felt as though there were more pressing matters to focus on.'

'That's true...'

'I was going to wait until our wedding day. As an extra surprise.' She paused. 'Hopefully a nice one?'

'Of course!'

'Not heart-attack inducing?'

'No. Not now, at least...' He still looked a little put out, but one look at her big blue eyes and her face with the charming new haircut melted his heart. 'It's just that as surprises go I feel like I'm the only one who *is* actually surprised. Neither your mum nor dad seem the least bit!'

Green laughed. 'I think mum worked it out almost at once.'

'Uh-huh. Even Eddie had suspicions...' Simon Howerth gave a rueful smile.

'An observant lad.'

'Meanwhile, muggins here, never had a clue...' Howerth stopped. Why on earth was he complaining when Laura needed rest, recuperation and his support. 'Sorry. It really is wonderful news, Laura. I just wish you had not put yourself at risk like that.'

'I had to. I had no choice. At the darkest point, my only concern was to find a way to get dad out of that fatal fix. Telling you about the baby and having you fawning and fussing over me and stopping me investigating the truth would not have helped one jot.'

'Me, fawning and fussing?'

'A little. But I like it. Best be careful, though, I might want to make a habit of it.'

* * * *

For Vignoles and Mellor the whole sorry story was going to take many months to fully resolve. There was a mountain of paperwork to deal with, made more complex by weeks of tedious work with other constabularies to find appropriate solutions that mollified everyone where areas of jurisdiction had been over-stepped and processes had not followed strict protocol, albeit with the best intentions. The dusty 'missing person's file' of Rosie Tustain, was now recast as a murder investigation. One small detail of the case they explained was the torn page from the Loughborough telephone directory.

'The investigating officer back then was a Superintendent Dumbleton.' Mellor explained. 'It was a page of names starting with 'Du' that Grimes had kept. He was looking to see if Dumbleton was still in the area.'

'And was he?' Vignoles asked.

'His widow is. The old man snuffed it ten years back. She remembers Grimes telephoning, but of course, she had no knowledge of this nor any other case, for that matter.'

'Another corroborative detail pointing to Grimes being the innocent party. Grimes was trying to prove Cartwright was the killer.' Vignoles felt a twinge of sadness as he recalled the image of the unattractive, and apparently unloved, Grimes lying sprawled in the inspection pit.

This further underlined the timescale this curious

investigation covered. Unlike the crimes which fictional sleuths such as Miss Marple unpicked in a matter of days to amuse their readers, many unexplained disappearances could take decades to resolve, and sadly, many would never find a resolution.

Furthermore, this was work far outside the reach of the Transport Police, a fact reinforced during lengthy sessions when both Vignoles and Mellor were grilled about their actions away from the railway where, as they were repeatedly reminded, they had no legal jurisdiction.

There were times when these tiresome meetings, obsessed with bureaucratic procedure and rules, grew fractious and both detectives wondered who was actually being investigated. Cartwright's murderous actions seemed to play second fiddle to pedantic questions of where the boundaries of the Transport Police's reach could be drawn.

Common sense prevailed eventually, but this peripheral nit-picking took any shine off their brave actions and neither received any thanks for preventing the death of a young woman and her unborn baby.

However, after some tense days when Cartwright mounted a strong fightback in defending his corner, they were at least able to witness the release of David Green and announcing this good news significantly improved personal relations within the Detective Department at Leicester. Pent up emotions were let loose and the decks further cleared by a memorably riotous night of drinking down at the Great Central Hotel when the news came through that David Green had been given back the keys to his signal box. It was just a shame Green could not have explained matters more clearly and accurately at the time, thereby possibly saving a lot of trouble, but Green was not a man about to change the habit of a lifetime, even, it seemed when facing a murder charge.

Discussing the case a few days later, Vignoles explained how the release came about. 'We've had our differences, but

DCI Thornbury and his DS are good coppers. Well versed in interview technique. They worked Cartwright to perfection.'

'Yeah?' Mellor remained sceptical. He'd found their questioning of his actions and motives particularly offensive.

'Cartwright mounted a strong defence and you could say he landed a few counter-blows against Green in the opening exchanges. He had a plan to set Green up and exploited it to the full.'

'But he's guilty of everything? He killed Grimes and probably Tustain and tried to kill Laura Green…'

'No doubt in my mind about his guilt. Thornbury thinks the same and Cartwright has been charged on all three counts. Cartwright is clever, but like many clever criminals, he'd got to the stage when he thought he was invincible. He believed he had all the answers and could evade even close questioning. Now, whereas Green did himself no favours by believing saying as little as possible was the way out of his predicament, Cartwright was the opposite.'

Mellor grinned. 'A talker?'

'Couldn't shut him up. Once he got going, he had an opinion and an answer for everything. Elaborating his story and repeatedly coming back with more embellishing details that he thought proved both Grimes and Green guilty.'

Mellor nodded appreciatively. 'Those are the best. Just sit back and pay out the rope…'

'And watch him tie himself in knots. You could say the noose was formed, tied and strung up by his own actions. He knew too much and didn't know when to stop. Describing things and trying to lay blame for actions he should know nothing about. That's the trouble with lies. They have to be watertight, and they have to be consistent.'

'He should have come up with one simple story and never deviated. The less you say, the less can trip you up.' Mellor agreed.

'That was Green's philosophy. Green believed his school

friend was an abductor and possibly even a murderer and yet didn't have the nerve to speak out and test his fears in the hands of the law.'

'Sayin' that, guv…'

'Yes?' Vignoles heard something in Mellor's voice.

'He fixed that big white beast of an engine. He held her over until she blew her top. Deliberate.'

'Really?'

'Yeah. I checked the signal box logs. Cross-checked and plotted the timings. True, there *was* a delay and some backing up along the line, but he could have let her through.'

'Would Grimes have been clobbered if it had gone through and not placed in the engine shed overnight?' Vignoles furrowed his brow.

'Cartwright would have nobbled him somewhere else. He had to kill 'im, just a case of where an' when. I reckon Green's paid a big-enough price as it is. I'm for letting this pass.'

'You're getting soft.'

Both men laughed.

* * * *

David Green was safely back in the secure and familiar environs of the family home in Woodford Halse, and on the surface, appeared untroubled by his dangerous flirtation with a trial for murder and the hangman's noose. His wife was still prone to reaching for a handkerchief as tears welled up, especially when any one of a succession of neighbours called in, ostensibly to wish Mr Green well, then demand the full story from start to finish in every heart-tugging detail. At these moments, David Green made his excuses and slipped away into his beloved garden and let his wife make however many pots of tea and tell all with floods of tears at appropriate moments.

Usually, this escape into the safe familiarity of his beloved garden was enough to push aside the more distressing moments of his arrest and his wife's repeated retelling of his ordeal was slowly reducing its impact and power to shock, but he was not completely immune. One warm summer's evening, a few days after his release, he was idly was checking his vegetable patch whilst the smell of his wife's baking wafted from the kitchen to mingle pleasantly with the smell of the warmed loam of the well-tilled garden, when without warning an icy chill ran down his spine and he found he couldn't stop trembling with the sudden recollection of the tragic fate he avoided by a hair's breadth. His fate and the appalling aftermath for his family and friends had been in the balance, not unlike that of a heavy wrench in the hand of man long used to handling heavy tools. His future son-in-law had been perceptive and alert to spot this anomaly, and David Green realised with a painful upwelling of emotion that he owed Simon Howerth his life…

Although a naturally self-contained man long trained in maintaining the 'stiff-upper lip' mentality that so many of the wartime generation were used to, he was shocked to find himself suddenly gripped by a quaking spasm of fear that made him tremble uncontrollably. It lasted just a minute or so and he was able to hide his weakness from his wife by leaning heavily on his hoe whilst partially hidden by the stand of runner beans entwined around a set of canes.

From this day on and for the rest of his days such uncontrollable spasms occasionally overwhelmed him, but always when alone at home, and most powerfully, during the long watches of the night shift in his signal box. His foolish pride and stubborn belief that his innocence would win out over evil had seen him come close to losing his life whilst allowing a dangerous and unbalanced killer to walk free. It was a particularly harsh lesson to learn.

*   *   *   *

The excavations to extract the human remains from the ancient tump close to where the Soar met the canal were taking an inordinate amount of time to complete. The mound was considered Bronze Age or possibly even Iron Age, and therefore all manner of permissions needed to be sought before the police could make any kind of excavation. No such undertaking had, as yet, been given in spite of a considerable amount of paperwork (almost as big as the tump) being generated.

'Cartwright just dug a bloody hole...' Mellor was unimpressed by the heel-dragging of the many experts and specialists weighing in with their opinions. 'Thankfully not our problem now. Let someone else sort it all out. She's lain there so long I suppose a few more weeks won't hurt.'

Vignoles agreed. 'Perhaps it's best taken cautiously. The whole sorry affair will stir up a lot of repressed emotions and it will be hard for some folks in Woodford having this troubling memory reawakened. One day, her family will at least be able to lay her properly to rest. I just hope that will offer them some crumbs of comfort.' He stopped, then sat upright and faced Mellor. 'However, before that, we have a different and far happier event to look forward to in Woodford. I presume you got your invitation?'

'I have.'

'And chosen a suitable present?'

'Lansdowne decided that a whip-round in the office would be best. That way she and Benson could find something suitable.'

'Very wise. The girls will know what to get. I always let Mrs Vignoles take care of such matters. Did you find something suitable to wear for the day?' He need not have asked. Mellor was always pin-sharp in his turn out and in spite of moaning at length how the tussle with Cartwright had ruined his suit, Vignoles knew Mellor had been shopping in a particularly fine gentleman's outfitters for something far better than the one dirtied and singed on the *Blackbird*.

'Of course. An' my shoes will be shinin' like glass. Got to do the Department proud.'

'Quite right. Then let's repair to the pub. PC Howerth is standing us drinks in anticipation of tomorrow's big event.'

Mellor was already reaching for his hat.

The End

Postscript

The Difference Engine settled down into months of trouble-free running before being transferred to the East Coast mainline. Doris Lessiter issued encouraging press releases suggesting the decision to give the engine a chance to show its potential along the prestigious run from London King's Cross to York and Newcastle was a sure sign it would not be long before an order followed for a production run.

'I fear her optimism was misplaced,' Vignoles explained one quiet afternoon to Mellor.

'I heard it was performing well?'

'Faultlessly. Once they ironed out the overheating problem it has proved to be fast, powerful and responsive. The crews love the warm and comfortable cabs and excellent forward vision. Sadly, the bean counters studying the data uncovered flaws Tomkins-Dunkler had not been given time to address. When running at high speed over long distances the engine was acceptable regarding fuel consumption, however, when asked to stop and start frequently as is the way on our crowded railway the consumption figures made grim reading. It cost a small fortune to keep her tanks full.'

'Bit like a 'Roller? Very flash and comfortable but guzzles fuel like a thirsty steelworker downs beer.'

'Something like that.'

'Then steam lives on another day! I'll drink to *that*,' Mellor looked pleased. Vignoles sometimes forgot that Mellor liked a good steamer as much as he did.

'I fear your celebrations may be short-lived. The British Transport Commission has decided to nail its colours firmly to the mast of the 'infernal combustion engine' burning heavy fuel oil. More of those overweight, underpowered and unreliable diesels, be they diesel-electric or diesel-hydraulic will be the order of the day.' Both men pulled disapproving faces. 'They cost a lot more to make than a steamer and there's no guarantee they will last long enough to pay back their build cost, but despite these obvious failings they have decided burning oil is the bright clean future we've been promised.'

'The death of steam?'

'I am afraid so, and well within our lifetimes.' Vignoles struck a match and lit his pipe, then blew a blue smoke ring which rose silently, wobbling in the air before shredding apart and fading to nothing.

Author's Note

The Signalman's Daughter is the twelfth title in the Inspector Vignoles Mystery series, although the eleventh book in the sequence. Ideally, it should be read before *This Transient Life* although the pleasure of either should not be affected unduly by reading out of sequence. I shall now take a short break from writing before commencing book thirteen. After amassing a significant volume of work, it would do good to re-fill the tender with coal and water... Please do not expect the next installment until 2023.

This book proved hard to write and whether the effort was worthwhile is for you to decide. Perhaps the difficulty lay not just in the arrival of a global pandemic, but because I also wanted this book to be quieter and deliberately not so much about *who* committed the crime (it should be quite easy to determine 'who did it') but about mistakes, about wrong decisions and things not seeming to be what they really are.

Whether it succeeds, I find hard to judge, but you will meet some favourite characters and there is a welcome return to Woodford Halse where this series began with *Smoke Gets In Your Eyes*, and sees the reuniting of old chums for one (last?) time to fight crime...

The Brush (now Abela) Falcon Works in Loughborough actually exists and continues to this day. There is no connection whatsoever between the fictional characters and events in this book and the real workforce and business. All characters in this book are fictional and the trains run to an imaginary timetable purely to satisfy the story's needs.

A number of gas turbine locomotives did run in the UK. *GT3* was a notable example of these and was built in the Brush Falcon Works and ran on the same former Great Central Railway as in this book. *GT3* was very reliable and gave some impressive performances but proved costly to run. However, even if this had not been the case, it had already been decided at the highest level that diesel fuel was to be the primary solution to eradicating steam on Britain's railways by 1968.

Inspector Vignoles will be back in
A Return to Broadway.